Flower Terror

SUFFOCATING STORIES OF CHINA

Pu Ning

HOMA & SEKEY BOOKS
Dumont, New Jersey

Copyright © 1999 by Pu Ning

Publishers Cataloging-in-Publication Data

ISBN: 0-9665421-0-X

Flower Terror: Suffocating Stories of China by Pu Ning
1. Wu-ming-shih, pseud
2. Authors, Chinese-20th century
I. Title

PL2824.Z5   1998   895.1'352-dc21   98-87238
                                                CIP

Published by Homa & Sekey Books
P. O. Box 103
Dumont, NJ 07628
Fax: (201)384-6055
Email: homa_sekey@yahoo.com

Editor: Shawn X. Ye
Cover Design: Judy Wang

Printed in the United States of America
10 9 8 7 6 5 4 3 2 1

TABLE OF CONTENTS

Acknowledgements

I would like to express my sincere gratitude to the two translators, Mr. Richard J. Ferris Jr. and Mr Ardrew Morton, who have made it possible for the book to be available to the English-speaking readership.

My thanks also go to Dr. A. Owen Aldridge for his Preface and to Mr. Luoyong Wang for his introduction to me and my writing.

I am also indebted to Professor Judy Manton for proofreading the translation.

Pu Ning and His Writing

Working as a professional actor in New York, I had not had much chance to read books in Chinese for quite some years till last summer when a friend of mine dropped me one such book in my backstage room in Broadway Theater where I was playing the role of "Engineer" in <u>Miss Saigon</u> musical. It was a collection of stories by Pu Ning (better known by his pseudonym Wu-ming-shih or Mr. Anonymous) about life in China from 1950s to 1970s. The stories helped bring back memories of my Chinese experiences over 20 years ago when I was a young boy receiving Peking opera training in a small city called Shiyan in China's Hubei province. It was during the Cultural Revolution and we were sent to countryside to "mend the earth" with hard labor and hot sweat. To motivate the working enthusiasm of young people like me, our teacher would hand-pick each day those of us whom he considered "hard workers" to come to his place in the evening listening to his serialized story-telling of one of Mr. Anonymous' novels *Woman in the Pagoda*, then a banned book but very widely circulated in hand-written form among young men and women across the nation. I was so fascinated by Pu Ning's love story of a young man desperately courting and finally hopelessly abandoning his girl that I decided to work hard every day in order not to miss any part of it.

There have been numerous stories about this legendary writer and his other remarkable books. It was reported that after 1949 Pu Ning found it hard to accept the new ideology then prevailing the country and one thing he did to keep his free mind afloat was practicing civil disobedience. For over thirty years he had been willingly unemployed even though he was twice put into labor camp and prison. In a space of twelve years he secretly completed his 2.6-million-word masterpiece *Book Without a Title*, a six-volume epic-like roman-fleuve portraying a young Chinese intellectual seeking truth and meaning in life. What was equally marvelous was that, risking being imprisoned again, he managed to smuggle the manuscripts of *Book Without a Title* and other writings to Hong Kong, where his brother lived, in about 4,000 disguised letters and had them all published in Taiwan later on.

Pu Ning's *Book Without a Title* has been acclaimed by many critics as one of the masterpieces of modern Chinese literature. A noted professor of Chinese literature who wrote the all influential *A History of Modern Chinese Fiction*, Dr. C. T. Hsia of Columbia University regards *Book Without a Title* as "a work of unprecedented ambition and scope in modern Chinese literature, far superior to the famous trilogies of the acknowledged leading writers, such as (Lao She's) *Four Generations Under One Roof* and Pa Chin's *Turbulent Stream.*"

Having read the first two volumes of *Book Without a Title*, the only ones available to him at the time, Suma Chang-Feng, famed critic and author of *A New History of Chinese Literature*, could not help asserting that "*Book Without a Title,* with its unprecedented originality, is no doubt the greatest work of fiction since the birth of new Chinese literature."

An even more enthusiastic view was expressed by Professor Chen Sihe, one of the towering Chinese literary critics of today and author of *A History of Chinese literature in the 20th Century,* who hails *Book Without a Title* as "an extraordinary book for all time" that "crowns modern Chinese underground literature in its literary accomplishment, filling a blank in the twentieth century Chinese literature ... *Book Without a Title* is comparable to such Western classics as Goethe's *Faust.*"

Running the gamut of full literary spectrums, Pu Ning criticism has grown voluminous among the Chinese letters, ranging from thousand-word newspaper and magazine articles to book-length Ph.D. dissertations. Pu Ning has in a sense become a "phenomenon."

Having labored on the above, I feel a little despondent that such an extraordinary writer with such inconceivable works has not been made known enough to Western readers and scholars. It is a pity and chagrin that jewels like *Book Without a Title* are not shared by the Western literary world. I can imagine how fantastic it would be if they also glitter in the eyes and minds of English book lovers. For that matter, any publisher of the English language who takes upon herself the task of rendering Pu Ning's works into the world's most popular language deserves my salute and respect. I hope that the day will not be far when Pu Ning's *Book Without a Title* enters the bookstores, libraries and even families of the American people who take a fancy to China and books.

Luoyong Wang
Backstage
Broadway Theatre
New York

Preface

The average American has great difficulty in comprehending the ideals, internal conflicts, atrocities, agonies, and reversals that have marked the history of the Chinese people during the past century from the downfall of the Ching Dynasty at its beginning to the reintroduction of capitalism at its close. Ever since the auspicious proclamation of the Republic of China under Sun Yat-sen in 1911, China has suffered one setback after another. Provincial generals or warlords conducted a civil war between 1914 and 1924, the Communists seized power in 1949, introducing a series of catastrophic assaults on individual lives and liberties, including land confiscation under the guise of reform, wholesale political purges, wars with minorities, and a so-called Cultural Revolution that came near demolishing the nation's precious heritage of arts, letters and social decency.

Pu Ning in a number of earlier publications has vividly depicted the persecution he suffered under these various political disasters. In 1958 he was subjected to hard labor and ideological purification at a self-criticism camp; in 1960 he was forced to join labor activity in countryside and in 1968 he began serving a prison term lasting over one year. He has described his ordeal at the self-criticism camp in *The Scourge of the Sea* (1958), and has vividly narrated in a companion book, *Red in Tooth and Claw* (1988), the day-by-day persecution that a fellow victim suffered under communist rule. The present book is not a continuous narrative, but a series of vignettes indirectly portraying the oppressive atmosphere of the period. Pu provides enough of his own background and experiences to assure the reader that his portrayal is authentic, but he writes as an impressionistic observer. His other works reflect personal grievance. Here he presents social criticism from an esthetic perspective.

In his sketch, "Flower Terror," Pu merely alludes to the period of incarceration which he has endured in order to concentrate on his mental condition after his final release. He even pretends that the protagonist of the story is a poinsettia that he purchases as a symbol of his freedom and return to normal social life. There are two separate plants that provide the symbolism in the title "Flower Terror," which neatly, but perhaps not intentionally provides a contrast to the "Flower Power" of American hippies at about the same time. The first flower was a pot of chrysanthemums that before his arrest Pu bought as a symbol of the joy, freedom and zest for life prior to the Communist takeover, a parallel symbol to the music of Mozart which he listened to in secret on a forbidden radio. The flowers seemed so alien to the oppressive atmosphere in which he lived that they evoked a kind of terror in his mind and in the hearts of his neighbors. But at the same time they represented a terror to the regime itself as a reminder of spiritual values that could not be suppressed. The second flower was a poinsettia that he purchased some time after his release from forced farm labor. The months on the farm had dulled his sensitivities, including his feeling for flowers, and it took him several months to regain his normal equilibrium. Like many other couples under the regime, he and his wife lived in separate communities and were reunited only for brief holiday visits. Attracted by the "Christmas Red" of the flower and its fragile beauty, he treated it like a woman. He describes at length his efforts to keep the plant alive during the frosts of January until his wife's anticipated visit on the Chinese New Year. The red of the flower represented Christmas rather than the bleak red sea of Communism that surrounded him. He nourished the flower against the cold weather to make it last until the New Year just as he nourished his ideals and values against the stultifying presence of the Communist regime. Pu carries on the flower image in the subsequent story "A Glass of Water," comparing himself to the affectionate fallen flower that meets the unfeeling flowing water.

The story "A Glass of Water," apart from its intrinsic message of condemning the cruelty and ruthlessness of the Communist regime, has the literary function of introducing the major characters of Pu's household and immediate neighborhood. While Pu is serving his prison sentence, his neighbors are kept in a constant state of panic by the pervasive atmosphere of fear and suspicion created by continual inroads upon the individual privacy considered inseparable from normal social relations. Pu's erstwhile friends, including some who have previously benefited from his generosity, refuse to give his invalid mother a glass of water lest they be reported and accused of consorting with the enemy. The hostility created in the day-to-day social environment is shown to be almost as terrible as the physical atrocities carried out in the prisons and on the battlefield. The powerful climax of the story, however, shows that a spark of benevolence still remains in the human heart even when it has been subjected to the psychological ravages of the totalitarian state.

"The Fossil" reveals that the malignant influence of artificially-created social hostility extends even into the very heart of the family. Here the first-person narrator is not Pu himself although the circumstances of the story fit his life closely. He could have escaped from China at the outbreak of the revolution, but chose to remain because he needed to take care of his ill mother and his cousin. His cousin became his wife, but twenty years later he was forced by the regime to endure a separation of three years followed by divorce. The protagonist of the story differs radically from Pu, however, in having at one time joined the Communist Party, whereas Pu himself remained aloof at all times.

Whether partly autobiographical or not, the story is a further portrayal of alienation brought about by the public ostracism and humiliation by local communist officials, The protagonist's wife is metamorphosed, like a character from Kafka, not exactly into an enemy, but into an indifferent object.

A similar theme is pursued in "Reunion." Two men who were once colleagues and close friends feel constrained on meeting after a separation during the Communist takeover. They are afraid to express even perfunctory feelings to each other lest they be interpreted as counter-revolutionary. Their conversation resembles dialogue in the theatre of the absurd. Nothing is neutral. Even that which is apparently nonsensical or perplexing could be construed as dangerous. In this milieu, becoming "a Plato" means speaking cryptically or communicating exclusively by means of signs and glances.

The plethora of autobiographical details in "Silken Veil" indicates that the protagonist or voice of the entire collection is Pu himself. The year is 1951, but the perspective is of the 90s. As a consequence of the revolution, Pu is forced to move from his home by the side of the West Lake in Hangzhou to a district on the Grand Canal. Venturing one day to stroll in the neighborhood he chances upon a lane leading to a factory where its owner had just committed suicide. The authorities refused to allow any reporting of the death or funeral ceremonies of any kind since it was inconceivable that anyone would have wished to depart from the happy surroundings of the communist utopia. Suicide was considered a non-existent phenomenon under the "Silken Veil" of artificially imposed silence.

The further significance of the year 1951 is indicated in "The Duck's Tongue Cap," the Chinese expression for something of a baseball cap. Any departure in dress, behavior or speech from the imposed norm of the "Counter-Revolution-Suppression Movement" of that year would be instantly noticed and reprobated. Wearing a Western-style cap was an open violation of standardization, but as Pu's vision needed protection from direct sunshine and as no law had been specifically passed about headgear, he continued to wear his cap even after China had "come under new management." By so doing he became an octopus among a school of sharks.

Nostalgia is mixed with humor in a story about the year 1950, "Flower Play," the title referring to the impressions one may have of a flower or a woman. While still a bachelor Pu accompanies three young girls on an excursion by rowboat on the West Lake. The girls have little interest in anything but eating snacks although they listen attentively to tales that he tells for their amusement. Another humorous tale, "The Turtle," mixes farce with the macabre despite the accompanying theme of the shortage of food and services in Red China. A short man riding on a crowded tramway and carrying a live turtle is forced to hold it over his head to avoid the crush of standing bodies. The turtle bites the ear of a fellow passenger who is tall and thin. Since the turtle will not let go, both men are forced to make their way inch by inch through the packed tram to dismount. At a clinic the turtle is given an anesthetic, the victim is released, and the owner of the turtle pays the victim four days' wages for the medical attention. After his wife cooks the turtle, she and their two children lose consciousness because of the lingering anesthetic in the turtle's body. Apart from its humor, the story is intended to reveal the overcrowding of all public transportation of the time and the hunger and starvation in the countryside.

"A Type" has the same theme as "Reunion"—the blanket of silence imposed upon the nation—but it deals with an earlier period, the year 1956. In this story, members of the Communist Party are symbolized as a "type of steam." The protagonist is a "speechless person," so afflicted because of fears that any words that he utters may cause him trouble with the authorities. While visiting his relatives for a stay of several days, he listens, laughs, plays with the children, but never utters more than two or three intelligible words. In describing his psychological muteness, Pu serves as a belated spokesman for all the people in China who were also deprived of their speech by circumstances.

In a similar vein in "Onto the Bridge," he uses an engineering marvel to symbolize the effect of the political regime on his thoughts and behavior during his residence in Hangzhou. After balancing a description of a river from a sixth-century classic poet with his own metaphorically-charged prose, Pu explains that for a variety of personal and political reasons he had not ventured upon the bridge for a number of years. When he finally did so, he felt an exalted awareness of being free, but was almost immediately brought down to reality.

In "The Day Mao Died," Pu does not underscore the coincidence that the date of Mao's death, 9 September, was the same as that of his release from prison seven years previously in 1969. In addition to expressing his own joy and relief, he records that he encountered no tearful eyes on that eventful day. For him, Mao's demise symbolized his release from prison, and for the Chinese people the liberation from a reign of terror. In a flicker of humor, he remarks that Mao has gone to join Marx, destination unnamed.

Pu originally earned literary fame with two romantic novels published under the pseudonym Wu Ming Shi, which means literally Mr. No Name or Mr. Anonymous. Both novels were made into hit motion pictures in 1940s. These were followed by a massive contribution to serious literature, a six-volume narrative of epic proportions, combining philosophy, religion, visionary speculation, and all the human emotions, including love and sex. The literary style of this work, *Book Without a Title*, is Proustian in its versatility and sensitivity, and its protagonist rises to Faustian proportions in the quest for the meaning of life. Critics have compared the novel to the classic of Chinese fiction *Dream of the Red Chamber*, and it is generally considered as unique in modern times. Not a narrative of adventure or intrigue, *Book Without a Title* resembles the English *Everyman* and *Pilgrim's Progress* except for its epic proportions, its sophistication, and its philosophical depth. Each of the six volumes of the collection has a separate title. Since Pu is a great admirer of Mark Twain and other humorous writers, I interpret the paradoxical title of *Book Without a Title* at the head of a collection of six volumes, each with a carefully chosen title, as a huge practical joke. Pu himself has declared that he devised the name of the set as well as his own pseudonym because "anything nameless is long-lasting." Pu's penname Mr. Anonymous acquired a grim symbolic meaning during his years under Communist domination, for he refused to register as a member of the Writer's Association, even though by doing so he would have guaranteed for himself a small amount of income. During this entire period he supported himself almost entirely; supports derived from relatives outside the mainland were very limited. Pu, despite his label of Mr. Anonymous, presents a highly subjective view of existence. He hides his name, but exposes his heart. As a distinguished scholar, I-Chun Wang has said, Pu's "moral earnestness for a harmonious world is exhibited in his vision for a new territory based on love and beauty."

A Chinese expatriate now living in the United States, Xiao Xiaoda, was also locked up during the Cultural Revolution. His only offense was that at the age of 19 he wiped up a spilled drink with a poster bearing the likeness of Mao Zedong. As retaliation against his persecutors, Xiao has contributed short stories to the "Atlantic Monthly" and other journals reliving his prison ordeal. In an interview for the Associated Press, he reveals that he "writes for personal revenge, for the memory of others who died behind bars, and simply to tell the truth to the world." (Taipei *China News,* 9 November, 1995). Pu also writes to inform the world, but not at all with a spirit of revenge. He wants the rest of the world to be aware of what happened in China so that politicians and statesmen may learn from their mistakes. He preaches neither revenge nor forgiveness. In an indirect reflection of the Christian message, Pu wants his own suffering to be counted toward the future deliverance of humanity.

Although his books are filled with Christian symbols and metaphors, Pu is not a Christian himself. At the age of 20 he was introduced to Western religion. He has studied its historical influence in depth, has celebrated its ethics and borrowed its literary iconography, but has never adopted its theology. He is Buddhism-oriented and regularly practices Qigong, or slow motion calisthenics, one of the reasons for his outstanding health and mental agility at the current age eighty (that is, eighty when this book will presumably be published). He does not directly propose the dichotomy, but his writing suggests Buddhist resignation rather than revenge.

Despite the prevailing somber tone of Pu's stories and reminiscences, Pu today maintains a humorous outlook on life and an optimistic attitude toward the future of the China mainland. His record of personal suffering and national tragedy is intended as a historical record, not an outpouring of woe and defeat. Most importantly, it is a triumph of literary style and imagination.

A. Owen Aldridge
University of Illinois

Dr. Aldridge was formerly president of the American Association of Comparative Literature.

The Fossil

I

Night. Like an ebony dye, spreading out on a canvas to form an enormous bear's paw. It was as if Walt Disney's brush was at work.

The steamy darkness weighed heavily upon me and made me pant as if out of breath. I had to lie down, to stretch out and embrace sleep in my five-foot long, coir-rope bed. My sleeping place was my refuge in an overly large universe that revealed itself every evening.

It was summer. At this time every evening, I had to recline at the side of a large fossil which emanated a cold that permeated my body. The petrified object I refer to is a woman. This woman is my——wife. When I wrote this word, I felt compelled to first draw a long dash. But I hesitated as my pen formed the line. Should I have written it this way?

It was the two-year anniversary of her fossilization.

There was no special celebration. In fact, my own commemoration was the result of beginning to view my wife in this way, a realization that has battered my subconscious mind like a violent surf. She had not spoken one word to me in the past two years, not even a "Hmm" of acknowledgement. She had achieved a level of silence more complete than what existed at the bottom of the Dead Sea that brushed past the shores of Palestine. A stillness more complete than that portrayed in Arnold Bocklin's famous painting "Dead Island." It was as if she wished to use this muteness to smother me, to stop the irritating sound of my breathing.

Women who are both attractive and compulsively clean are sometimes the most subtle of snares. You do not dare to disturb their rigidly imposed order, like a fly fearing to alight on a peony, or a mosquito recoiling before a lotus. Those who aggressively maintain silent surroundings are no different. You are unwilling to break the pristine quiet for fear of fatally wounding them. My wife's silence, however, was not pathological. It was an incredible act that became real with the passage of time. The palpable silence was what frightened me. This is when I began to feel that she had become a fossil, like those of the Triassic dinosaurs and their aquatic predecessors.

This fossil was quite different from the "Husband-Watching Rock" in Hubei Province, which has passed into Chinese folklore. The latter represents a hallowed object, a testament to the endurance of love. The former, something utterly inimical.

This was no fiction. For two whole years, it seemed like the family had been a captive audience at the openings of innumerable exhibitions of petrified curiosities.

Faced with gallery upon gallery of sights at these exhibitions, I was forced to develop a particular skill. Before long, I was the most experienced of collectors. Not of antiques, but of sufferings. To each of these was attached the image of a particular fossil, the ghost of something that was once alive. And I hid them deeply—deep enough so that no one else would discover them.

That night, the exhibition of the human fossils was celebrating its two-year anniversary.

I should have had some way of memorializing the event. It just so happened that it was the seventh day of the seventh month according to the Lunar Calendar—Chinese Valentine's Day. The day when the constellations formed the legendary magpie bridge, allowing the spinning maid and the cowherd to spend their one precious night together. This cowherd was lying next to his gelid spinning maid. Her wintry aura was my only indulgence. Even in her deepest sleep she continued to emanate a benumbing chill. It was little wonder that I awoke frequently, awash in her vapors.

It was a torrid night. The autumn tiger (a spell of hot weather after the beginning of autumn) had chased back the cooler weather. Summer would not pass very easily. The fossil's presence, however, created an atmosphere which covered me in cold sweat. About an hour earlier, that giant bear's paw had penetrated the room and pressed down on me until I convulsed for lack of air. I could stand it no longer! I reached over and turned the light on. A dim light shone on her fine, pale face, and her breasts which rose slowly with each breath. I glared at her with increasing anger. The light disturbed her sleep and I could see that she had awoken. Like so many times before, however, she just lay there with her eyes shut. My fury had passed the point of tolerance. I tore at the porcelain buttons on her silken undershirt and exposed the two large persimmons that lay beneath, and then pulled off her panties. I quickly shed my own clothing and climbed on to her body, like some kind of feral beast.

History was repeating itself. I cannot count the times that we had reenacted this primeval mating dance. She was always like an automaton, her only movements being those that I created. Even if bedewed at the approach of a climax, she would lie there like a stone, as still as I was frenzied. She made only one voluntary movement: no matter how wildly I kissed her, she would clamp her teeth and lips tightly together, never allowing my tongue to touch her own.

I was not yielding to sensual pleasures. It was just a means of releasing the built-up pain, a means of revenge.

Every time I lay on her body I felt like a lecher, as if I were raping a recently expired body.

I wanted revenge.

Maybe this vengeful episode was my pleasure. Maybe it was my way of commemorating our time together. All my actions to this point, however, appeared to be just fruitless attempts at assailing the enemy's fortifications, like Don Quixote attacking his windmills.

Her soft body and my virility. They did not complement each other. We were both covered with sweat and she was panting faintly. This was the first and only sound she emitted for me. Only at this particular moment did she reveal a glimpse of her humanity.

Damn it! The rock had finally emitted a sound!

All this time I had been waiting for a sound.

I continued my actions with renewed fervor. That night, I was incensed.

My body was surging with adrenaline. I was like a stallion bolting into an open field. I climaxed three times that night. I wanted to commemorate that damn anniversary—that damn rendezvous on the magpie bridge.

I had to retaliate.

I had ridden the crests of the waves and was soon washed ashore. I finally collapsed on her and lay silently, as silently as she. I, too, was fossilized. My heart felt as if it had been consumed in a fire.

Suddenly, I burst out in tears.

II

I remember our days together too, though she was the same, irrespective of the location of the sun. She forced me to imbibe the Dead Sea's mordant water. I knew I had to struggle to avoid going adrift on this lifeless pool. To see more than the occasional shards of past life floating by.

"Mama! Today's the first day of the Lunar New Year! Are we going to Grandmother's house to celebrate?" said little Congcong, my daughter and a sixth grader. She had excitedly bounded into our room at the first light of dawn to ask this question, rattling her pigtails as she spoke.

My wife glanced out at the courtyard. It had finally stopped raining. She nodded her head at Congcong and emitted a faint "Mmm" of agreement.

Mingming, my other daughter, then added in a soft voice, "Are we going to take Papa?" She was in the fifth grade. She stood there, waiting for my wife's reply, her eyes wide with curiosity.

My wife leaned over and whispered something in Mingming's ear. I knew the meaning of these secretive actions. Before Mingming left the room, she made a face at me. This wasn't the face of a daughter flirting with her father. It had the effect of a slap in the face.

My wife seemed to have anticipated the consequences of Mingming's actions. My blood had surged to my face. I could feel my skin growing warm. She forced herself to look at me. At seeing my reaction, I could have sworn that her face momentarily lost its adamantine sternness.

Maybe she realized that this was a special moment—something out of the ordinary. I truly thought that I had seen the faint spirit of a smile brush past her cheeks. In one long year, she seemed to have allowed herself a three-second surrender to humor. This was my New Year's Day gift.

Deep inside, I knew that smiles could be flowers or deadly poison. Many people had willingly fallen before this kind of deception. I did not wish to be one of those. The poison in this woman's glass, however, was not very potent. But it was still poison, because it was used arbitrarily, outrageously, and often kept hidden from view.

Out on the street, every person thought himself a champion or a philosopher, full of Socratic confidence and a Napoleonic eagerness. Most of those I observed, however, were forced into these roles.

It was now five months and eighteen days after the two-year anniversary of our home's fossil exhibition. About nine hundred days in all. Every weekend or public holiday, I would depart from the village commune in Lin An County to go to my home in Hangzhou. I should have been enjoying a day or so of "homely" warmth but in truth had no choice but to return to Lin An and take my role as veteran visitor of the permanent show.

My house seemed like a vast cemetery, somehow imbued by life. The tomb-like, oozing silence was an earthly punishment for me. It seemed to pierce my veins and enter my bloodstream, overwhelming my whole body. At this time of year—during the Lunar New Year, most families were gathering around the table for celebrations. The moribund silence was the trademark of our holidays, another gift to me. The house, so crypt, was filled with a silence potent enough to fill my soul with dreadful expectations. I expected a hair-raising sound to issue forth from the place at any moment.

The person creating this atmosphere and these feelings did not contemplate the serious results of her actions—and their scarring effects on the children.

The day before, on New Year's Day, while other families were reunited for the annual feast, my family was making a similar attempt. I looked around our table, at the dishes placed there, and filled a little glass with wine and placed it in front of my wife. Then I filled my own.

"Yaling," I said, "I apologize. I have made a mistake and you have had to suffer the consequences. I have burdened you with taking care of our home, our children, all by yourself. Thank you for your patience and diligence. I'll try to change my views of the world—of society. My labors on the village team have been promising. I hope to be able to regain the trust of my comrades, to be able to finally discard the bad name I've been given." [1]

I stared at her delicate face and said, "Tomorrow is New Year's Day and our family is finally sitting together at the table. Let's drink a toast to the health of you and the children—and to my early release from my labors!"

She continued to eat, not making a noise. It was as if she hadn't heard a word that I said. She pushed the glass to one side.

She may have been trying to dampen my spirits, but my heart had already been reinforced against most of such attacks. I turned toward the children and dried my glass.

"Congcong! Mingming! Papa's drunk a toast to your health, to the New Year, and to your studies! How about wishing Papa an early release from his labors!?"

---

[1] The narrator of the story had been criticized by the Chinese Communist Party and subjected to reform through labor.

The two children glanced at their mother, and then at each other. They made no sound and simply returned to their eating, shoveling the rice into their mouths.

Two minutes later, I collapsed on a nearby bed and let the tears stream down my face.

The three of them remained seated at the table, silently eating their New Year's meal.

The next morning, after we had all had a cup of brown sugar tea and a bowl of New Year's soup, the three of them went out to make their holiday round of visits. I knew that none of the households were welcoming someone branded with the label of "anti-communist." My going out to make New Year's visits would be taken as a sort of malicious joke, like calling the funeral home to have the hearse driven over to the house of someone you hated.

In college I had studied biology. I spent New Year's Day reading Darwin's essays to kill the time. His essays served as a sort of salve on my wounds, temporarily soothing my nerves and calming my emotions. The night before, I had had my fill of the bitter salt from my tears. I couldn't bear that taste again. I wasn't willing to acknowledge that I was like a young girl who suffered continual indignities at the hands of others. But it was always this way.

I had, after all, already endured almost two and half years of these harms. New Year's Day was like any other. And time was just an insult. Willing or not, I had to learn to live with my fossil.

Early the following morning, I had breakfast with her. At lunch and dinner, I was staring at her cold exterior. On the bed, she was a fossil. Out of bed, still a fossil. There was not a minute of the day that she fell out of her role. The impenetrable lack of noise that she maintained could outdo that achieved by the rocks that lay in the fields nearby. But even the cliffs at the seashore, in contrast, were able to echo the sounds of the wind and surf. While at home, she and the children rarely spoke a word. When they did speak, it was only in a muffled whisper.

As soon as I returned home, the whole house fell mute! The children had been taught well.

She was the director of each of the household drama. Our two daughters obeyed her every word. I imagine that, if I were absent from the scene, our traditional-style house—measuring only seventeen square-meters and surrounded on all sides by other households—would be bubbling over with happy sounds. Children are naturally free-spirited and full of vitality, like young saplings growing in the forest.

Let me be present, however, and I affected my surroundings like a carrier of scarlet fever. The three females who were originally glowing with life, lost their natural ebullience when I was near. My surroundings took on the guise of a somber, autumn landscape, impressing the viewer with the feeling of faded vigor and a foreboding of bitter days ahead. What shocked me to the core was how my children, having just shed the down of their infancy, observed a mode of conduct worthy of the young members of England's Royal Family.

It was difficult to not feel some respect for the "carpet bombing" approach of China's ideological training at that time. That sort of sweeping attack could be devastating enough to reduce all of Berlin's gothic edifices to rubble; it was capable of producing effects much worse than those exhibited by my wife! It had already leveled centuries of the ingrained traditions and social concepts of millions of Chinese. Even elementary students were taking part in games of "seek out the Taiwan spy." Simply directing the occasional smirk at an anticommunist like me amounted to commonplace etiquette.

My memory is still imprinted with images of so-called "anticommunist" being pelted by rocks thrown by elementary school children as they passed the school entrance way.

But my children were the products of my wife's own educational system. Yaling had expended great effort in preserving a fair and reasonable atmosphere during the successive fossil exhibitions at our house. She had been an elementary school teacher, and Congcong had been one of her students. It was not difficult, therefore, to get the children to act according to her directions. I could perceive that, in order to suppress the children's innate reactions to the world around them, their mother had no choice but to incessantly threaten them—to frighten them into total compliance.

This kind of treatment was necessary because they still loved their papa. Even though their mother meant the world to them, the thread that bound together as family refused to unravel. As soon as Yaling left the house, the children would drop their guard and visibly soften toward me. One day, I held Mingming in my arms and said softly, "Didn't you used to love to go with papa to play at the park by the West Lake? We haven't gone there in over two years! How about my taking you and Congcong there right now?"

Eleven year-old Mingming widened her lively black eyes and looked at me warmly, perhaps even a little anxiously, and then glanced at her elder sister's round face from the corners of her eyes. Her expression belied any malevolent purpose. These simple motions had thawed the film of frost that normally obscured her spirited features. She then said in a hushed tone, "Papa, I want to go with you, but Mama—"

Her voice trailed off without forming the words that should have finished her sentence. Just then, Yaling returned from the market. Mingming sprang up and headed for the courtyard. I couldn't stop a tear or two from trailing down my cheek. When she spoke the word "papa," it seemed so natural, sweet and pure. This was a pleasure that I longed for, but scarcely experienced.

More than equal to this great pleasure were my constant sufferings. Even though Yaling fulfilled all of her wifely responsibilities, she did so in a way that left me with the feeling that my tonsils were being abraded with a huge toothbrush. She also displayed the obedience of a camel, completing each task with a steely countenance. The abrasion continued, and was becoming unbearable. She washed and mended my clothes, bought and cooked my food, cleaned my dishes. She did all that a traditional wife in a Chinese family was supposed to do. I used to work for the Government, in a cultural organization situated in Hangzhou. I was a middle-level cadre and earned a comfortable salary. I was later sent to a Lin An village to undergo labor reform. My earnings dropped to a meager 30.00 yuans (about US$ 10.00 by the then exchange rate) a month for living expenses. I was set on giving Yaling one-half of this amount but she would only take 10.00 yuans. She preferred to use the 40.00 yuans she made as an elementary school teacher to support the household. This attitude—or way of thinking, perfectly complemented her fossilized physiognomy.

Her large eyes rarely looked at me, as if I were a non-existence. If she was compelled to communicate with me, she was not even willing to use sign language. Instead, she wrote her words to me down on a piece of paper with a pencil.

"Mrs. Huang, the Team Head of Public Security from next door wishes to speak with you. Go see what she wants."

"Someone at the Police Bureau wants to speak with you. Go see what they want."

"Go and buy a jin (roughly a pound) of soy sauce and a jin of salt."

"Take the bowl of braised pork with preserved vegetable in the cupboard to work."

"Give me your seal."

"I washed the winter clothes. They are in the bottom drawer of the bureau."

Sometimes, she merely asked one of the children to relay her speech to me.

I had gradually become accustomed to letting my visual organs substitute for my aural senses. If I suddenly found myself in the North Pole, I would be forced to communicate with the natives by means of body language or pictures scratched on paper or wood. In my own special circumstances, I could only try my best to refrain from speaking, and only vocally express myself when all other attempts at communication failed. A sense of self-respect is normally like a scalpel, able to remove tumors of the soul—and the aberrant growth of communication. I had no such instrument. The children and I grew gradually further apart. If we didn't, my suffering would just have increased. I had to forgive them for their ignorance. Even their mother was unable to handle the pressures and temptations of the era. How could they?

III

Sometimes our passions take on the role of a steamer trunk, packed with provisions to help us cope with the needs of life's travels. The contents don't necessarily have to be of practical use. Some may simply be packed to nurture the spirit. The illusory antibiotics, painkillers, creme-filled cookies and fresh fruit juices may help temporarily ease the wounds of the heart, but they are still unable to allay the disease, pain, hunger and thirst of our journeys in the real world.

My miseries at that time, however, were more than a match for anything in my own steamer trunk. I really had no use for such a thing. Soon, I discarded it. When I returned to my house on the weekend, her presence surrounded me again like the walls of an ice cellar, and the children averted their eyes. At these times, the symbolic banishment of my trunk seemed to help placate my spleen. Long past midnight, I sat listening to my heart bleed, and talked to myself silently.

Though painful and melancholy, I had to return from my labors in the country to this very real and permanent place each weekend. Gold is still gold, whether in its purest or an alloy. My family was of the alloy type. But it was still a family.

After returning home from six days of slavery in the fields, I felt that I was freed from at least some of my shackles. Even though my entrance was accompanied by the usual frosty disregard, I was still able to vicariously enjoy the inner warmth that still passed between mother and children—long after the umbilical cords had been broken. This was truly my last refuge. Without this familial hostel, the world would have to tolerate the existence of another of life's orphans, a spiritual nomad.

Threatened by the steely exteriors of the large and small fossils in my home, my only defense was to be equally as adamantine.

Even under these circumstances, I patiently nurtured the spark of a hope—that one day my fossilized wife would resurrect, and speak to me.

My glimmer of hope was constantly on the verge of fading to ash. The problem lay not with the fossil herself, but the thin wooden walls of our house and the carefully watched courtyard outside. We shared the right wall of our home with Mrs. Huang, the Team Head of Public Security. I can remember her standing outside, with her legs slightly bent. She was a corpulent woman many years my elder. She reminded me of Old Mistress Wang in the classic *Outlaws of the Marsh*, who liked nothing more than to meddle in other's affairs. Every time she saw me returning from my country labors, she would run over to speak with me, to "understand" how things were going with me—and my family. Each of these "understandings" lasted at least twenty minutes, or the time it took to smoke two good cigarettes and drink a cup of Dragon Well tea.

China has three major traditional holidays, all falling on specific days of the Lunar Calendar. These are the Mid-Autumn, the New Year's and the Dragon Boat festivals. On each of these days, I naturally had to pay my respect to our inquisitive cadre, "Mistress" Huang. Even though the walls which separated our two dwellings appeared to be of solid wood, they might as well have been thin sheets of gauze. Even if those in our house took care to speak in a barely audible whisper, like hens reciting Buddhist scriptures, each word could be heard next door with the clarity of a ringing bell.

Mistress Huang had a son and a daughter-in-law. They had a big one-room house the size of ours, but it apparently was not big enough for them. As a result, she followed the examples of those imperialists whose faults she kept criticizing to expand the territory. She and her family occupied a fifteen square-meter piece of land abutting the east end of our courtyard to build another tiny dwelling. The neighbors dubbed the building "the Earth God Temple."

In this "temple," "Mistress" Huang's son and daughter-in-law placed a small, coir-rope bed. There was nothing wrong with the bed, but when the husband and wife opened their window which looked out over the courtyard and onto the front of our abode, we were allowed no privacy. "The Earth God Temple" seemed to have taken on the disturbing appearance of a sentry post.

Things soon turned for the worse. On our left lived the Zhangs. They were all model workers from the Du Jinsheng Silk Factory, and respected members of the Communist Party. A rough wooden wall also separated the living quarters of our two families. Menacingly, these boards afforded us the privacy of a patchwork of newspapers.

It was as if any of the words uttered by a member of my family were immediately packed into a truck and transported into the next household. And the conversations that took place in our neighbor's homes were like missiles that routinely intruded upon our living space. Not much time had passed before the Zhangs also captured a small area of land bordering the courtyard to afford some of their family members a little breathing space. The new "Earth God Temple" became a complementary sentry post, which could observe in great detail every event that occurred in our house.

One day, a sense of foreboding fell over the dwellings that encircled the courtyard. The local police and the neighborhood cadres had gathered at the Huang residence. I returned home that evening and was overcome with a familiar, sickening fear. So many eyes and ears, like an impressive radar installation, were focused on me—the sole target.

Two families—all respected laborers—lived above us. The addition of the two new "Earth God Temples" to the courtyard had blocked all but one means of egress for these families. Therefore, whenever a family member had to leave the house, the only open ground left for them to walk to and from their errands was located right in front of our door. Living under such intense scrutiny, the urge to move was naturally very strong. But such an action was impossible. Not only was our abode "government property," but we had no recognizable reason for moving! Moreover, as soon as we mentioned the word "move," we would elicit the intense suspicion of our neighbors and so place ourselves in an even more uncomfortable and dangerous position.

In this atmosphere, it was of course not surprising that Yaling assumed her fossil-like disguise. But I felt that she had gone too far. She was overreacting to these pressures and experiencing horrors where fears would suffice. The devil just asked for her nose, but she had offered him her whole face. Yaling had come to equate the wrenching of my heart, my sufferings, with a kind of security. I can hardly imagine how I felt and coped with such fossilization in my first few weekly home-returns about two years ago.

At the beginning of the fossilization, things were vague and desensitized with Yaling. Gradually I came to realize the reasons for her odd behavior. I couldn't help feeling astonishment. But my surprise soon gave way to anger.

One day after dinner, my Vesuvious erupted.

"Yaling! Yaling! Yaling! What's wrong with you? Are you a mute? Are you human? Are you a vegetable? Or a rock? Why haven't you spoken a word all day? Not even reply to one question? You've been playing dumb each time I've returned home for three weeks now! What's the matter with you! You're as unresponsive as a boulder! Did I do something wrong? Tell me what day, what time, I did something that made you react this way! Tell me! Tell me!!"

I shook her violently. Her delicate body looked like a small shrub buffeted by a storm. I could feel that she was frightened.

As before, she remained taciturn—a fossil.

No matter how I jolted her body, she kept her silence.

My cheeks were flushed with the heat of passion. I couldn't stand it any longer! I lashed out and slapped her twice across the cheeks, muttering "Goddamnit!" under my breath.

Silence.

No sob escaped her lips. I didn't even see the misty beginnings of a teardrop. She had somehow developed an infrangible resolution.

I couldn't hit and curse at her again. It didn't matter in any case. She was a first-rate student of Ghandi's school of passive resistance. And I lost every battle. I could not continue my offensive attacks. Neighbors on each side were her allies in disguise. If they discovered my hot-headed actions, a disaster would ensue. No matter how I looked at it, her rigid silence was my private anguish. If a neighborly "cataclysm" truly occurred, my suffering would be many times worse. Her silence actually saved me during those outbreaks of domestic violence.

The households to the left and right of our own were actually tiger's dens and snake's nests. I had to be careful not to beat the grass and startle the snakes, or lure the tigers from their dens.

Our confrontation continued, painfully, for two hours in all—without any result. Then I broke down and cried, quietly. I was exhausted. I had labored in the country for six days, only to return home and labor again. It was too much. No more! At day break I had to rush to the countryside to toil again.

IV

Memories are like anesthetics, suppressing emotional hunger pains.

In the summer that I met Yaling, Zhejiang University had just let out for summer vacation. I had taken refuge in my uncle's simple tiled house located near the Mist and Cloud Cave of the Southern Mountain. I wanted to lose myself in the invigorating mists of the highlands.

I had been studying at the University for three years. Even though through two of those years the nation had been submerged in the blood of the Sino-Japanese War, I was safe from the fray. My alma mater hugged the Full Moon Mountain on the right side and girded by the Flourishing Springtime River on the left. The billowing peaks and threadlike waterways were like frame after frame of far-off scenes painted with other worldly colors. I felt like I was sailing away on the billowing clouds. I was in some immortal land, like one of the Chinese gods, holding a holy scroll. Even in the intolerable heat of summer, the area around the Mist and Cloud Cave was cooled by the underground vapors. Sometimes, before sunrise, I would hike up to the peak of the South Mountain and let my eyes slowly take in the West Lake's nine thousand plus acres of emerald water. I also often passed into the Stone House Cave's inky darkness, and went spelunking, or just observed the strange white bats that hung among the stalactites. I can still hear the music created by the cascading waters of the Happy Water Cave as they ricocheted against the golden stones. The rocks were like Vulcan's drums and Persephone's bells, creating a rhythm that was moving, yet peaceful.

I was happiest when, at daybreak, I could take a brisk walk along the small, undulating mountain path that took me over the Weng Family Mountain and down into the valley of the Lion Peak, all the way to the Dragon Well Temple. In the Temple was a square pool from which the holy site got its name. The pool was decorated with a stone dragon's head. Pure, invigorating water continually spouted from the beast's mouth. Tiny, red lizards thrived in the pool's waters. The monks called these "little dragons." I liked nothing better than to stand on the large, man-made rock formations which decorated the area around the Dragon Well and sing. My repertoire consisted mainly of western songs popular at that time, like "Home Sweet Home," "My Old Kentucky Home," "The Last Rose of Summer," and "Ave Maria" etc. These were songs that never seemed old or common-place no matter how many times I repeated their lyrics. In college, I was known for my melodious voice.

I saw her early that morning when I had just finished my song. She appeared suddenly from among the man-made rockeries. I immediately bounded down from my lofty stage.

"I hope I didn't scare you! I just walked over to enjoy your beautiful singing." She smiled as she said this.

She had a petit, oval face that perfectly complemented her delicate figure. There was an alluring and refreshing feeling about her. Her large, raven-black eyes mesmerized me, like the undisturbed surface of a pond in the twilight. Her every word and movement was unfettered by feigned shyness. I felt immediately at ease.

"Aren't you afraid of being bitten by snakes, hiding in the crags of these mountains so early in the morning?" I asked her softly.

She grinned and replied, "I arrived at daybreak. You come here every day to practice, don't you? Before you arrived, I decided to slip into the cave and listen to your songs. In any case, this is a temple; no snake would dare linger on holy ground! After listening for a while, I found your singing has grown all the more beautiful." She laughed lightly as she said, "I thought perhaps I'd enjoy the songs even more if I listened to them in the light of day...."

She lived with her family in the district bordering the temple. She often took early morning strolls that took her through the temple grounds. She had heard my singing many times before, but had at first thought it best to keep out of sight. Thus, as of last week, she started secreting herself in the cave to await her private concerts. Then that morning arrived, when she was listening to my strains of Shubert's "Ave Maria," and she was suddenly overcome with emotion. Unawares, she had revealed her presence to me. She spoke in an unaffected, clear tone of voice that left me stunned. Her words flowed freely, like the waters that filled the mountain streams around us.

Our small talk slowly resulted in the exchange of introductions. I found out that, next semester, Yaling would be a junior at the Hong Dao Girl's High School.

"To commemorate our first meeting, I'd like to sing for you. You pick the song." I said to her.

She answered, "Sing whatever you wish. All the songs you sing are classics from the West. They're all beautiful. There's no need for me to choose."

I sang a time-honored love song from Flotow's famous opera, Martha.

After I finished, I explained the meaning of the German lyrics to her. At first, her face remained serene and pale. I soon noticed, however, the faint tinge of a blush fill the edges of her cheeks.

I sang three more songs before escorting her home. She asked me to stop and took her leave when we were about two hundred meters from the door of her family's Western-style house.

The evocative strains of a piece of classical, expressive music can transport the listener into an illusory realm. It was summertime. Every scene from our first meeting seemed to have been taken right from Mendelssohn's "Midsummer Night's Dream." I felt like we had acted out "Scherzo," "March of the Fairies," "Ye Spotted Snakes," "Nocturne," "Dance of the Clown," and "Wedding March."

After that day, we continued our meetings. Failing to appear only if the weather had forced us to stay home. My songs were our conversations and our strolls an indispensable accompaniment. After summer turned to autumn, and the school year started afresh, our meetings still continued. But we met every week or two, on Saturday morning or afternoon, and sat together for a few hours, enjoying the beauty of the West Lake's scenery.

In the district where she lived, you still had to rely on pedicabs or rickshaws for transportation. They would take you at bone-bruising speed along the narrow paths that ran along the mountain streams.

Her father was a wealthy tea merchant. His tea plantations were located on a nearby mountain. By living in the Dragon Well district, he was able to effectively oversee his business operations. He owned a large, old, Western-type car, which he cared for meticulously. Still, when he had errands to run, he would take a pedicab, or the bus which stopped at Nine Springs.

In the city, she had an uncle who owned a jewelry shop. He lived in a Western-style home, larger than her own. He lent two of the rooms to her father to use as offices.

One Saturday, as we had made plans to go to the movies, she gave her parents some excuse for staying out that evening. When the movie got out, it was already too late to return home. She stayed at her uncle's house, and left for Dragon Well the next morning.

About a month and a half later, the time of year arrived when the air was filled with the heady scent of cassia blooms. I remember sitting in Cassia Pavilion on a Tuesday afternoon. The Pavilion was located at the foot of the mountain, beneath the opening of the Mist and Cloud Cave. We ate bowls of the area's famous broth, filled with chestnuts and sweet osmanthus, and then walked through the groves of thickly packed and fragrant osmanthus trees.

As we strolled, the air would sometimes be filled with the pungent, earthy scent of the golden chestnut trees. After we emerged from the coppice, we followed the rising land to the South Peak and looked out on the majestic vista of the West Lake that had unfolded below us.

I sang one or two lines from the song "Rainbow on the River."

"Let us hold hands and stroll by the ripples...."

I warmly grasped her slender hand and noticed that her cheeks were blushed like harvest apples.

The following week, on the eve of the Mid-Autumn Festival, we went boating on the West Lake. I pulled the boat to shore near the Center Lake Pavilion. The moonlight shone on the many pointed little boats that were moored in a row along the water's edge. In that light, the shoreline looked as if it were sporting a silvery butterfly skirt. The boat-mistresses, who made a living plying couples back and forth across the lake, were exercising great tact. One would turn in our direction for only a second and then, realizing the sensitivity of the moment, go back to their business.

I sang Shubert's Serenade. As the last lyric faded into the night, I leaned over, bringing my face close to hers.

"Are you afraid?" I asked.

She just waved her finger slowly, expressing that she was not.

I put my arms around her and held her closely, and then kissed her.

In May of the next year, the time when green finches filled the air south of the Yangtze River, I felt especially carefree. My studies progressed without difficulty, and I felt that I would not have trouble with my graduate exams. She and I still found time to relax and revel in nature's embrace. Our surroundings were so overpoweringly beautiful that we had to hold each other to keep from falling down, intoxicated by what we saw. We became hopelessly addicted, returning often to toast the creator of this awe-inspiring landscape.

One day that month, after visiting famous spots such as Solitary Hill, Crane-Releasing Pavilion and Autumn Moon on the Calm Lake, we lingered on the grass at the foot of the Solitary Hill, surrounded by a ring of peach trees, finding it hard to leave the wonders we had seen that day. We had lost our sense of time, and day quickly passed into deep night.

It felt like we were floating among the soft and soothing vapors of a universe that was pulsing with the stirring melodies of our increasing ardor.

Youth is sometimes like a spout of fire, like Stravinsky's Fire Bird, creating a conflagration wherever it alights. The two of us had ignited and the sparks from our fire shot into the heavens. I felt like I had been drawn into a magnetic field and could no longer resist its pull. I thought I had taken on the form of a Tanganyika lion as we joined body and soul on the wild grasses.

It was very late when we lay in each other's arms, resting from the night's passion. She didn't return to her Uncle's house. We stayed at an inn for what remained of the hours before dawn.

V

The modern-day Adam and Eve had tasted their apple and immediately wanted more.

The world was sadly lacking a means, however, by which a secret could be safeguarded—eternally.

Her father was soon aware of the fact that she sometimes did not return to her uncle's house until the early hours of the morning, if she returned at all. After making this discovery, he began to slyly observe his daughter's every move, her expressions, and the way she carried herself about the household. He thought himself quite knowledgeable in the affairs of young hearts. It was not long before he had decided that there was indeed something different about his daughter. One day, he hired someone to keep track of her weekend travels. At long last, he was to receive proof of my existence.

Her father reacted to this information with remarkable alacrity. The very next weekend, on some excuse, he forbade Yaling to stay at her uncle's on the weekends.

Yaling soon graduated from High School. After the ceremony, her father suddenly confronted her with the details of her relationship with me. It was like a thunderclap. Both father and mother disclosed their knowledge of what they deemed was disgraceful conduct. Yaling was given an ultimatum in which she was to observe the ways of a filial daughter in the future and consent to the match that her parents had arranged. Her parents informed her that her future husband was to be the son of a wealthy milliner. He had attended Shanghai Technical College and was next-in-line to take over the family business. They also assured her that his family background was many times more dignified than that of "the other boy's," with his poor, commonplace, middle-school teacher of a father. They contended that the milliner's son was the best-match for the daughter of a well-to-do tea merchant.

At that point, it appeared that we would have to go our separate ways.

Her father then announced her punishments. The worst of all came first. She was to be married to the promising young milliner's son in three or so months, on October 10, the National Day. Second, she was to be incarcerated in the family house until the day of her marriage. The whole family, including the house servants, were to help enforce her sequestration.

Luckily, her younger sister Qiaoling was sensitive to her sufferings. Qiaoling was true to her sister and had a valiant heart. She was eighteen, two years younger than Yaling.

Qiaoling understood the transcendent forces of the universe, such as the growth of love between a man and a woman. She knew that the love that both Yaling and I shared had reached its apex. It represented a burning pine whose glow was a beacon for all to see.

Qiaoling found the opportunity to inform Yaling that she was willing to be her "Red Maid," the character from the classic novel *Romance of the Western Chamber*, who helped her mistress rendezvous with her forbidden lover.

Like the Chinese knights errant of old, I felt that my sword stood ready at the table, and was glowing with an anticipatory magic. I had no choice but to join this battle and return victorious. Any other scenario was unthinkable. I had to meet this challenge, to see this barbaric contest through to the end.

I could not harness my charging emotions. I sat down and wrote a lengthy letter to Yaling, expressing my undying love for her. This missive would only enhance the already strong sense of rebellion that was simmering within Yaling. Shortly after finishing the letter, I began planning a means of escape.

Three days later, after Yaling secretly received my letter, she knelt perfectly rigid before her parents. Weeping, she said, "Mother, Father, I apologize for all the troubles I have caused you during my upbringing; for deceiving you; for not telling you about my meetings with Mr. Shen. I have been reflecting on my conduct for many days now. I realize that I have not acted as a woman of this family should have. From now on, things will be different. I will try my best to be a filial daughter. I hope with all my heart that mother and father will give me the chance to prove my change of heart."

She went on in this self-deprecating fashion for an hour or so, both she and her mother shedding bitter tears.

Her father showed no signs of compassion. He just rubbed the Japanese-style beard that grew on his plump face. Finally, he spoke, "Well—I'm glad you feel that way. But you'll have to follow up these words with actions!"

She soon altered the inspiriting chrysalis that represented her playful, ingenuous and stubborn youth, making it an unassuming, conventional shell, protecting her from predators. She used to be an excellent actress. As a member of the school's drama club, she would always excel in the role of the lead character. My presence at this period of time would illuminate her life like the burning fires of the Solar System. My inspiration and her nascent talent easily changed a Catherina de Siena from Shakespeare's *Taming of the Shrew*, into Othello's dutiful Desdenona.

She no longer read the popular novels of the period. She now concentrated on the Chinese classics, mostly annotated versions of Confucius and Mencius, as well as the *Canon of Filial Piety*, translated into the common speech. She made a point of asking her sister to buy a copy of the Yuan Dynasty book *The Twenty Four Examples of Filial Piety*. She was like a tiny field mouse, watching and waiting patiently for the right opportunity to move. At the time of year when the air was stiflingly hot, her father would return from work with his body issuing heat like a dumpling-steamer. As soon as he entered the house, she would take off his Panama hat and his shirt, give him a cool towel and cup of tea, turn on the ceiling fan and hand over his grass sandals.

She would appear and disappear without a sound, all the time discreetly assessing her father's mood, his expressions and his reactions to her tending of his needs. She was so thorough in caring for her father that the family's servants were able to enjoy more than the normal share of idle moments.

She often acted as if she was very dissatisfied with the work of the household help. In order to assure that her parent's sleep was undisturbed by the biting of mosquitoes, flies, lice, bedbugs and other pests, she took it upon herself to spray her parent's room, as well as the rest of the house, with DDT. She used a stepladder and covered even the ceiling with the pesticide. When she finished, the tears were streaming from her eyes as a result of the potent chemicals.

She never displayed any anger to the family's servants, but always spoke respectfully and with a smile.

One day she was pacing to and fro in the courtyard, and had just passed by the opening of the family's large, black-lacquer front gate, when he heard a voice from Ah Gao, the family porter, who came out from nowhere.

"Mistress! Don't open the door!"

"I'm sorry, Ah Gao. I was only admiring the canna lilies over there. I was not going to open the front gate. Thank you for your concern."

She had been acting like this and living under these conditions for a month when her father looked at her one night and again began rubbing his carefully groomed Japanese-style beard.

Softly, almost under his breath, he said to his wife, "Yaling is truly the daughter of a wealthy household. She has the grace and bearing that befits a lady."

Her mother replied, "Our little Ling-ling has always listened to us. You're treating her like a convict! I never agreed with your method of punishment."

Ah Gao then whispered to the cook, and some other servants, "You couldn't find a filial daughter like Mistress even if you lit a lantern and searched every alleyway in Hangzhou!"

It goes without saying that Qiaoling supported her sister's master performance with incredible stealth.

On the seventh day of the seventh month in the Lunar Calendar, families in China were observing the Zhongyuan Ghost Festival. This was the day when Yama, the god in the Underworld, opened the gates of Hell and allowed the ghosts to walk the earth. Buddhists knew this as the day when the dead followed no divine rules, and the world of man became their playground. Yaling's family had been practicing Buddhists for many generations. Her father and mother, therefore, made their annual trip to the Ling Yin Temple to observe the ritual Buddhist rights for the ghost festival. The service at the temple consisted mostly of the placing of fresh flowers and fruits, etc., on the sacrificial altar in front of the shrine's deities. In addition, the worshippers would make donations to the temple and ask that the monks recite the appropriate scriptures for the festival, aiding those ghosts that have no family members to see to their needs in the afterlife to be released from Hell and achieve a speedy reincarnation.

After a long, weary day of worship, her parents returned home. That evening, the cook prepared a vegetarian repast for the whole family, including the servants.

Qiaoling opened two bottles of vintage rice wine made in Shaoxing and poured the wine into two attractive tin wine decanters. In one of the decanters, Qiaoling furtively dropped a small amount of sleep-inducing powder that her sister had given her earlier. The sisters placed the decanter that was free of the drug at their end of the table. After dinner, the family's two male servants, Ah Gao and Old Zhang the cook, had only just finished clearing the table when they felt the drug's influence. Normally these two exhibited an impressive alcohol tolerance. They were sturdily built men, and rarely tired. That evening, however, they didn't even make it to the washroom to clean their faces before they, like the rest of the household, had fallen into a deep slumber on their beds.

At around eleven o'clock that evening the moon was still shining brightly. Qiaoling led her sister slowly down the stairs. Before taking each step, she would first place a thick, woolen sweater on the wooden stair to absorb the noise of their footfalls. Like cats, they slunk through the house, never letting their feet touch the ground without the padding of a carefully placed sweater. After exiting the front door, they looked back. The house remained silent and dark, like a forlorn mausoleum. The only sounds the two could hear were the insistent "Pom Pom Pom" of their hearts, which were threatening to leap out of their throats at any minute.

They had already prepared an excuse in the event that someone in the household awoke and discovered their absence. On a beautiful night like that, what was more natural than two young women admiring the moon?

That night, I had no choice but to take the role of an itinerant Buddhist monk. As I waited for her at Dragon Well Temple, I occasionally dipped into my jute bag filled with sacrificial paper money and artificial silver ingots and pretended I was making sacrifices to appease the hungry ghosts that were wandering the countryside that evening.

My wild swan finally arrived. I very quietly expressed my gratitude to Qiaoling. Yaling and I then departed, passing over the Weng Family Mountain, following the mountain road that skirted Mist and Cloud Cave, and making straight for Four-Eye Well. Only after we passed the Well did we finally reach the Qixia highway. During our journey, when the path became dark and treacherous, I would light some of the sacrificial money in my jute bag. We maintained a quick pace on the highway until we got to Lake Side, where we were able to hire a pedicab for the journey into the city. We made into the city just in time to make the 2:30 Guangzhou express train which was heading north. We got off the train in Shanghai.

Just in case the train was full, I had reserved a sleeping berth. To our great relief, we were the only two persons in the compartment. The rest of that night was filled with long, passionate kisses. The sparks from our heated embraces seemed to free our souls from their earthly moors. We awoke still tired from our night of ardent tumbling, enhanced by the train's own pitching and rolling. The dawn had broken and colored the landscape with a warm, red glow.

Two weeks later, we took our I.D. cards and went to the Shanghai Courthouse to get married. We didn't tell anyone about our marriage. Even my own parents did not receive the news until a month later.

Before our marriage, I had already accepted an offer of a position as the teacher at a private high school in the area. That winter, Yaling also accepted an offer to teach at a local private elementary school.

We were like two swallows, building a nest on the sweet, dry rafters of a large house. Our household was permeated with the feeling of matrimonial bliss. While not wealthy, we were very comfortable and wanted for little. We were both able to truly enjoy the youth, beauty and pure joy expressed in the Midsummer Night's Dream. It was not long before our lives were both blessed and happily burdened with two daughters, adding two more sweet strains to Mendelssohn's "Dream."

VI

In March of 1949, a few days before the vernal equinox, I prepared a feast for the family. After dinner, feeling the warm tingle of too much wine, I turned toward my wife and said softly with a serious expression, "Yaling, I can't hide this from you any more. I'm a member of the Communist underground. The year we won the Sino-Japanese War, I was recruited by the Party. They were attracted to me because I had excelled in my studies and was well-known for my talent to sing. Even though I loved my country and aspired to work for its betterment, I had a free spirit that would not be tied down. Therefore, I was not as earnest in my work for the Party as I should have been. I had received the Party's instruction, however, up through the time we arrived in Shanghai. My increasing ire at the developments within our country caused me to fully embrace the Revolution. When I was finally admitted to the Party as a full member, my life naturally lost its formerly simple character. It is no wonder that you had difficulty understanding why I was often busy with the errands of "friends," sometimes not returning until the wee hours in the morning. I must confess, Yaling, the reason why you were able to find a job so easily once we reached Shanghai was because of the Party's help. I have many comrades in both your school and my own."

I stopped for a moment. I felt relieved after telling her all of this, and continued in a happier, albeit softer, voice.

"The Liberation Army recently won a battle in the Northwest. According to the latest secret reports from our headquarters, after fighting for over thirty hours, from February 29 to March 1, the Liberation Army defeated four garrisons—over two hundred four thousand men—under the command of Hu Zhongnan in the Shan Bei area. In addition, our troops overcame the Twenty-ninth Corps under the command of Liu Kan, and the Ninetieth Division under the charge of Yan Ming. As a result, the Shan Bei area is now under the complete control of the Communist Party. The Liberation Army has also been victorious in many of the battles fought in Henan and Shandong Provinces, as well as many areas in the Northeast. Our troops have been fighting with a fervor that the soldiers of the other side cannot match. If we continue this wave of enthusiasm, we will be able to liberate the whole country within two years.

"When that day arrives, our luck and our lives will take a dramatic turn for the better. For your capitalist father and uncle, as well as the son of the owner of that textile mill, however, the future looks very bleak. The policy of the Party is primarily focused on the breaking down of class barriers through the unification and redistribution of the people's wealth. Therefore, attacks on the well-to-do are unavoidable." My tone was repentant. I tried to lessen the perhaps painful impact of my words. "Dearest Lingling, I have waited until now to tell you all this, all the events that have so influenced my life. Can you forgive me?"

Yaling gently picked up her chair and placed it next to me. She then sat down and embraced me, saying softly, "Cangming, there is no need for either of us to ever beg forgiveness. Won't I always be yours? And won't you always be mine? Aren't we one person, body and soul?"

We both smiled and laughed warmly. Then Yaling continued. "If you believe in what you're doing, I will always approve—give my support. Hasn't it always been that way?"

I grinned and said, "Wonderful! Wonderful! Let's drink a toast." We then lifted our glasses and clinked them together.

My foresight turned out to be as accurate as Ji Cang's arrow, which could pierce the heart of a louse. Like tidal waves which follow earthquakes, victory upon victory followed the Liberation Army's initial successes on the battlefields. In August of 1948, our forces won the Battle of Jinan; in October, the Battles of Liao-Shen; and in December, the Battle of Huaihai. By the end of the year, our begonia-shaped nation flashed with the bright-red color of the Communist Party.

The Party was finally able to reap its harvest after years of careful cultivation. In the summer of 1949, there was no longer any need to work as a member of an underground movement. I was therefore given the honor of being appointed the vice president of the Science and Technology Publishing Company in Zhejiang Province. Yaling was hired as the director of student affairs at a public elementary school. She soon became a member of the Communist Youth League. We had both adopted the ideals of the new society. We had severed our feudalistic roots. In the past, we had lived our lives like timid marmots, darting in and out of our holes. After the liberation of the country, I thought that we were finally able to enjoy our lives, even though my workload had increased substantially.

Each Party and Youth League member took on the burdens of Greece's mythical Atlas. The man-made globe that each of us bore weighed down on us until we all gasped for air.

I often waxed philosophical during those transitional years. There were times when I felt that the practical demands of life were too wearisome. I therefore concentrated the energy that would otherwise have been used to fulfill these dreary demands on travel and my love of music. In this way, I was able to fend off that dreaded fatigue. Later, these pleasures were replaced with lengthy obedience to Marx and his teachings. It was not long before I wholeheartedly embraced the Communist Party and all that I thought it stood for. Now, however, I realize that, in my quest to avoid life's taxing burdens, I had only added to those the average person has to endure.

The Counter-revolutionary Suppression Movement of 1951 left me exhausted. Day and night I was as tense as a bow string. At times, I only got two or three hours of sleep. My fatigue didn't really stem from my job, or the daily struggle meetings. It was the result of the endless executions that occurred each day, blood gushing from the victims' temples, or the napes of their necks. Never in my life had I been exposed to such an onslaught of murderous news. According to internal sources, during the months in spring and summer of that year, the number of daily executions of counterrevolutionaries authorized by the authorities reached two or three hundred.

Later, when I paged through several of the daily district newspapers from Zhejiang Province, one or two whole pages would be black with the names of counter-revolutionaries slated for "suppression." Sometimes I would count one thousand names, sometimes two thousand.

It was at that time that I finally awoke from my dream. The true meanings of "liberation" and "revolution" were blood-curdling revelations.

As a Party member, I was unable to exhibit even the slightest dissatisfaction with the status quo, let alone independent observation. The Party's discipline was like an incredible, single-edged razorblade, removing any sign of individualism from its members. I had to play the model Party member, loathing to alter a single pre-determined step. In those days, having been admitted to the Party as a member meant that you had to be a leader. You were expected to ignite the sparks that led to the deadly anti-revolutionary movements. Even though my head had not yet been penetrated by the brass bullets of some Party executioner's rifle, my heart often bled secretly. I feared that the people would eventually come to take the fresh blood that covered the ground so often lately as a sort of daily necessity.

During the "Three Against" and "Five Against" Movements of 1952, which were essentially large-scale struggles against corruption, waste, bureaucracy within the Party and the government; against bribery, tax evasion, theft of state secrets, cheating on government contracts, and stealing of economic information as practiced by owners of private industrial and commercial enterprises, those labeled as "capitalists" by the Party were sent alive into the deepest pit of Buddhist hell. My wife's father and uncle fell victim to those life-endangering struggles at an early date. Their crimes were simply the association of their family names with "wealth." Yaling and I could only sigh in the face of our relatives' great hardships. We were unable to lift a finger to help them.

In 1953, during the further suppression of anti-revolutionaries, rightists and corrupt cadres, the mounting anger and hate represented by the movement created a juggernaut that finally collided with me. I was unaware that my father had been a member of the Kuomintang Party. Therefore, I naturally did not mention this when filling out my Party application, nor did I bring it up during my interviews with the Party officials. In that horrible era, however, my ignorance was an unforgivable crime. I became the focus of acrid criticisms during Party struggle meetings. Soon after that, I was sentenced to seven months in prison. The Party suspected that I was an undercover agent for the Kuomintang, a mole planted within the Party to learn its deepest secrets.

The incessant struggle sessions and self-criticisms were like an infernal whirlwind threatening to pull me apart. It was as if I were sentenced to undergo the ancient capital punishment of being rent apart by five horses.

Perhaps this was heaven's revenge on one who had aided in creating this earthly hell. My own flesh had been seared by the fire and brimstone.

When the Party was finally convinced that I had been ignorant of my father's involvement in the Kuomintang Party, I was released. After leaving prison, my father's past continued to haunt me. I was demoted to associate editor-in-chief of the publishing company. Fortunately, I didn't lose my life-saving membership in the Party, though I was subjected to almost unbearable scrutiny. Both of these factors were intimately connected with the fact that I had professional expertise that the Party needed, and had a working knowledge of English. I remember that vulgar president of the publishing company. He was like a half-empty bottle of vinegar, which made a lot of noise when shaken up, but consisted mostly of air. He didn't finish college and relied heavily on me for everything, including all of the company's business.

During the "Hundred Flowers Movement" of 1956, I was able to spit out all the bitterness that had been building up inside of me for so long.[2] I expressed my criticisms of the Party's organization, as well as my bitterness over the wrongs it had done me. My father was a middle school teacher in Chongqin when he joined the Kuomintang. At that time, he was also doing his part to defend the nation in the Sino-Japanese War. Because I was attending school in an area occupied by the enemy, I never received news of his new political affiliations. Even my mother, a junior high school teacher in Hangzhou, was unaware of his membership for a long time. After the Sino-Japanese War ended and our family was reunited, my parents never talked about this again. Moreover, from that point on, my father seemed to have washed his hands off all political activities. I told the Party officials that, being completely ignorant of these events, I should have been guiltless. My imprisonment by the Party,

---

[2] The "Hundred Flowers Movement" was fostered during the period of May-June 1957 and was aimed at exposing anti-Communist Party members and intellectuals. On May 1 of that year, the Chinese Communist Party announced that all people should feel free to voice their indignation against the Party so that the Party could make progress in correcting itself. In May and June, the criticism campaign became widespread, first in writings and later in demonstrations, leading to a deluge of anti-Party sentiment. Infuriated and alarmed, Mao Zedong later initiated a series of anti-Rightist struggles labeling and suppressing those who had criticized the Communist Party as Rightist.

which was effected without taking the trouble to discover the possible reasons for my not having revealed my father's political history, was manifestly unjust. I also wanted my former position and salary back.

While I was making these "contentions," a great many of my comrades empathized with me and agreed with my manner of expression. With the start of the "Anti-Rightist Movement" at the latter half of the following year, the authorities seized the opportunity to attack me. The associates who had originally supported me underwent a chameleon-like change and turned against me. Their words and acts were swords thrown violently against me.

The struggle sessions became like violent monsoons, lasting months and months. Each raindrop was like a macabre bullet piercing my soul. In the end, I was labeled a "Rightist" and sent to a village in Ling An county to undergo labor reform. Once there, I was under the supervision of the whole village. Yaling was soon demoted from director of student affairs to a simple teacher. Luckily, she was then too old for the Communist Youth League and had distanced herself from that sort of Party affiliation.

We were forced to leave the Western-style housing provided by the publishing company. Soon after that, we moved into our present, cramped but ever-vigilant living quarters.

VII

The vermilion moon was obscured by the evening mists as it climbed into the empyrean. It looked as if someone had hung a warmly glowing lantern far off in the distance. The red light which shone over the earth, however, gave the earth a fearful and ghastly appearance. I quickened my pace toward the direction of the red moon. I could feel my wrath building as I moved along. No matter how much I wished to run away, to escape that madness, I knew that I would be unable to break free of the powerful communist aura that then ringed the country.

Spring was drawing to a close. In the lands to the south of the Yangtze River, nature had reawakened and, like an enormous orchestra, was in the midst of a crescendo. Even though the sweltering heat of summer would soon arrive, I could still sense the warmth and promise of spring. It was odd that these beautiful surroundings made me feel all the worse for the contradiction that they represented.

I was surrounded by acres and acres of farmland. I could see quite far. Nothing grew on the flat fields that was tall enough to block my view. The sweet potatoes that had been growing in long rows had been harvested quite some time ago. Now, the earth was dry and cracked, and overturned in the places where the potatoes had been pulled up. It gave me the impression that I was standing on the scales of some long-dead fish. The whole scene filled me with despair.

I remember my first experience at labor reform in this place. I was forced to carry two huge baskets of potatoes slung from a pole that bore into my shoulders. The weight of the baskets was more that I had ever lifted before—about two hundred and eleven pounds.

I was always hurrying along the paths that crisscrossed the fields. I had to rush. Work could no longer be accompanied by periodic rest, nor accomplished with moderation.

While engaged in my toils, I felt the echoes of an abhorrent sound reverberating in my heart.

"Shen Cangming, I've decided to divorce you. It's best for the children, for me—and for you. I have to break all ties with you. You have to leave us and live by yourself."

This was the chilling sound of Yaling's voice. Her expression was stern and full of the resolve associated with Western knights, just after they had thrown down the white glove of challenge.

I wasn't an idiot. I knew that any attempt to argue the issue with her at that time would simply exacerbate the already deteriorating situation. I could only utter eleven words in a very low voice. "Please let me think about it for a while, okay?" My words were more a plea than a question.

Yaling replied, "Fine. Think about it. When you return next weekend, give me your answer."

She had waited until the morning, before I left to return to my labors in the country, to announce this horrible news. But she was not devoid of kindness. If I had heard those words the night before, I would certainly have gone without sleep, agonizing over my fate. Yaling was able to foresee such a reaction, and had prevented it for a short time. She knew that I worked like an ox in the country and would not be able to cope with the heat and exertion without a proper night's rest. She also feared that, if I remained in the house too long after hearing that statement—without having the chance to get away—I would react violently.

My one-and-a-half hour ride to the countryside over uneven roadways had diluted my feeling of intense anger that had welled up within me after hearing her words. Overturning the endless clods of earth with my large rake helped lesson my ire even further. But at night, when all was silent, I could not bear being left alone with my thoughts. The village dormitories afforded me no solace. I felt the need to rush out of my sleeping quarters into the fields. I felt that that was the only way to dispel Yaling's haunting words.

I had borne the label of Rightist some six months before she made that horrible decision.

Memories can also be like tiger's teeth, gnawing at you until you cry out in pain. We had a love that had brought us to heights unmatched by the Himalayas. For what seemed like thousands of nights, we clung to each other's bodies, only to be buried in this avalanche. Twelve years of the deepest love between husband and wife! The sudden severing of our relationship was an intolerable pain. I felt like I was being skinned alive, without the benefit of some numbing drug.

In moments of indescribable suffering, Einstein's Theory of Relativity sometimes provided inspiration for my mental escape.

I would lie down and his writings would propel me into the cosmos, my body and soul pulsing with the rhythm of the stars. Only when we are in touch with such awesome and mysterious forces do our mortal troubles appear truly miniscule. The Soviet Union had recently launched man's first satellite into the heavens. This was only a beginning, but it presaged our ability to physically leave the earth by means of rockets. My present difficulties might pale in the face of the troubles that the future could bring, but these thoughts were able to temporarily free me from painful reality.

My reveries lasted for only about two hours. The wood-plank beds in the dormitory near my worksite creaked horribly and made it impossible to fall asleep.

The result of my night's insomnia was "No! No! I absolutely cannot leave her and the children—until I leave this earth!"

After hearing my decision, she spoke only two sentences to me in a detached voice, "Fine. If that is the way you feel, all the consequences will be yours to bear."

After she finished speaking those words, it was three years before she added a third sentence. No. Before she added another word.

Each scene from our family's lengthy fossil exhibition surpassed the famous Western sculpture Laocoon for its anguish and wretchedness.

She could pass the entire day without looking at me. If she did hazard a glance, it would only be from the corners of her eyes. When she spoke with the children, she would walk up to them and whisper in their ears, as if she were afraid that I would hear what was said. And whenever I hugged the children, or started to play with them, she would find some excuse to shoo them away. No sounds issued from our household.

All of its occupants had apparently been struck dumb. It was like the serene plays of the symbolist Maurice Maeterlinck, or France's acts in mime.

It required all of my strength to abide with these bizarre events. At times, I felt that I could stand it no longer. But I had to. The two treasures of my life were in her control. Incredibly, she was able to play her part quite naturally and almost with zeal.

I threw myself into the household chores. I chopped the wood, lit the coal stove and cooked the rice gruel. Before noon, I'd help with the house cleaning. This included sweeping and mopping the floor, wiping the furniture and carrying the large metal pail to the public pump to get water to wash the vegetables for the evening meal. In the afternoon, I'd go out to the market and carry a large bag of rice home on my back. I'd also go and buy baskets of coal, which I'd hang from a pole that I carried on my shoulders. Then I'd bring the loads of wood that I'd cut that morning into the house. Lastly, I'd empty the privy bucket outside—

No matter how hard I toiled, she never spoke a word of thanks. Unless we were entertaining a guest, our house was devoid any noise. It was like the silence, I thought, that existed at the dawn of time.

I still find it hard to believe that this stillness lasted three years.

I don't know exactly when it started, but one day I perceived the slightest change in her.

The color of her face, the way she carried herself, her movements and moods, were all like the surface of a body of water. They were indistinct and mystifying to all but my eyes, which I had trained to reflect the sensitivity of a hydrologist's.

Three years was a long time. I decided to risk confronting her, speaking with her. I sensed that the changes I saw in Yaling were a sign that this time, my efforts might not fail.

VIII

It was after two in the afternoon on a beautiful Mid-Autumn Festival day. Our neighbors on all sides had left their cages to go to the banks of the Qiantang River in the town of Yanguan to take in the tidal sights. Our children had gone to their school to take part in the holiday activities. We were the only two left in the compound. She had finally sat down and had picked up a Lu Xun novel. It was a love story recounting the past trials and tribulations of a Chinese family.

I couldn't sit still. I got up and paced to and fro. I had long ago come up with the outlandish idea of seeing how far her act would go, and since that time it had been smoldering in my breast like some hellish bed of sulphur—

The five major faculties of my body had been charred by this internal fire. The heat varied with the intensity of my rage. Right now, the veins in my face were protruding and my whole body was suffused with the wrath that had been seething within. Suddenly, I charged to the table where she was reading, grabbed her book and threw it aside. My actions were like those of Othello when, in a frenzied jealousy, he came upon Desdemona in her bed, intending to smother her. I screamed at her, my face streaming with tears.

"Yaling!! Yaling!! In fifteen years of marriage, when have I wronged you? Tell me! When have I been unfaithful to you? Tell me! What is the reason for your treating me so cruelly? Did Chairman Mao instruct you to act this way, to mimic a pre-historic fossil? Or was it the Party? Why must you be so hateful toward me? Simply killing me would have been less vicious! If a person is murdered at least you can see the blood, know the act for its savageness. You've killed without letting blood! You've turned our home into a stone nest, occupied by two large stones and two small ones. Is there any humanity left in our household? You're not human! You're just a sort of punishment, a humiliation! Yes! You're the humiliation of our family! I'm a rightist, but I feel no shame because I'm still human! But you're not! You're definitely not! I ask you, in what era of history, in China or elsewhere, has such a bizarre phenomenon occurred in a peaceful society, in a peaceful household? When has such a tragedy, such a comedy been enacted before? Tell me!! Tell me!! Tell me!! Think about it. In the past fifteen years, do you know how I've loved you? How I have given my heart to you?

You're not blind, deaf or an idiot! You can see, hear and think, can't you? Just close your eyes for a moment and think. Can you continue doing this to me? You've filled three years with your cruelty. If we hadn't eloped, if I hadn't freed you from your father's feudalistic control, you would have been married to that capitalist boss's son from the Gao Xintai Cloth Shop and been suffering untold miseries. After the 'Three Against' and 'Five Against' movements, what kind of life would you have left? That year in Shanghai when you fell ill after giving birth, do you remember how I cared for you? During the day I taught classes and at night I was busy with work for the Party. But morning, noon and night, I made time to return home and care for you, and the children. When was there a night that I didn't get to bed until the early hours of the morning? After you recovered from your illness, you had lost only about six and one half pounds. I had lost about ten and one half. During the 'Three Against and Five Against' movements, after your father died in prison, no friend or relative volunteered to help the family. I was the only one who appeared at the prison to make the funeral arrangements, bury your father and help your mother. Because of your uncle's frequent trips to Hong Kong between 1949 and 1950, he was suspected of being an informant for the Taiwan-based Kuomintang. As a result, he was sentenced to labor reform, spending his days breaking rocks into gravel to build new roadways. Because of this, his relatives refused to acknowledge any connection with him. I was the only one who, every month, would bring him basic living necessities and see to those of his needs that I could. Your aunt was isolated from society, and spent her days waiting to die. After her passing, I made the funeral arrangements. In my dealings with your family, never did I consider politics. I only wished to help them. I have done nothing that I regret.

"You are my only love. These fifteen years, there has never been another. Why, then, must you be so heartless? Each time I return from my labors, where is the warmth that should be associated with hearth and home? I have endured the living agony of your bloodless whip, your silent punishment. You never even look at me, never even breathe a word. Our innocent children have learned from their mother. Their pure hearts have been tainted with the cruel reality of the times we live in. They now look at their father as if he were a stranger, even an enemy of the people! Is it surprising that my heart has shattered? Yaling! Yaling! Speak to me! Why are you doing this to me? Why have you been as lifeless as some prehistoric fossil for the past three years?—A horribly cruel, unequalled fossil! You have to give me an answer today! I've endured this for three whole years now! I can't stand it any longer! If you don't answer me, don't speak with me today, I won't forgive you! If you don't answer, I'd rather that we both die, and the children become orphans, do you understand?!! Damn it!!! I don't care about the consequences! If you don't resolve this, then I will! Or we both will!!"

She cried as she listened to my words. After I finished speaking, she broke down and sobbed loudly, leaning against me. She had cried like this for some time when she spoke through her tears.

"Cangming! Cangming! My dear Ming! My dear—Yell at me! Curse at me! Hit me! Even kill me! But don't look down on me! Everything I have done was for the children—for you! Listen to me—You're right that I'm inhuman. I'm so sorry! I'm ever so sorry! But tell me, how could I dare to be human!! For the past ten years, each street, each lane, each household was devoid of anything resembling a human! No person acted like a human! If no one else dared, how could I all by myself? Only by not acting human and looking human could I continue living! If I had kept my compassion, my humanity, how could I have fended off the suffering, the pain? Everywhere people are being struggled against, imprisoned, forced to labor! Is this a humane world?! It doesn't even resemble a primitive world! In the wild, tigers do not eat tigers, wolves don't eat wolves, tigers and tigresses can love their cubs. In this world we live in, however, people are treated like garbage. Sons struggle against their parents and parents hate their sons. They're worse than wild animals. The authorities give us orders, and we must spend night and day carrying them out, like puppets. And these puppets are unbelievably cruel and cunning. They spend their time cursing and struggling and killing. They act according to the directions of the leaders who reside in Zhongnanhai. I'm just such an unfeeling puppet. What else could I be?! How else could I use the role of puppet to protect my family, the children, myself, even you? Cangming, my dear Ming! These three years, you've suffered enough! I've smothered you! I've smothered myself!—I haven't allowed you to breathe! I haven't allowed myself to breathe! There was never a time when that 'bloodless whip' struck at you that I didn't feel its lash myself. There was never a time that your sufferings were not my own. Each time you returned to the countryside, I would hide from the children and cry. I couldn't let the neighbors find out. Even in my grief I had to play dumb, had to force you to look into my stony face. Do you think I willingly took on the guise of a fossil? I'm also a living person! I'm also of flesh and blood! I hate myself for being so cruel to you, for not having spoken to you these past three years, not even one word. I've been more callous than a stone!! At least stones can produce sounds when moved by other forces!! But I'm not a stone, I'm absolutely not a stone! What could I do?! The apartments to our left and right, even over us, were filled with ravenous wolves and leopards. When these radicals struggled against others, they were more ferocious than wildcats. How could I help but be cold and heartless toward you? If I played the role of a fossil, then the family would be safe. The more resolved to be distant, unfeeling, a mute, that I was, the more satisfied were the wolves and leopards that things were going their way. Intellectuals like us have always been the focus of their enmity. It was not long before I became notorious for my activities of the past three years, breaking all discourse with you, always taking the viewpoint of the Party, and especially my stony, silent act. The principal of my school was constantly trying to get me to divorce you. After news of my fossil-like conduct reached him via our neighbors, however, he praised me publicly. He said that my actions were exemplary, but hoped that I could also say a few words to you with the goal of accomplishing some thought reform—

"When I heard the principal say this, how could I tell whether she was telling the truth? Maybe she was being honest, maybe not. Perhaps it was some sort of scheme. In this society, where plots are thicker than hairs on a ox, if I fell prey to one of their traps, not only would I probably be extinguished, but little Congcong and Mingming as well. And you would only be brought one step closer to oblivion. I could only see everyone as an assassin. It was the only way to protect myself. We have been forced to board a sinking ship. Our ability to flee in the last moments before she submerges depends entirely on our ability to maintain this noxious suspicion and this rock-like heartlessness. Thus, I had no choice but to play the fossil.

"My dear, dear Ming! My darling Ming! My darling Ming!! I was forced into this role, securing their faith through our suffering. It was the only way to protect our family. I was worried that little Congcong wouldn't be allowed to enter middle school because of our family background. But because of my politically acceptable behavior, this summer she finally was allowed to take an entry exam into middle school, and I could let my stony exterior fall away. Three years ago when I said that I wanted a divorce, I was only acting. I secretly planned that even though we would be legally separated, I would never marry another. I would wait until you were able to clear your name and then remarry you. This was the safest way—How could you understand? It was my last line of defense. I knew that if I could prevent those wolves and leopards from severing this last means of protection, they would have nothing to criticize. Ming! Ming!! My heart! My dear Ming! My dear husband! I love you! I love you! I will always love you! I've already eaten out my heart for you! Strike me! Hit me!! Take my life!! I won't strike back!!—"

I listened to her words, then suddenly started hitting myself in the face. If she hadn't quickly reached out and grabbed my arms, my face would have been boxed redder than Guan Gong's, the Chinese god of war.

We hugged tightly, and cried for a full hour.

That night, I slept soundly for the first time in years. But not before we experienced love—passion like that of our wedding night, when primordial desires overtake the senses with the force of a bursting volcano.

The heat from our eruption finally dissolved the fossil.

As we lay next to each other, our heads sharing the pillow, I quietly sang again the strains of Flotow's love song.

IX

Two weeks later, my old publishing company requested that I return to Hangzhou to attend a large meeting and listen to the reports that would be given there. At the meeting, a senior cadre relayed the words of Chen Yi, which were spoken that summer in Guangzhou and directed at the country's literary circles. Chen Yi was the Secretary of the Ministry of Foreign Affairs. During the civil war, he had been promoted to Commander of the Third Combat Troop Battalion. It was significant that such a high-ranking individual was chosen to announce this news. The words that left the deepest impression on me were the following (according to my own memory):

"During the past few years, our intellectuals have suffered many wrongs. From this day on, the Party will not undervalue this precious resource. Intellectuals labor with their brains, and as laborers, they are part of the proletariat. Just like the country's other laborers, they are leaders in the People's Democratic Dictatorship.

"In this way, they are given the recognition they deserve. In the future, the Five Bad Elements (including landowners, wealthy peasants, counter-revolutionaries, villains and rightists), will no longer include 'rightists,' and will be amended as the 'Four Bad Elements.' Within this year, several rightists who have been exemplary in their accomplishments will be able to shed the appellation 'Bad Element.'"

The head of our publishing company met with me and praised my four years of labor in the countryside. He told me that this year, before the National Day, I would be reinstated at the company and given editing work.

I knew why this change in policy had taken place. Relations between China and the Soviet Union had broken down. Our "Big Brother," the Soviet Union, had terminated its one hundred fifty commercial contracts with our country. As a result, our economy nearly collapsed. North of the Yangtze River, nearly twenty or thirty million people starved to death. At the same time, General Chiang Kai-shek was initiating his plans to "retake the mainland" from Taiwan. Each time troubles arise, the Government in Zhongnanhai has no choice but to turn to the people—especially the intellectuals—and make temporary concessions in their favor.

It suddenly became quite clear to me. About a month ago, Yaling had heard the news from higher up, and had received some hints from the school principal. It was then that I began noticing subtle changes in the water marks.

These matters are of little importance now. In any case, the curtain has finally closed on this act of our miraculous domestic play, which, I believe, has had no equal in the history of human kind.

(Translated by Richard J. Ferris Jr.)

A Glass of Water

I

One midnight, late February 1969.

Creatures hibernating in their burrows had yet to be awakened by the first spring thunder. It was the week before "The Waking of Insects," still in the latter solar term "Rain Water."[1] Over the past two days the steady downpour had eased, yet a chilling dampness permeated into the veins of the earth, releasing wave after wave of cold. Meanwhile the tingling caress of the wind scything through the willows testified to a last cold snap before the appearance of spring's welcome warmth.

For the past two years, from Hangzhou, City of Buddha, across the entire mainland, one might say that multitudes of people had been dashing madly around like hornets angrily winging their way from an overturned nest, furiously bent on stinging their opponents to death. The countless ransacking, accompanied by beating, smashing and robbery, recalled hornets in action. Ironically, "Operation Hornet" was the code-name given to America's first bombing raid on Tokyo in World War II, which was led by a warship of that name. That was a single surprise attack on Japan, whereas during the past three years the Cultural Revolution had brought numerous surprise attacks.

Nevertheless, even the wings of furious hornets grow tired from flight. Amid spring's bone-chilling dampness, midnight's darkness and the wan phosphorescence of street lamps, even hands and tongues that had beaten, smashed and struggled with

---

[1] The twelve months of the lunar year are divided into twenty-four solar terms, with each month having a "former" and a "latter" solar term. "Rain Water" begins in the middle of the month, and so is a "latter" solar term.

insane zeal were obliged, in obedience to biological laws, to call a temporary halt.

Tonight in this storm-tossed city many a courtyard could, at least briefly, hold the revolutionary animals at bay thanks to the enveloping blackness of night, allowing its residents to recover their breath in their dark, sweet lair. Ultimately life so thirsts for peace, and the world has such need of tranquillity.

Naturally there were exceptions. One of these was No. 15 Lower Huaguang Bridge of Hushu District.

"Help!... Comrade Sun Junlun!... Help!... Mrs. Fu!... Help! Comrade Wu Jingan!... I'm dying of thirst! I'm dying of hunger!... Help! For pity's sake!... Give me a glass of water!..."

A sharp female cry edged with sobbing rent the night, quivering in the darkness, and trailing a resonant echo.

At this hour such a cry was grossly shocking, intolerable to any normal ear.

And yet in answer to this poignant midnight cry there was only silence, darkness, and the sound of the wind.

Beyond the gateway, the waters of the ancient canal flowed lazily from Hangzhou down to Suzhou. But its rippling surface was answering the sound of the wind, not her cry.

"Help!... Help!... I'm dying of thirst!... I'm dying of hunger!... I haven't had a drop of water or eaten any food for two days and two nights!... Help!... Help! For pity's sake!... Give me a glass of water!..."

At nearly one o'clock in the morning her cries issued again, only at a weaker pitch and volume.

The great courtyard's response to her remained nothing but silence, darkness, and rustling wind.

II

As in some disaster at sea, this "S.O.S." was first emitted at around six o'clock the previous morning.

In the gathering light of dawn everyone was initially transfixed with shock, but soon fell silent again. This was like a huge ball of tangled yarn, complex and awkward, which no one was willing to unravel. So many tales had been spread in this society with the message that all balls of this kind are in fact not tangled yarn, but a mass of thorns, capable of pricking any who touched them until they were bleeding all over.

Around the courtyard no one dared mention it openly. Even in their own homes, characters who normally counted as "Black Tornado" Li Kui types now sobered down all of a sudden and purposely played it cool.

Yet Grannie Pu's cries, issuing again and again from the west room downstairs, grew steadily more insistent. Like a fierce tiger, her suffering hurled itself against each family's door with overwhelming force. Faced with these bitter assaults, however, people put up a shield of perfect rationality. We must go off to work and "grasp revolution!" We must busy ourselves with washing, cooking and eating breakfast, hurrying off to the vegetable market basket in hand, attending to something or other! All were swept up in this urge to be busy.

Before long, most of the thirteen households had gone out. The mountainous weight of "revolution" had actually crushed Grannie Pu's cries for help to fine powder.

At 85 years of age, Grannie Pu was an "old native" of the courtyard. She had fallen ill with a fever one morning three days before, and was all alone with no relative near at hand. Grannie Xue, a neighbor from the adjoining courtyard and like herself a native of northern Jiangsu Province, had come over to see her and brought her something to eat and drink. But from the following day onwards no one had been in to visit. After a day of hunger and thirst, yesterday was her third day of sickness, and, unable to bear another whole day without food and water, she began to cry out for help. Her temperature must have gone down, or her cries would not have been so spirited. Yet the old lady was still too weak to climb off her bed; she could only call for help. People with high temperature break out into sweats as their fever recedes. So she was extra thirsty.

To give her a glass of water, or a bowl of rice gruel, would appear to be a simple matter, but—

This weird era teems with a multitude of "buts" which act like countless crocodile's mouths, liable at any moment to devour all forms of life. People cannot but pull up short in front of them.

From her cries, people seemed to arrive at an even deeper insight into a strange fact which might be termed the "Pu Ning phenomenon." Imagine a Zhou dynasty sacrificial vessel of great antiquity, which time had long since encrusted with a thick layer of venerable green patina, transforming it into a redundant object to which no one any longer paid the slightest regard. Now the sound of her cries was like a great piece of sandpaper constantly rubbing away at it until finally it was polished to a brilliant sheen that caught the eye. Only then did it occur to people that although the bright red flag with five stars had been flying over the Gate of Heavenly Peace for twenty years, Grannie Pu's son Pu Ning was still an unemployed good-for-nothing. He was still only fifty or so, in good health, had, so it seemed, once been a writer of some repute, and was even more highly cultured than a university graduate. Yet as a born idler he had whiled away a whole twenty years at home.

In capitalist countries, "being unemployed" means just that, something brought about by a dark system. In the People's Republic of China, where all systems of exploitation have been eradicated, "being unemployed" has a connotation of criminality, implying as it does "disaffection" from the People's Government. Yet Pu Ning had resolutely remained unemployed for twenty years. Ten years ago he had served thirty-seven days of labor correction at Lower Sand, and was later sent down country for a year and three months for another spell of labor correction, yet still it failed to budge his grotesque determination to remain unemployed. This time, in June of last year, he must have been mixed up with some villains in Shanghai and was arrested by fleet-footed undercover agents on the train back to Hangzhou. He was still detained in Little Cart Bridge prison now, under isolated examination for "counter-revolutionary" crimes. Grannie Pu's daughter-in-law was in trouble too, so it was said, and had stopped mailing money back home. Her eldest son in Hong Kong, a reactionary figure no doubt, helped out his aged mother from time to time, but nothing had been heard of her youngest son for years.

The "Pu Ning phenomenon" was rare indeed; no other case existed in the whole of Hangzhou. And the above account is based mainly on the strict interpretation of the public security office; not every household in the courtyard necessarily had such thorough knowledge. It was just that a day and night of the old lady's cries forced them all to dredge this "phenomenon" up from the depths.

In short, Pu Ning had now become an "evil individual."[2] That place of his was an "evil individual's home." Once he was condemned, the whole courtyard seemed to be tainted in some sinister way. People scurried desperately to get out of the way, for who dared be touched by that taint?

Privately everyone thought: What a pitch of desolation Grannie Pu has reached in her declining years—but—

Another "but!" Truly, this world is under cruel occupation by "buts!"

Lying on her five-foot coir-strung bed, the old lady was wrestling with these "buts."

No one could fail to admire her intelligence. For all her advanced years, and despite three days of sickness plus two days of hunger and thirst, she still knew the importance of choosing the right moment, and selecting the right target, for her pleas.

Her cries for help were most frequent at first light, over lunch time, and in the period between supper time and bed time especially, when the residents of the courtyard were generally home from work and their time was more their own. She cried out virtually every half-hour, sometimes even twice within thirty minutes. Adopting a strategy akin to the Allied carpet-bombing

---

[2] The Chinese Communist authorities labeled "landlords, wealthy peasants, counter-revolutionaries, bad elements and rightists" as the "five types of evil individuals." Pu Ning fell into this category at the time.

of Berlin, she directed her cries at all thirteen households around the courtyard, not sparing even grade school kids—luckily she had an excellent memory. Meanwhile the majority of her pleas were aimed at the families of Mrs. Fu, Sun Junlun, and Wu Jingan. The first two had known Pu Ning the longest and were normally perfectly friendly, while the Wu's were her immediate next-door neighbors.

III

"Help!... Help! Mr. Wu! Mrs. Wu! For heaven's sake! Give me a glass of water! I'm dying of thirst! I'm dying of hunger!... Mr. Wu! Mrs. Wu! For pity's sake! Give me a glass of water!..."

Wu Jingan, nicknamed "Limpy Wu," was around sixty years old. During the War of Resistance against Japan he was in a crash in which his vehicle overturned, severely injuring his left leg, and leaving him a cripple. At this moment he was sitting on an old wooden chair four feet from the Pu family's door, smoking a cheap Flag & Drum brand cigarette. With a dark gray, lantern-shaped corduroy hat covering his wizened cranium and a dirty old gray cotton overcoat wrapped around his scrawny frame, he looked shabby enough to be a wartime refugee. His sideburns were silvery; his face, like a faded old calf-leather shoe-upper with a hint of the opium addict's gray pallor, was crisscrossed with wrinkles; his cheeks were as lean as stretched hide. A few short white strands of beard hung from his pinched chin. His bovine eyes alone dimly shone with the steely glimmer unique to natives of Ningbo.

Like a frog sucking in water, he drew deeply on his cigarette before slowly emitting rings of sapphire smoke, silently watching each wreath of pale blue dissipate in the golden sunlight. Inwardly he was muttering: That witch-incarnation of an old woman! For indeed she had detected from the spreading scent of tobacco that he was sitting by her door. Those cries, like so many hand-grenades, were being tossed directly his way.

Despite himself he peered to the right. The Pu's door was left unlatched; one gentle push and it would swing wide open.

For once it was a fine day after the long rainy spell. This afternoon he would enjoy a pleasant bask in the sun and smoke a couple of cigarettes in comfort. If only –

Perhaps his guts were a little knotted, for Limpy's dry gray face was unusually cold and forbidding. He seemed to hear nothing. From time to time he took a leisurely drag on his cigarette, raised a covered glass from the little bench alongside him and calmly sipped a mouthful of green tea. Old, doddery and shabbily dressed though he was, at this precise moment every drag, every sip nevertheless seemed as precious to him as life itself. He was utterly impervious to anything going on in the outside world.

Inside the doorway to his right, Grannie Pu seemed to have spotted her target amid the encroaching aroma of tobacco smoke, and taking close aim lobbed her hand grenades at him from time to time.

The cigarette-smoker and tea-sipper did not consider himself to have been hit.

The sharply echoing cries from her doorway were frenziedly calling his and his wife Chen Yueying's names. To any normal ear this may have been an explosion, but to them it was like wild billows dashing against a rocky reef, with no aftermath beyond automatically turning into spray.

The Wu's had lived next door to the Pu's for eleven years. Their friendship could be said as very good, if not excellent. Relations were generally harmonious. Strange to say, this fellow Pu Ning was like some thousand-armed, thousand-eyed Bodhisattva Guanyin with an eternal expression of benevolence who seemed able to discern people's emotional reactions beforehand and to know in advance when to quietly extend his hand to smooth away all traces of their inner woes. As to the Wu's, they were a fiery-tempered duo known far and wide as a couple of powder-kegs. Yet no matter how the pair lost their tempers and clashed with Pu Ning, he managed to bring his verbal skills and quick mind to bear, devise some concession and finally defuse the confrontation, all without sacrificing his own dignity. To be honest, Pu Ning had helped the Wu's a good deal, virtually satisfying their every demand. But from Grannie Pu's first cry for help this morning, Limpy Wu and his wife had, as if in unspoken agreement, decided to play in auditory terms the role of the two stone guardians at the gate of Shanghai's City God Temple.[3] No matter how piercing her cries were, not a single sound could penetrate the narrow whorl of their ears.

At lunchtime, though, it was their second son, Wu Yaozong, who wore a solemn look; his name began to feature in her entreaties.

"Wu Yaozong, good boy! Help! Save me! Give me a glass of water! I'm dying of thirst!..."

He couldn't help saying softly, "Mom! Poor Grannie Pu … let's give her a glass of water!"

"Wretched devil! You'll be the death of us! The whole courtyard has it in for us. You forget how they criticized us the other year! How can we afford not to take a firm stand now?..." Mrs. Wu's eyes opened wide like a panther's and an angry flush suffused her puffy brown face as she sternly scolded her son.

There is a strange type of person in the world who can only survive day by day on the logic of the firing-squad. Mrs. Wu seemed to belong to this queer tribe.

The Pu's and the Wu's apart, the entire courtyard young and old numbered 78 eyes, almost half of which were trained like searchlights on the relationship between the Pu and Wu families, illuminating it as brightly as snow. Ever since the Wu's moved into this large courtyard nine years before, their dirt-poor family circumstances had been the Pu's burden. Mrs. Wu was on the wing all day long, borrowing money all over the courtyard. Sometimes the loans were repaid; sometimes they weren't. Things got in a muddle and in the end no one would have any more truck with her. By now the Pu's were the only ones who still consented to have money dealings with them. When the

---

[3] These two stone guardians are said to bestow good fortune upon worshippers at the City God Temple.

Wu's first moved in, there had been nothing which they did not borrow from Pu Ning—from a galvanized iron bucket for drawing water, iron tongs for gripping coal briquets, a banana-leaf fan for fanning the coal-fired stove, to the leather slippers on old Wu's feet and the envelopes and writing-paper on his table. In due course Mrs. Wu borrowed money, raw rice, cooked rice, oil, salt, cigarettes, matches, soap, coal briquets, postage stamps—virtually everything—from the Pu's. Fortunately Pu Ning was endowed with the patience of a camel, and he never minded obligingly acting as an abacus whose beads old Mrs. Wu was allowed to flick around to her heart's content. Even when he was slammed in jail, the Wu's still continued the "tradition" of many years and borrowed as before from Grannie Pu. Many a time their eldest son, who worked in the countryside, came home late at night, at nearly 11 o'clock when Grannie Pu was already sound asleep, and Chen Yueying would beat on her door like peals of thunder, insisting on waking the old lady up and dragging her out of bed just to borrow a catty of rice to cook a meal for him.

Why Pu Ning had humored the Wu's at every turn was possibly a personal secret of his. This secret would no doubt have to wait until twenty-four years later, after he had left Mainland China, to be revealed. As to Grannie Pu sucking up to the Wu's these days, this was mainly because the entire courtyard regarded her as a "counter-revolutionary" family member and generally gave her the cold shoulder. Only the Wu's felt they had something to gain from volunteering to keep up contact with her. On the surface they were lending her a helping hand, but in reality they were taking advantages. Anyway, help from the Wu's was indispensable and came in handy. When Grannie Pu paid her monthly visit to the prison at Little Cart Bridge to take the convict Pu Ning daily necessities such as soap and toilet paper, Wu Yaozong was always ready to go out into the street and hire her a tricycle cab. Sometimes when the Wu's went out shopping they would buy a few items for her at the same time, or place her orders for rice and coal.

Now Wu Yaozong was thoroughly perplexed: for the past nine years, right up to when Grannie Pu fell sick the other day, the Pu's and the Wu's had, to all appearances, blended like milk and water (although they had not been without their disagreements), and his mother had been forever dropping into the Pu's place every couple of days like a hungry rat. Why now suddenly this bolt from the blue and insisting on "taking a firm stand?"

That phrase of Chen Yueying's was in fact a profound expression which, if diligently dug down into, might reveal a darkness almost as stygian as the bottom of a mineshaft, far beyond wide-eyed junior high school student Wu Yaozong's ability to penetrate. Furthermore, his own character formed a high barricade closely fencing it off so that he could not enter. To their neighbors the Wu's place was like a porcupine's lair, and the only one untainted by porcupine ways was this straight-nosed, honest-natured junior high school kid.

In Mrs. Wu's eyes he was a dutiful son. No matter how his mother spat at him at the dinner table that day, he bit his tongue and said nothing. Only, as he recalled all Pu Ning's kindness to his family in the past, he couldn't help inwardly reproaching himself every time he heard the cries from next door.

During these past three days Wu Jinan and his wife had suddenly turned extraordinarily silent at the urgent cries for help issuing from the Pu's place. What lay behind this was an open book to several neighbors in the courtyard including Sun Junlun. One reason lay in the tense situation in the courtyard over the previous two years. Once the furor of the neighbors' criticism-struggle against the Wu's had swept past, many households would have nothing further to do with them. Pu Ning alone remained as friendly with the old couple as ever. At the time of the criticism-struggle, even normally civilized Principal Lu and Sun Junlun from across the courtyard donned helmet and armor and stood in the ranks, not to mention that busybody Xia Shuimu from the third floor. Once again Pu Ning alone, citing a severe illness and firmly insisting that he would not get out of bed, declined to take part in the criticism-struggle meeting and remained strictly neutral, thus winning the Wu's respect and favor. As this favor reached its Himalayan peak it became a veritable love affair. Whenever she saw Pu Ning going over to the Sun's, Chen Yueying would straight away put on an injured look and make some sarcastic remark. In time, Pu Ning didn't venture to stay long at the Sun's unless the whole Wu family were out. In a likely manner, Sun would never drop by at the Pu's except in a real emergency. Even in that situation, he only came for a hasty word or two at the door, never parking his bum on Pu's bench. Other neighbors, such as Mrs. Fu, took a similar attitude.

Way back before the Cultural Revolution, a time when for once the political barometer showed clear weather, there was one occasion when, taking advantage of the entire Wu family's absence, Pu Ning quietly went over to Sun's place for a chat. Sun asked him: You've lived next door to the Wu's for six or seven years now so you must know more about their family affairs than any of us. Why are they so overbearing toward all of us—especially old Mrs. Wu and her eldest daughter Wu Peizhen? You know I'm always polite to people and never like to offend; why do they regard us and their other neighbors with such hostility, bristling the moment they open their mouths?

This was a top-secret conversation. For the very first time Pu Ning poured out to his good friend Sun all the information he had collected, as he had been thinking of using it in the discreet composition of an extended short story.

IV

After demobilization from the Anti-Japanese War in 1945 Wu Jingan became a section chief in the Zhejiang Central Bank when, in the power-play of "section member politics," he landed a plum job at the Zhejiang Central Trust Bureau expropriating enemy real estate throughout the province. One can imagine how many Zhejiang businessmen were just licking their lips to lay hands on shops and houses in all the counties and

municipalities that had once belonged to the enemy. All it took
was for Wu to nod his head or say the word, and those gold-
diggers' daydreams of opening up in business would soon come
true, the road to riches stretching before them. Needless to say
he was amply rewarded, whether the pay-off came in company
shares, in gold, or in U.S. dollars. In less than a year Limpy Wu
had shot into the stratosphere, turning himself into a "fat cat"
overnight and instantly becoming a figure to be reckoned with
among the provincial capital's movers and shakers. To curry
favor with him, the concubine of Xi Baoqi, a former Secretary
of State in the Northern Warlords period, ceded to him her
grand residence in Shuilu Temple Lane, with its magnificent
grounds in the style of the Jia family's Great Prospect Garden as
described in *The Dreams of Red Chamber*. He happily took it
over and enjoyed it without hesitation. In those days he lorded it
over a domestic staff which at one time numbered as many as
eleven: a nursemaid for each of his three sons and three
daughters, who later became live-in babysitters, together with
five male and female domestics, chauffeurs and cooks. His
entire family regularly patronized all the biggest restaurants and
hotels in Hangzhou, never paying cash but signing the bill and
settling up at the end of the month. The cigars he smoked were
the same Luzon Number Two brand favored by the British
premier Winston Churchill. At cards his initial stake was one or
two "little yellow fish." When he had an impressive hand it
would rise to ten, and once he even flung down twenty.[4] There
was an expensive new type of all-purpose lightweight bicycle
from Holland which could be folded up and carried by hand, and
his favorite daughter Wu Peizhen was the first person in the
whole of Zhejiang to own one.

From May 4, 1949, the red flag flew all over Hangzhou. He
had the nous to speedily offer the "Great Prospect Garden" he
had been occupying for the past four years to the revolutionary
city council, which praised him as an "enlightened gentleman"
and rewarded him with a nice three-story Western-style house,

---

[4] A "little yellow fish" was a small gold bar weighing one tael. A "large
yellow fish" was equal to ten small gold bars and weighed one catty.

as well as retaining his services and appointing him head of the general affairs section of the Central Bank printing plant. In his new home he held a splendid ball, to which all the important revolutionary big potatoes in the plant were invited.

When the "Three Against" and "Five Against" campaigns finally reached its climax in 1952, for the first time in his life he couldn't cope with such an absolutely crazy experience. He had the honor of being listed as a "great tiger" of the Hangzhou business world, locked up in Little Cart Bridge prison and compelled to "confess all his crimes." This lame "tiger" who had tasted every gourmet delicacy in the world could hardly swallow down the frightful prison food, for in his day even sesame seed cake and fried dough sticks were strictly banned from the house as "too unhygienic." Those red Party thugs didn't need any lengthy criticism-struggle either, since to get things over with he willingly handed them his entire family fortune altogether. Not to mention yielding up all the huge sums stashed away in the bank, he even "made a clean breast" of the big yellow fish and little yellow fish hidden underground alongside the water meter and under the pipes, around 100 bars in all, totaling 100 catties (one catty is roughly a pound) of gold and worth fifty or sixty thousand U.S. dollars at the time. In addition he had also squirreled away an enormous amount of foreign currency, shares and company stocks.

A front page headline in the Zhejiang Daily extolled his "thorough honesty" and called upon all "big tigers" in the province to "emulate his example." Limping along holding a black lacquered walking-stick, he was led out of Little Cart Bridge by Mrs. Wu. Once back home, his wife wept and railed, tearing a proper strip off him. "You dutifully handed over the very last tael of gold, the very last dollar bill—how on earth are we all going to manage from now on?" The printing plant agreed to his "honorable retirement" and in their boundless graciousness the revolutionary authorities granted him a monthly retirement allowance in Renminbi of 22 yuans, roughly equivalent to US$ 11.00 at the prevailing official rate, enough for him alone to scrape by on the basics for the rest of his life.

Don't forget that in those days a peasant laborer shed a big bowl of sweat every day for an average monthly wage of only around ten yuans! He thanked the Party a thousand times over for taking care of him; Chairman Mao's mercy was truly higher than the sky.

That summer vacation his eldest daughter Wu Peizhen had to discontinue her studies at the end of her sophomore year at Shanghai's Tongji University and was forced to return to Hangzhou and be a bus ticket seller. Known as "princess" at college, this gorgeous girl had grown accustomed to an alluring style of dress which inevitably drew male admirers. Sometimes she stayed at the transport company's dormitory. At midnight one night, having ascertained that her female colleagues were out, Wang Zhiyuan, a young male bus ticket seller who was just out of high school, entered her room on a pretext. Raising a generous wine glass in one hand as if drunk, he fondled her with the other. Having grown up in a hothouse since childhood, how could she resist his intimidating advances? In the end she let him do what he desired. Her belly gradually swelled and she finally had to marry the little squirt. Later "big little master," the eldest son Wu Yaozu, went into the countryside to chew mud on a farm. The two pampered younger daughters went off to be an apprentice and a child laborer, and only the second son and youngest son stayed at high school. Limpy Wu's modest income wasn't enough to feed a family of seven. To supply their needs, Chen Yueying had no alternative but to go out on the street selling fried dough balls stuffed with shredded turnip from a vendor's stall. If only they had used their remaining assets astutely they would still have avoided being reduced to grinding poverty. But in the wake of this catastrophe it never occurred to Limpy Wu and his wife to smarten their ideas up; they continued their gourmet ways as before. It was bad enough that they ate and drank their way through all the jewelry, antiques, china and furs in their possession; but when they moved house for the third time and moved in next door to Pu Ning, all six of them were squeezed into a 16-square-meter (about 170-square-foot) room with virtually nothing but four bare walls. Yet in winter they sold off their summer mosquito nets and in summer their winter cotton quilts. Comparatively new summer clothes were sent away to the auctioneer's in December and perfectly good winter clothes sold to second-hand dealers in July, all in exchange for the baked crucian carp with shallots, stewed chicken, and pickled specialties at which Mrs. Wu was such a dab hand. And so the vicious circle went on until he ended up, as Xia Shuimu from the third floor once jocularly described it, "as poor as a man with a naked butt."

As his narration of the rise and fall of the "Kingdom of Limpy Wu" came to an end, Pu Ning, hearing voices in the courtyard, immediately stepped outside to take a look. Seeing that it was his neighbor the workman Wang Tongqing, his wife and their son Xiaojun, he breathed a sigh of relief and went back inside the room.

"I told you that long story in answer to the question you raised just now." he paused. Afraid that Sun did not fully understand, he slowly added, "In the old days the Manchu Qing emperors banished mandarins guilty of offenses to the desert wildness of Xinjiang. The eighteenth century Bourbon court used to exile criminals to a French colony beside a river in the wilds of Mexico. Those criminals, Chinese or French, were able to vent their anger neither by taking revenge against the Qing emperors or King Louis, nor by avenging themselves on the desert or river; they just had to accept their fate. Old Wu and his family moving into the pigeon coop next door to mine looks for all the world like banishment or exile in another guise. What they see before them is not desert, wilderness, or a river, but a courtyard of Aunt Sallies upon which they can vent a bellyful of resentment, spleen and fury, like the Indian cobra which spits its venom four feet through tiny holes in its fangs. So in time all of us have come to feel that they really are a family of porcupines, with the sole exception of Wu Yaozong. Since they were at one time owners of a "Great Prospect Garden" and put on aristocratic airs, they still can't help retaining a sense of superiority even now, seeking to lord it over people at every turn. By delving into all this with you today, I want you to understand why I have accommodated his family in every possible way over the years?"

Having said all this, Pu Ning gave a long sigh.

Sun Junlun's oval face showed its habitual kindly smile. Nodding his head gently from time to time, he swayed his elongated body slightly on the bench. Then he said extremely quietly, "So that's it." Rubbing his scrawny chin with one hand, and still speaking extremely quietly, he added, "Quite a few families have ended up like theirs in the Hangzhou and Shanghai area, but they don't necessarily act the same, as if their bad luck in the past was all our fault...."

"It's a question of breeding."

This secret Pu-Sun dialogue had taken place three years earlier. Ironically, on this very afternoon three years later Wu Jingan's "breeding" was truly at that height of perfection where he could virtually "remain unperturbed if Mt. Tai collapsed in front of him."

"Mr. Wu!... Good Mr. Wu!... Good Mrs. Wu!... Save me!... Save me!... For pity's sake!... Give me a glass of water!... Give me a glass of water!... I really am dying of thirst!... I really am dying of hunger!..."

Like a statue of Qingtian stone, Limpy Wu's head showed not the slightest movement. His brownish-gray face was every bit the "Poker face" of his gambling days, seemingly bereft of all trace of human warmth. Having finished leisurely smoking his third Flag & Drum and leisurely drinking his third cup of green tea, he appeared to be a little more contented. Of course this contentment was a chameleon which could change with circumstances at any time. Overall, he still projected an image of stern inviolability. By now the sunshine in the courtyard had lessened in warmth and, clearly declining toward the west, no longer shone on his skinny body. His gaze ceaselessly swept those walking in the courtyard as if reconnoitering their movements.

He was glad Grannie Pu's hand-grenades were no longer being lobbed his way; now they were aimed at the Fu family next door.

Inside, Mrs. Wu was standing at a large round wooden bowl with the broad sleeves of her buff-gray quilted cotton jacket rolled up, grating shredded turnip ready for tomorrow morning's trading stint on the quayside. As she grated, her mind seemed to wander slightly. Every time Grannie Pu called out her name, the smooth grating action of her hands slowed a little as she sank into thought. But she decided to grate a little less filling today and only go to the main canal quayside for the early morning market tomorrow, not the noon and evening markets. Although just a rank-and-filer, her feelings now bore a modest resemblance to the emotional state of Yelhonala, the Empress Dowager, 70 years before, when she learned that the Guangxu Emperor was about to attempt a coup. She sensed that beneath Grannie Pu's big coir-strung sick-bed next door there might be lurking a time-bomb. And-whether it exploded before or after old Mrs. Pu's death, the Wu family would get the full blast. She must be on high alert. At this point in her train of thought, a cunning smile flickered across her slightly puffy brown face.

V

"Help!... Help!... Mrs. Fu! For pity's sake!... Hu Zhilin!... Give me a glass of water!... I'm dying of thirst!... I'm dying of hunger!... Dear Maodi!... For pity's sake!... Give me a glass of water!..."

The first stronghold to be bombarded by Grannie Pu's cries for help was the Wu's home. This having withstood repeated raids, she now trained her sights on the Fu family downstairs on the east side, not even sparing their fourth daughter schoolteacher Fu Maodi. Elementary schools in the city had suspended classes due to the political upheaval, and as a sufferer from chronic kidney disease she took the opportunity to return home to recuperate. Her mother Hu Zhilin, a woman of fifty or so, never normally went outside the courtyard except to go shopping for vegetables. Hu Zhilin had formerly been a residential cadre, but because her husband was in Taiwan she had been stripped of that position by the Neighborhood Committee since the Cultural Revolution.

Grannie Pu's cries sounded as horrible as if they issued from the Buddhist Hell of Solitude beneath Mt. Cakravala, the iron mountain of Jambudvipa. The Wu's unusual silence was even more horrible. It was like the stillness of a catacomb piled high with white bones. These two types of horror were like the Yangtze's treacherous "pincer-barrage waters" which threatened to close in and engulf her boat, at least spiritually. Since hearing the first cry this morning Hu Zhilin's heart had seemed to be tightly constricted by a rope. It felt so suffocating, so oppressive.

For some time Hu Zhilin had been the landlady of this courtyard of two buildings, collecting rent from all living in it, but the buildings were confiscated by the government following the 1958 "socialist transition through joint state-private management." Ever since Pu Ning began renting a room on the west side downstairs, the two families had always been on friendly terms. Everyone knew of Pu Ning's warm sincerity, and when her elder sister's husband died and she wanted to lay him to rest in the top-class Nanshan Public Cemetery, it was he who found the necessary contacts to arrange for a nice inexpensive burial site, and a double tomb at that. Frankly, she felt that Pu Ning was decent in every respect, only he was permanently reluctant to take a job. This, however, was purely a men's business. It was no concern of hers. Her own teeming abundance of mundane affairs was enough to reduce her to panting exhaustion. Her husband had gone off to Taiwan twenty years before leaving behind six daughters, and like a mother hen with her chicks she had struggled to bring them up and arrange jobs and marriages for each of them. Hacking her way through thorns and thistles, the arduous path she had traveled through life was almost on a par with the Tang monk Tripitaka's pilgrimage to India to fetch

Buddhist scriptures. The burden that had weighed on her shoulders for so many years was just about to be made worthwhile when, two years before, the Cultural Revolution had suddenly burst upon her. And early this morning Grannie Pu's cries for help suddenly burst in upon her too....

At this moment her attitude was identical to Chen Yueying's; right under her nose there could be a time-bomb hidden beneath Grannie Pu's bed.

Come dinner time, mother and daughter were alone at the table. Maodi's large pale face with its square features showed a slight flush of embarrassment.

"Mom! Surely we can't just listen to her going on like this!"

Her name issuing from the mouth of the 85-year-old woman next door was no mere name but a scimitar-sharp blade stabbing straight down at the young heart in her tall, well-built frame.

Mrs. Fu looked down and continued eating in silence for a while until eventually she emptied her bowl of rice, at which point she raised her pair of patterned light-brown bamboo chopsticks and sharply tapped the bottom of her bowl, making a "du! du! du!" sound.

"Damn you! Eat up your dinner, won't you! What on earth is it to do with you?..." The sound of her voice was suppressed to the utmost, only circulating around her throat.

Normally admired for her self-control, it was unusual to find this woman scolding her daughter so sharply and severely. Her sweet pale face showed a hint of anger. To tell the truth she wasn't actually annoyed with her daughter, she was releasing the guilt which had haunted her in the past two or three days. As a friend of Pu Ning and Grannie Pu of eighteen years' standing, when Grannie Xue visited the Pu's place the other day she ought, no matter what, to have gone in with her to see the old lady. After all she was eighty-five years old and deep down we are only human, but—.

Seeing Limpy Wu obstinately perched by the Pu's door made going in there quite out of the question.

The central apartment occupied by the Wu family lay to the north facing south, while the Pu family's door lay to the west facing east. On the right-hand side of their door stood a large seven-gallon water-tank and a smaller one-gallon tank. The left-hand side originally formed part of the Pu's territory too, but the Wu's forcibly occupied this with a wooden table, slowly but surely squeezing the Pu's coal briquet stove into the corner. In between there remained a narrow little passage barely wide enough for one person to get through. For the past two days Limpy Wu had sat right across the mouth of this passage.

Now the Pu's home had become like a legendary cricket's nest. In popular belief, the most highly prized fighting crickets are the so-called "centipede cricket," "scorpion cricket" and "poisonous snake cricket," whose nests are guarded by centipedes, scorpions and poisonous snakes. Right now old Wu seemed bent on playing the role of these reptiles.

Hu Zhilin's thoughts went back to the criticism-struggle meeting of two years before. As it so happened, she was away in Changsha at the time visiting two of her daughters. Maodi in all innocence let it slip out at the meeting that the Wu's had denounced their large curtained brass bedstead upstairs as a manifestation of the "four olds" because of the feudal dragon and phoenix motifs carved on it, while in reality it was ethnic art of the laboring people. After that, Wu and his wife turned against the Fu's. Upon her return she wanted to make it up between them, but to no avail. Whenever they ran into each other they would exchange a few perfunctory words, but there was an underlying bitterness which meant that at the first opportunity the Wu's would surely stab them in the back. Against this background, plus the Warring States atmosphere of mutual wariness which already dominated the whole courtyard, how could she now walk into the home of this "evil individual" Pu Ning ... this cricket's nest guarded by a poisonous snake?

"Mrs. Fu!... Good Hu Zhilin!... For pity's sake!... Help! I'm dying of thirst!... Give me a glass of water!..."

The daughter regarded her mother with a look of pity, her slightly short-sighted eyes beginning to moisten. Her expression, however, assumed an air of scorn as she snorted gently through her nostrils.

"Hmph! The Wu's!... They're after a plump fish!..."

This time, though, her mother did not scold her. She couldn't help inwardly breathing a sigh of relief that her daughter had at last seen the crux of the problem. But the relief was only momentary. Soon those same cries once more tightened around her like a rope, binding her left and right. Her eyes grew wet and gradually overflowed.

She gave a lengthy sigh.

VI

Like that of a wounded beast, the sound of Grannie Pu's cries flung itself against every familiar hole. Finding the Wu's and Fu's doors firmly shut, it dashed off elsewhere. But the ferocity of the previous two assaults had lessened. Evidently Grannie Pu had understood that many residents in this old western-style building of solid green brick might well not feel interested in her cries. She was simply clutching at straws like someone who has fallen into the sea, doing everything humanly possible and trusting to luck.

"Comrade Wang Tongqing!... Dear Wang Tongqing!... Comrade Chen Yumei!... Good Xiaojun!... Help!... I'm dying of thirst!... For pity's sake!... Give me a glass of water!..."

Wang Tongqing, the Pu's diagonally opposite neighbor, occupied a small cubbyhole of some 13 square meters (about 140 square feet) on the ground floor next door to the Fu's. He was a boiler factory worker of around thirty, a powerfully-built, stocky man. His wife Chen Yumei, with her pretty face and nicknamed "Red Date," was the "sassy" woman of the neighborhood. She was only twenty or so, yet at every opportunity she put on the airs of someone older and more senior. She was said to have had various romantic affairs before her marriage, and she was still without a job.

"Dad! Poor old Grannie Pu ... she wants a glass of water." Thirteen-year-old schoolboy Xiaojun, hearing someone calling his own name, couldn't restrain a naughty smile as he softly spoke.

All three of them were sitting around the table under the weak electric bulb after dinner. For some unknown reason, both husband and wife felt averse to talking. Wang just smoked in silence. As he was smoking he caught his son's remark, promptly reached out with his left arm and gave the child a violent shove on the shoulder.

"You idiot! Another word and I beat you to death!" Taking a deep drag, he went on quietly, "For the next two days I forbid you to go poking your nose in the Pu's door. If I catch you, see if I don't fetch you a hell of a slap!" He slowly exhaled a mouthful of blue smoke. "It's the hand of fate that Grannie Pu had such a baby for a son, and a writer too! Now he's brought his old mother to a pretty pass!"

For a time all was quiet in the room, the only sound to be heard being the soft exhalation of smoke.

Wang Tongqing had something up his sleeve. Although he didn't speak out at that criticism-struggle meeting two years back, he mentally took sides and lent support to the general thrust, making the unrelenting and jealousy Wu's extremely unhappy. Moreover, for the last six months or more there had been tension between the Wu's and himself over a certain divisive issue and he had to be constantly on the alert, while Wu and his wife were also on their guard against him all the time.

After a while, Chen Yumei quietly went to the door and peeked out. Seeing no one in the hallway she came in and closed the door, saying in an undertone, "That Limpy guards her door like an iron general all day. He's determined to be a dog blocking the path, the bastard!" She made a face at her husband, winking her lovely eyes. "They say 'even the poor have three pieces of property.' Do you think the Pu's have only 'three pieces'?... That wicked old wife of his is so hard-hearted; she can't wait for all the Pu's to die so she can have everything to herself! Hmph! And that big room of theirs, 25 square meters (about 270 square feet)...."

Wang interrupted her with a "shush" and pulled a face as he softly said, "Pipe down a bit!"

Chen Yumei had always admired Pu Ning's dashing air. He looked young for fifty, and with his genial, cultured manner he was so different from Wang. Alongside that proletarian trash he was a crane amid a flock of roosters. No doubt that was what they meant by capitalist pro-Westerners! Western chic! But how she adored it! Infuriatingly, though, this counter-revolutionary pro-Westerner Pu Ning, out-and-out capitalist as he seemed, was never willing even to ogle her properly! Truly "lovingly the blossom may fall, but unheedingly the water flows on."

She glanced at Wang Tongqing, the cigarette-end in his mouth having already accumulated a length of ash.

"I bet old Pu gets at least twenty years of imprisonment," she said coldly.

"He's got it coming to him!" Wang shoved his cigarette butt into the hole in the glass ashtray, cocked his ear to listen out for a moment, and gave a single dry cough. "Huh! The old witch is going for Xiaosu on the second floor now. No use!" He spat a gob of phlegm on the floor and said quietly, "What the hell is it to do with me! The old witch has gotten her just deserts, and the sooner she dies the better! Damn it!" After a pause he added darkly, "And then see if I don't have a final settling of scores with Limpy Wu!"

"Comrade Zhao! Comrade Shi Xiaosu!... Help!... Please help!... I'm dying of thirst!... Give me a glass of water!..."

As Wang Tongqing had said, her cries were now raining down on the Zhao family on the second floor with the same impetuousness as her previous assaults.

Apparently Grannie Pu still cherished high hopes of Shi Xiaosu. Thinking back, Xiaosu had been poverty-stricken as a child. Her schooling came to an end with higher elementary school at the age of twelve or thirteen, as her family couldn't even afford to send her to junior high school. With her hair let down all day long she used to labor for her father Shi Abing raising vegetable seedlings for a living. In snowy weather her bare feet were like a pair of frozen tomatoes, and it was Pu Ning who gave her some old shoes and socks to ward off the cold. In those days Pu Ning used to call her over to his place at monthly intervals to do some cleaning up, mopping the floor, humping sacks of rice, carrying loads of coal. Besides paying her money, he would offer her plenty to eat and drink. So the Shi family always looked up to Pu Ning. Later, when some ruthless high-ranking cadres in Shandong Province sent people down to "pick out" attractive girls in the Yangtze Delta area, her elder sister, a great beauty, was selected and married off to a regimental commander in Jinan who a few years later rose even higher up the ladder to divisional commander. Now that the Shi family had struck it rich they rapidly invaded their neighbor Yin Jinsong's vegetable garden. When their high ranking son-in-law showed up to give them his backing, as they particularly asked him to do, the neighbors were dumbstruck and intimidated into inaction. Even the chief of the local security bureau gave way to him to some extent. Unfortunately this divisional commander was grossly obese; his whole body was one round ball of blubber like a great pumpkin, weighing 170 catties at the very least. Everyone said the Shi's had planted a lovely flower on cowshit. How could she bear this great pumpkin pressing down on her roselike body? But with this nepotism, all chickens and dogs rise with Buddha into heaven. Everyone in the Shi family, young and old alike, now found employment. Xiaosu herself was promoted as an "active element" by a local state-run hardware factory. She wore a woolen overcoat and an Enicar Swiss watch, rode a Phoenix brand bicycle and married Political Instructor Zhao, a deputy company commander in the Air Force. It was a complete turnaround.

"Comrade Xiaosu!... Comrade Zhao!... Help!... I'm dying of thirst!... For pity's sake!... Give me a glass of water!..."

In the darkness of night these cries rang out with even greater poignancy, taking on an element of solemnity. Comrade

Zhao, a native of Shandong and a man of kindly disposition, was shocked at the sound and couldn't help feeling uncomfortable.

"Xiaosu, Grannie Pu's cries sound so wretched. We can't just stand idly by. It's only a matter of a glass of water. What harm can it do to take it over to her?..." At which point he abruptly swallowed his words. In the light of his many years' experience in political work, the silence of the entire courtyard in response to these cries was a major lesson for him. He could not but consider the truth of Mao Zedong's dictum "situations can overwhelm mankind."

Traces of a wry smile showed on Xiaosu's plump round face.

"When I was small, old Pu and Grannie Pu were good to me and looked after my family too. On that basis I ought to help her." There again—she pondered a moment before recalling the freshly-learned revolutionary term. "According to 'revolutionary humanitarianism' we ought to sympathize with her. But—" she directed a pout at the floor beneath her feet, "even her next-door neighbors the Wu's are adamant about not helping her, so what can we upstairs neighbors do? It's beyond our reach!"

She analyzed the situation for her husband. She didn't move in until after the criticism-struggle meeting in the courtyard the other year. She had no dispute with the Wu's; their relations weren't bad. But because she was unwilling to string along with Mrs. Wu and side with the Wu's against the Sun's, the Wu's had always been a little bit peeved and she had to tread carefully. There again, one mustn't block the path to riches, and if she went to the aid of Grannie Pu she would indeed be blocking someone's way to wealth.

"What 'way to wealth'?"

"You blockhead! You really are a numbskull through and through! You can't even see what makes these few families tick." With a wry grin she said, "If Grannie Pu really does starve to death, there'll be some fighting over her property. The Wu's want it all for themselves, but I'm afraid it won't be so simple. Xia Shuimu and old Wang will take the lead in stirring up trouble. On the surface old Wang is indifferent and makes out it's nothing to do with him, but in fact he's already hinted that he is a member of the working class, and that little cubby-hole of his, that cockle-shell of a place, is a demeaning insult to the working class. If Pu Ning gets put away for fifteen or twenty years, old Wang won't wait for Grannie Pu to kick the bucket; he'll approach the Housing Bureau and ask to be allocated her house. And what clout will old Wu have? He's a hold-over from the KMT! As for Xia Shuimu, he was a hoodlum in the old society. Toward the end of the Japanese occupation he was traveling around trading on his own account at the age of twenty with the backing of that traitor Wang. Now he's joined a light-bulb factory, but he's an inferior worker; only he makes out he's a decent worker, a genuine worker! Still, Xia Shuimu told me on the quiet that his place on the third floor catches the afternoon sun and heats up to forty degrees Celsius (104 degrees Fahrenheit) in the summer. It's only good for steaming buns of human flesh. How can a human being live there? He is a member of the working class, and as soon as Pu Ning is sentenced, he will demand to switch places with Grannie Pu. The Wu's, however, have the advantage of living right next door and are bound to make the first move and grab the Pu's possessions and occupy their house before anyone else. You'll see! There's sure to be fireworks." She tried hard to keep her voice down, as if leaking some top-secret intelligence report.

As if receiving enlightenment from above, Zhao finally saw her point and kept saying, "How silly of me! How silly of me!"

Stepping across to him, his wife once again quietly breathed into his ear, "Even when nothing's happening the Wu's go around to the Neighborhood Committee and the police station laying complaints, cooking up secret reports and stirring up trouble. Who now would dare to enter the door of the 'evil individual' Pu Ning, that really would be...."

Xia Shuimu's inner desire was put in a nutshell in Xiaosu's brief words. Nevertheless, the latter had seen only the peel and flesh of the fruit, not its kernel. Xia after all had knocked around in Shanghai and was worldly-wise enough never to let his innermost secret leak out.

As soon as word got out last summer that Pu Ning had been arrested he had a brainwave and went straight over to visit Grannie Pu to express his concern and take her some snacks and delicacies. He told her to let him or his wife Jinhua know if there was anything she might be needing in the future. After that, he and Jinhua made a habit of dropping by at the Pu's in the evenings after work every other day or so and taking her something to eat. After only the sixth or seventh time, that tigress Chen Yueying's roar suddenly burst out from next door.

"Who do you think you are! You little Shanghai urchin! You asshole! You ruffian, you hoodlum from a light-bulb factory! Why don't you look at yourself in the mirror before you come stealing our territory! Don't you know what place this is? Think an asshole hoodlum like you can come waltzing in and out of here whenever you like? What was all that stuff you did back then with that traitor Wang? We ought to make you come clean.... You come strutting around here again, and see if I don't fetch someone to tear your hide off...."

By "someone" she was in fact referring to her eighteen-year old younger son Wu Yalun, a senior high school student who practiced kick-boxing with a master. In an instant this young boxing instructor, known as "little black charcoal," was looming in the doorway furiously yelling.

"Get out of here, and fast! Get out! Get out! See if I don't beat you till you eat shit! Till your asshole points to the sky!"

Xia Shuimu and his wife had just emerged from the Pu's into the courtyard when they heard this barrage of foul language, and they went upstairs without uttering a single word. As Wu Yaolun scoffed later, "Those bastards scurried away with their tails between their legs."

Xia Shuimu was a resourceful individual for his ability to wriggle out of tough comers. Thereafter the two of them, husband and wife, still soldiered on doggedly, but with a change of tactics from positional warfare to guerrilla warfare. Every time the Wu's went out to the cinema or to enjoy themselves, they would tiptoe along to Grannie Pu's, and so surreptitiously maintain contact.

Xia Shuimu's course of action was crystal clear. As soon as Pu Ning was sentenced to jail, Wang Tongqing and the Wu's were bound to fight over the Pu's bigger apartment. Let two tigers do battle, for one is sure to be wounded; he would imitate Bian Zhuangzi in the old story of how he set about killing a tiger. Another analogy was that of the snipe grappling with the clam, in which he would play the fisherman who profits from the situation. The Wu's didn't have a penny to their name, and couldn't afford to win over friends with money. As for Wang, money was as dear to him as life itself, and he certainly wouldn't be prepared to bankrupt himself to forge friendships. Neither of them had any choice but to brazen it out. Only he, Xia Shuimu, had been willing to dig into his pockets, dance attendance on the cadres at the local Housing Bureau and make a determined effort to curry favor with them. He had treated them to dinner several times and quietly sent them Jinhua ham as gifts, requesting them to "open the back door." Having won their tacit compliance, once the crucial moment arrived they would naturally come to his aid.

Xia Shuimu had already worked everything out with a colleague at the factory. When the time came he would use a carrot and stick approach to persuade Grannie Pu to move into the colleague's small room, while he himself gave up his top-floor room to his colleague and moved into the Pu's. As he enjoyed the support of the Housing Bureau there was no fear of old Mrs. Pu not bowing to his demands.

But now the situation had changed, and changed for the simpler at that.

"Comrade Xia Shuimu...Old Comrade Xia!... Comrade Jinhua... Help! For pity's sake!... I'm dying of thirst... Give me a glass of water..."

He and his wife had just finished their evening meal and were sitting at the table over a cup of tea. Hearing the cries, they couldn't help exchanging smiles.

"The old lady isn't in such good form as this morning. Her short fat body trembling slightly, Jinhua kept her voice low enough for only her husband to hear.

"I think it's only a matter of three or four days now...." Xia Shuimu's habitually sallow face, its sickly pallor due to excessive love-making, was flush-red with excitement. As if struck by a thought he whispered softly to her, "I think you should take another Jiang ham over to Section Chief Wang's, a genuine Jiang Village ham to go with his wine."[5]

Jinhua nodded her plump head.

Xia Shuimu lit a Beauty brand cigarette and settled down for a smoke. Turning things over in his mind, Xia figured that the only person with any clout at all in the coming battle was old Wu's son-in-law Wang Zhiyuan living opposite, who was now a member of the revolutionary rebel faction at the public transportation company. But Xia didn't care. Wang Zhiyuan had risen from ticket seller to driver only a few years ago, and as a junior hanger-on there wasn't a lot he could do. Section Chief Wang headed the rebel faction at the Housing Bureau, so a mere driver was certainly no match for him.

His immediate neighbor on the third floor, Mrs. Xie, had been promoted to head of the Party Committee office at the municipal plastic factory, and as a high flyer she really did have some political capital. Fortunately she would soon be eligible for dormitory accommodation in the factory, where she would live in a large new suite of rooms. That place of Grannie Pu's was of no interest to her.

At this point in his deliberations he exhaled a mouthful of smoke, as on his face there once again appeared a chilling smile.

VII

During the Cultural Revolution, those who did not join any rebel faction but simply observed events dispassionately and maintained a neutral stance were uniformly dubbed the "non-

---

[5] The most famous brand of Jinhua ham comes from Jiang Village. It is also called "Jiang Ham."

committed faction." By the time of these cries for help from the Pu's, only three families in the whole courtyard could truly be considered members of the "non-committed faction:" the Xie's, the female worker Cuizhen on the ground floor opposite, and the Zhang's upstairs.

Mrs. Xie wanted to move, but not because her room was too small or too far from town as she claimed. Her hidden reason was quite different. Although she was plain looking, being short and dumpy like a dwarf winter melon, her husband Xie Yuqing was a man of good looks who stood straight as a ramrod. In the period immediately after his return from "resisting U.S. aggression and aiding North Korea," even as a mere platoon officer Xie Yuqing had been the hero of the courtyard. What with his grass green army uniform and his command of cadre terminology, he made a great impression. Everybody looked up to him. He was assigned to a unit of the local district committee with responsibility for local cultural and educational guidance work, which took him everywhere. Through a strange combination of circumstances he got to know a girl from a capitalist family with a taste for dressing flamboyantly. They fell head over heels in love, and eventually the inevitable happened in the shrubbery on the other side of the river. She was still a minor, and her family sued him in the municipal court. In view of the fact that Mrs. Xie had been a model worker or activist year after year and was one of the elite the Party was keen to nurture, a lenient view was taken of Xie's case: he was merely expelled from Party membership and sentenced to two years of education through labor. The case was kept absolutely secret in order to protect the reputations of the families on both sides. Mrs. Xie lied to her relatives, friends and neighbors that Xie had gone away on a long-term mission to Sichuan Province. Upon completion of his sentence, just a few months before the Cultural Revolution, he returned home and was assigned to work in a factory. By then he was nearly forty, but still with a fresh healthy glow to his face and looking as handsome as ever. The neighbors suspected nothing. Unfortunately no secret can be concealed for ever. Last year news about Xie came to the ears of

"Red Date" Chen Yumei from some unknown source, and one day she was quietly discussing it with her husband in the bedroom when she was overheard by her young son. Next afternoon this sixth grader, who normally addressed Xie with punctilious respect as "Uncle Xie," cheekily dashed up to him and called out,

"Old Xie!... Xie Yuqing!... You—hee hee hee hee!..." Xiaojun accompanied his jeers by wickedly pulling a face.

Mrs. Xie's jaw immediately dropped and without a word she quickly dragged her husband upstairs, with their two daughters hastily following behind.

To Mrs. Xie, Xiaojun's mischievous prank was every bit as sharp a reprimand as when a member of the British House of Commons is directly "named" by the Speaker.[6]

A single leaf spells autumn. At that moment in time the People's Republic of China must surely have been the most sensitive and nervous country in the entire world. And this whole courtyard, like countless others throughout Mainland China, was a highly sensitive place where a single pin falling to the ground could spark suspicions of conspiracy.

That night, with a face as black as fury, Mrs. Xie firmly insisted to her husband that they must move out as soon as possible. Luckily the new dormitory inside the factory was nearly finished and she only had to apply to be sure of being allocated a spacious apartment.

Xiaojun was merely the fuse for this decision, for in fact she already had a presentiment that the truth would ultimately get out in the courtyard; after all, where in the world was there paper that could wrap fire?

---

[6] The sternest reprimand the Speaker of the House of Commons can issue to a Member of Parliament is to order him to withdraw from the chamber. When this sanction is exercised, the Member concerned is directly named. Normally members of the House of Commons are addressed by the name of their constituency.

"Comrade Xie!... Comrade Xie Yuqing!... Mrs. Xie!... Big Miss Xie!... Little Miss Xie!... Help!... For pity's sake!... Give me a glass of water!... I'm dying of thirst!..."

In the stillness of night, these cries were markedly weaker but still clearly audible as they penetrated to the Xie's place on the third floor. Their two daughters were revising their lessons while husband and wife sat facing each other under the lamp, regarding one another in complete silence. The cries were like sounds from another planet being transmitted back to Earth by rocket-mounted instruments. They weren't the least interested. They could hardly manage to cope with affairs on Earth, let alone those of another planet. Soon they were drinking freshly-brewed Longjing tea and talking over their forthcoming move.

Their feelings were shared by the Zhang's who lived opposite. To the couple, Grannie Pu was like an alien: her cries were sounds from Mars or Mercury and their very content was all vague. They weren't even clear about Grannie Pu's having fallen ill. And no wonder. Both husband and wife worked at a local state-owned machinery factory, going out early and coming back home late. The cooped-up corner where they lived was like an isolated island in the Pacific Ocean where contact between the natives and outsiders was rare. Of course, the Cultural Revolu-tion was like a permanent force 14 typhoon whose buffetings engendered widespread fear. It plunged everyone into crisis and robbed their lives of certainty from time to time. Both of them sought only to protect themselves and shied away from any involvement in extraneous matters. Take that criticism-struggle meeting in the courtyard two years ago. Having found out about it in advance, Zhang simply fled to his father-in-law's home in the evening and didn't venture to return home to sleep. It was the only way to cope. Needless to say, their next-door neighbor Wang Zhiyuan's home was a tiger's lair they mustn't disturb. They must simply make themselves disappear all the time like shadows in the June sunshine.

"Dear Comrade Zhang!... Dear Mrs. Zhang!... Help! Give me a glass of water!... I'm dying of thirst!..."

Tucked inside their warm cotton quilt against the springtime chill, husband and wife let the "Martian" sounds from opposite wash over them as they weighed things up and discussed how to continue playing their "non-committed" role at the next day's criticism-struggle against the "evil demons" at the factory.

Although Cuizhen belonged to the "non-committed" faction, she wasn't as relaxed about it as the Xie's or the Zhang's. She had made up her mind to move next month and had already asked a colleague at the knitting mill to make arrangement for her. She was transferred to Hangzhou from Shanghai in the first place only as a "support the hinterland" worker. But by then she already had her heart set on a salesman at a large food store on Shanghai's Nanjing Road. After their wedding, husband and wife played a permanent "ox-herd and weaver girl" duo in a marriage that forever revolved around traveling, honeymoon-style—it was really quite unique. Every Spring Festival, the only time of year when she had any length of time off work, she would travel to Shanghai to be with her husband again. The rest of the time her husband would take advantage of his occasional business trips and such holidays as May 1st Labor Day or October 1st National Day to visit her in her love-nest and rekindle their dreams of married bliss. She had grown up steeped in the bustling atmosphere of a cosmopolitan city, and her attractive good looks and fashionable clothes naturally set her apart from the normal run of girls.

A month ago, after the Lantern Festival, at about 11 o'clock at night shortly after coming home from her shift at work, she heard a gentle knock on the door. Opening it, she was surprised to find it was her neighbor Principal Lu. He softly closed the door and, drooling with a big show of tenderness, quietly said, "Cuizhen, aren't you lonely all on your own? How about if I keep you company? Let me just spend an hour with you..."

Normally she was a timid creature, afraid of everything—even a mouse almost would petrify her. But now a burst of incisive courage came to her. In an instant she pulled down her face. Firmly pointing to the door with her forefinger, Cuizhen said with icy coldness, "Principal Lu! Behave yourself and get out of here immediately! Otherwise I'll scream at the top of my voice, and then see what happens to your reputation tomorrow!..."

"No, no, no!... I'll leave, I'm going! Whatever you do, don't scream!..."

The visitor was in a panic, not having anticipated that a girl who was normally as soft as a sponge would suddenly turn out to be as hard as a sheet of steel, and instantly fled.

Only the next day did she find out that the day before, a Saturday, Mrs. Lu had taken their two sons back to visit her own parents. After that, Lu never spoke to her again, and she ignored him too. Only when it was unavoidable did she exchange a few perfunctory words with Mrs. Lu in case she grew suspicious. She would never have dared to let this secret out at all, except that her next-door neighbor Sun Junlun, whom she respected more than anyone, once asked her why she was so anxious to move out. As Mrs. Sun and her three daughters were out, she quietly told him the whole story, repeatedly urging him at all costs not to let the cat out of the bag.

"Cuizhen!... Nice Cuizhen, there's a good girl! Help!... For pity's sake!... I'm dying of thirst!... Give me a glass of water!... Help!..."

At the sound of these cries, Cuizhen felt wounded to the heart by an inexpressible feeling of pity. After all, she was such a very old lady, and who does not have parents? All the more so since, as well as Sun, she also respected Pu Ning's regular decency of conduct. But, she quietly thought to herself, I myself have a wicked wolf for a neighbor, while both opposite and upstairs are two tigers' lairs. Since Wang Tongqing and Xia Shuimu both seem to be counting on the Pu's place, why should I get involved? To put it bluntly, she herself was but "a clay Bodhisattva crossing the Yangtze who could not come to her own rescue." If the risk to herself was too great, why bother to poke her nose into other people's business?

VIII

The neighbors in general were unaware of Cuizhen's story, and their impression of Principal Lu was naturally a good one. Lu came from a poor farming family out of town. Having completed his studies at an intermediate teachers' college he underwent a lengthy process of nurturing and testing by the Party before being promoted step by step to director of discipline and dean of studies, then finally clambering up into the position of principal of the local Qinfeng Elementary School. With his high moral airs and genial attitude this middle-aged man nudging forty embodied the perfect gentleman. Added to that was his nut-brown peasant's face which gave him an earthy rustic touch. Besides, his speech never betrayed a hint of capitalist literary language. All this immensely enhanced his authority as a Party member school principal. Furthermore, his wife, Teacher Wu, was elected as an activist at Fish Market Bridge Elementary School year after year. Of their two sons the one at elementary school wore the red scarf of the Young Pioneers while the other was in the Communist Youth League at his senior high school—a family red to the core. Unfortunately, though, in the past two years the winds of the Cultural Revolution had blown him dizzily off course. Big-character-posters stuck up in the school made the walls a mass of black, and the Red Guard rebels dubbed him an "inveterate feudalist" and "the school's number one capitalist-roader." Following a big criticism-struggle meeting they forced him to "stand aside." From being principal he slipped back to a teacher, and very nearly found himself tumbling to rock bottom. In his denunciation it was said that in marking sixth-grade compositions he would write one wrong character in every three or four essays, and that his corrections even included totally incomprehensible phrases. For this he was accused of "leading people's children astray." One big-character-poster revealed that he would ask older sixth-grade girls in for a talk, and while lecturing to them in person would sometimes stroke the faces of the prettier ones in the very act of delivering instruction, which was considered an immense loss of dignity on the part of a teacher and a derogation of duty verging on indecency. No sensible individual, however, took these wildfire criticisms at face value. After all, "you don't mince words in a cursing match, nor pull punches in a boxing match," and these were generally dismissed as the ravings of madmen. When word of all this came to Sun Junlun's ears, he too took them for "tall tales." But one afternoon in the dog days of last summer Wang Tongqing and his wife suddenly had a big row and come to blows in a terrible way. Chen Yumei screamed for help, and whereas none of the other neighbors would lift a finger, Lu took it upon himself to climb down off his bed and dash across to break up the fight. When Sun went over to mediate, he saw Lu with his arms around "Red Date" Chen Yumei as if to prevent Wang from punching her, except that he was clasping her a little too tightly. "Red Date" was only wearing a thin short-sleeved cotton print vest which left her arms bare, and a pair of shorts. Lu had on a sleeveless singlet. Each was squeezed against the naked flesh of the other. Even then Sun still didn't harbor any suspicions toward him. Only with Cuizhen's confidence last month did he recollect and begin to put two and two together.

As a fish knows of its own accord how warm or cold the water is, so Lu had been feeling distinctly uneasy for almost a month. Cuizhen's icy face was like an icy fist which seemed to strike him day after day. Not until he heard she wanted to move could he breathe freely again. Not that all his fears focused on her, as anyway it was only her side of the story against him, and without corroboration she wouldn't be able to press her case against him. Mostly he was afraid of the Wu's and the Wang's. If they should get wind of any rumor and spread it around, it would mean curtains for him. At the criticism-struggle meeting that year, he and his wife bitterly denounced the Wu and Wang families. They said that when Wu Peizhen mopped her floor it was as if it were raining on the three families below, and they had to put umbrellas up indoors. Cuizhen was the worst affected, while he and the Sun's also got soaked by raindrops. One time they complained about this to Wang Zhiyuan. They explained that the ceiling was not solid, being just a layer of planks with cracks in between, and asked them to take more care. But that very afternoon the Wu's elder daughter gaily sloshed a bucket of dirty water over the floor, drenching the three families below in a shower of filthy rain.

The three neighbors shared a water tub which was connected to their gutter. This was meant to provide clean water for cooking, drinking and brewing tea, but the Wu's daughter was in the habit of picking up a large greasy food bowl and scooping water from the tub to wash the dishes. Mrs. Sun politely pointed out her objections to her. Next day she went right ahead and tossed a pair of muddy plastic overshoes into the tub, then cleaned them off with a big scrubbing brush. As for Limpy Wu, he threw his weight around the place no less than his daughter did. At twelve o'clock at night, when all the neighbors in the courtyard were asleep after being at work all day, his darling son Wu Yalun would sing "Mao Zedong has appeared in the East" at the top of his voice, creating a terrible racket and shattering their peaceful dreams. If you said anything, he would accuse you of being opposed to singing the praises of Chairman Mao, which was what an active counter-revolutionary would do!

Also present at the criticism-struggle meeting was Feng Shaoqing, deputy chairman of the Neighborhood Committee, who stoked things up from the sidelines, fanning the flames and spreading waves. One neighbor after another enthusiastically denounced the rampant arrogance and offensive conduct of those two families, hammering home their criticisms until all of a sudden Wu Peizhen had a premature period and her menstrual blood seeped onto the floor, where it formed a small puddle. Only then was she allowed to go upstairs to change her trousers and apply a sanitary towel.

Having made enemies with both those families, Lu could hardly wait for Cuizhen to move out and give him one less worry on his mind.

"Principal Lu!... Teacher Wu!... Good Wu Daming!... Help!... For pity's sake!... Give me a glass of water!... I'm dying of thirst!..."

Short, petite Teacher Wu had just finished marking her
students' math homework under the light and gathered the
exercise books into a neat pile on the table. Her round white
face, strewn with freckles, wore a serious look. She quietly
addressed her husband in subdued tones.

"Old Lu! You've been a school principal and I'm a teacher
and we've both been studying Party policy for years. Pu Ning's
criminal offence is his own personal matter; each person's
crimes stop with that individual! The socialist system is no
feudal dynasty and we can't implicate innocent people. Pu Ning
may deserve imprisonment, but his 85-year-old mother hasn't
committed any crime. Now she is sick, hungry and thirsty.
Shouldn't we consider finding some way, based on Chairman
Mao's revolutionary humanitarianism, of taking her something
to eat?..."

"I've thought of that too, but the consciousness of the masses
isn't that high, especially—" Lu jabbed at the ceiling with his
forefinger, then pointed opposite. "If they go spreading lies and
twist the facts to the authorities, we'll be in for it. You know
very well what times these are. And I'm 'standing aside'." After
a moment's silence he added quietly, "I think the best thing
would be to go through the organization, to speak to the
organization first and ask the organization to decide. I'm still a
Party member and must respect the views of the Party
organization." He paused and looked at his wristwatch. "It's
past 10 o'clock. There's no time this evening. I'll talk it over
with Old Sun and Mrs. Mao tomorrow morning. Although Mrs.
Mao is retired, she was a Party member at the factory and was
an outstanding worker for many years. Now she's a member of
the neighborhood public security committee. I must get in touch
with her first of all and she's bound to take this matter up."

His wife nodded. "So that's it, then. All of you will discuss it
in the morning."

To her mind, in purely political and Party terms Lu was a
red-robed Catholic cardinal among the population of the courtyard, a cut above the ordinary masses. When the time came, he

would proudly stand forth and actively guide the courtyard's overall political direction.

IX

Gray-haired, strong and tall, Mrs. Mao was a manly-looking woman with a broad, deeply-tanned face which exuded a Buddha-like compassion. She enjoyed sorting things out and resolving disputes for people in the neighborhood. But Grannie Pu's cries, which had been resounding since dawn the previous day, presented her with the first really serious problem she had encountered in her life.

"Mrs. Mao! Senior Master Mao! Young Master Mao! Young Mrs. Mao!... Darling Yinfeng!... Help!... I'm dying of thirst!... For pity's sake!... Give me a glass of water!..."

All five members of the family had been addressed by name, but, like her, none of the other four made any mention of the sound at the dinner table. They had all had it drummed into them what the Wu's and the Wang's were like. The Mao's had moved in only a year before. Mr. and Mrs. Huang, the couple who exchanged homes with her, had waited until they moved away to spell out the evil deeds of these two families in no uncertain terms, quite taking Mrs. Mao's breath away and almost making her regret she'd ever switched homes in the first place.

Wu Peizhen had been strangely jealous of Huang's pretty wife and had concocted various poisonous rumors about her, as well as routinely bullying the Huang's at every turn. At one point Huang flew into such a rage that he grabbed a big eight-catty machete ready to split her head open, intending to fight to the finish. Luckily he was pulled away by his neighbors, otherwise it might have blown up into big news in Hangzhou. That August, two years ago when the Cultural Revolution first swept the country, Huang became a minor figure among the Red Guards. In early September he rapidly summoned a criticism-struggle meeting involving the entire courtyard. It was a baking hot Indian summer when the men were wearing sleeveless singlets. Old Wu and his wife, though, were tightly wrapped in thick cotton quilted jackets and still shivered with cold. They were verbally attacked until their faces turned clay-white as if they'd caught malaria.

Next day the two families found some Red Guards to back them up and mounted a counter-strike. After that, both sides sniped away at each other endlessly. Suddenly the whole courtyard turned into a battleground as in the Wu-Yue conflict of ancient China, sharply split into two opposing camps. The situation was as tense as a drawn bow. The strategy of the Wu and Wang families was first to capture the enemy leader, so they ignored the rest of their opponents and focused solely on Huang. He and his wife worked during the day but also had to stay up late countering these hostilities at night, which claimed so much of their time that of course they couldn't hold out for long.

Besides, they were overwhelmed by sheer force of numbers since there were only the two of them, while the other neighbors did nothing by way of active support, each being intent on minding their own business. In the end, Huang beat a retreat and exchanged apartments with the Mao's, allowing the Wu's to take the upper hand and giving a further boost to their arrogance.

Hearing this history of bloody warfare literally made old Mrs. Mao break out in beads of sweat, and from then on she had made a point of paying careful lip-service to those two families. In any case, though, since Mrs. Mao was a member of the public security committee and the head of a thoroughgoing "red" household of workers, neither of the two families would have dared to offend her. In view of the circumstances, even with her innate kindness of heart she felt constrained to adopt a "non-committed" stance for the time being toward this sudden occurrence with Grannie Pu—to be a turtle with its head drawn inside its shell, so to speak.

Tonight, as bedtime approached, she really could contain herself no longer. Before her husband, her son, her daughter-in-law and her daughter Yinfeng, she quietly revealed her inmost thoughts. No one spoke a word, which was tantamount to raising both hands in agreement. Her husband, a retiree, had long suffered from cancer of the esophagus. Being himself "at heaven's door," he really didn't have the energy to attend to extraneous affairs.

Her son was a pork butcher, and her daughter-in-law plucked duck's feathers at a poultry and egg company. As well as working at their tedious jobs they also had to interminably study, discuss and attend this or that explosive criticism-struggle meeting. Plunged into exhaustion day after day, how should they have any appetite for leaping into the fiery pit, the whirlpool in the courtyard? Her daughter Yinfeng was a vibrant character who pitied Grannie Pu from the bottom of her heart, but she was also a good girl who was accustomed to obeying her mother. When she heard her mother painfully confessing her true feelings, she quietly chimed in.

"Grannie Pu is a good person. I only hope the Bodhisattvas protect her in her old age and keep her safe from harm!"

"You little devil! People out there have already 'smashed the four olds.' The Bodhisattvas have been swept away and they no longer exist! Don't talk nonsense, and mind they don't overhear you next door." With a smile, old Mrs. Mao scolded her daughter in a low voice.

Actually, Wang Zhiyuan and his wife next door wouldn't have overheard her. They considered the Mao family as neutral and thus as people to be won over to their side. Although the two households were only separated by a thin wall panel the Wang's had no intention of listening in on the Mao family's doings.

"Comrade Wang Zhiyuan!... Good Peizhen!... Good Baoluo!... Good Naya!... Help!... For pity's sake!... I'm dying of thirst!... Give me a glass of water!..."

Deep in their hearts the true feelings of the Wang couple toward these miserable cries were rather different, though Wu Peizhen kept the lid on hers and on the surface stuck by what her parents and husband said. Secretly despised by all as an "evil bitch" and "female despot," this woman actually pitied Grannie Pu from the bottom of her heart. This was not entirely due to any regard for her, but more because she adored Pu Ning. She cared not a whit for anyone in this courtyard except Pu Ning. She had been captivated by Pu's writings, which had once enjoyed great popularity. Since moving into the courtyard she had been the chief admirer of old Pu's character and demeanor. Though she had occasionally lost her temper with the famous author, even turned hostile and scoffed at him, the storms would quickly pass and blue skies returned in no time. He had never nursed a grudge against her. She knew very well that of all the people in Hangzhou perhaps only old Pu, the sensitive author, could truly sympathize with and comprehend her personal situation: a queen, a princess of beauty at college, a fresh rose from some Alpine summit, who had been literally ruined and strewn on the ground by that bastard Wang Zhiyuan, as well as splattered with mud and ravaged by the political storms of the era. Finally she was assigned to the People's Life Pharmaceutical Works as a lab technician, where her monthly salary was less than the price of a bottle of champagne at a night's dancing in the old days. She had barely turned thirty, but due to overwork she had become shortsighted. She had developed a waxy yellow complexion and sallow bony cheeks, and white hair had even appeared on the nape of her neck. Now the die was cast, and besides she had three children on her hands. Apart from occasionally getting as angry as a turkey and bitterly tearing Wang off a strip, there was nothing she could do but accept her fate. Wang, however, had one lovable point. No matter how she scolded him or beat him, he never struck back or answered back. Her innumerable quarrels and fights with her husband never led to anything. At the most, his only recourse to violence was to restrain her from hitting him. Her little family already had a reputation: every three days a little quarrel, every seven days a big quarrel; once a fortnight a little fight, once a month a big fight. They had gone on fighting until after the Cultural Revolution broke out, and only when the two of them suffered a criticism-struggle did their civil war ease off as they united to some extent against the outside world. But deep down she was seething with incalculable hatred! She hated this world, and apart from her parents, brothers and sisters and her own children, she hated all people—especially Wang Zhiyuan. She believed Pu Ning understood and pitied her injured soul better than anyone else. This is what made her pay him such respect. All the more so as he extended such a generous helping hand to her parental family since they had moved into the courtyard. And on that night when the whole courtyard denounced them so viciously, he steadfastly insisted he was too sick to leave his coir-strung bed. Such great kindness was touching indeed.

Early on, she had given Pu broad hints as to her feelings quite a number of times, and had frequently gone out of her way to please him. To her dismay, though, his deeper feelings were entirely focused on his beloved wife, so he habitually made out he was as deaf and dumb to her as some rock on Mt. Lingyin's Flying Peak. Inevitably, in due course her ardor cooled, except that from time to time it would flicker back into life and, like a leaking gutter after rain, would drip intermittently, putting Pu into embarrassment from time to time.

All of this was absolutely her personal secret. No one in the family or outside had the slightest inkling of it. Only old Pu with his microscope-like eyes perceived every minuscule detail, but he never breathed a word.

Over the past two days, under pressure from her family, she had just had to flow with the tide and let things take their natural course. As to her parents' ulterior motive, she was as much in the dark as Yaozong.

"Mom and them are weird. Grannie Pu is begging so pitifully for a glass of water. What's the big deal about taking one over to her?..." she couldn't forbear gently muttering.

"You silly little creature! What the hell do you know? Two years ago at that criticism-struggle meeting you were treated so badly it brought on your period. If it hadn't been for me and Yaozong managing to maneuver to take the pressure off you, how could you have gone on living calmly until today? Your mom and dad have had their reasons over the past two days, and I totally support them. You can never be sure of people. They're all jackals, wolves and tigers in the courtyard. We've already suffered once at their hands and we can't let it happen a second time...."

Wang's voice was even softer, so low that only she and the two children could hear. In fact, though, neither Baoluo nor Naya—the boy and girl whose names Grannie Pu had called out—could make head or tail of the dialogue between their father and mother. Meanwhile little Xiaobo was by this time fast asleep.

Wang Zhiyuan glanced at his wife and children, then turned his gaze toward the Pu's place across the way downstairs. His pallid face with its regular features showed a grim smile. From time to time his short body rocked gently on the little old bench. His colleagues had been jealous of his having married a beauty, and despite having no evidence, they had somehow gotten wind of the roguish way he had plucked the flower of her virginity that night. On top of that, there were some occasional episodes of light-fingered dishonesty from his days as a ticket seller, which meant he had had to struggle along in the company for fourteen years before being taken up by the organization and rising to the rank of driver. But tonight he was truly satisfied with himself. After all, he had successfully enjoyed the entire youth of a college "princess" along with her gorgeous body, and had "planted his seed" by fathering three cute kids.

He only had a high school education, but he was a clever schemer. Two years ago at that great debate to right all wrongs, he and Yaozong found a squad of Red Guards from Hangzhou Number 3 Middle School to run the show. Before long the meeting site at Baoqing Bridge Elementary School next door was seething with a great mass of people who had crowded in to watch the fun. Determined to seize the initiative, he took everyone by surprise by obtaining a nod from the Red Guards to be first to speak. He deliberately took his time and launched boldly into a long tirade aimed at delving step by step into the very heart of the matter. First he denounced Huang's wife Wang Meiling as a "capitalist-roader" and "idler" who regularly dressed in a smart pro-Western style, and whose pleated skirts were now targets of the "smash the four olds" campaign. Her insistence on copying the corrupt mannerisms of British imperialist Hong Kong Chinese by dressing so outrageously seductively was an attempt to corrupt women of the proletariat. Her husband Huang habitually resisted Chairman Mao's "supreme directives." Chairman Mao's first big-character poster called for "bombarding the headquarters" and overthrowing "people in authority," whereas Huang regularly clung tightly to people in authority and struck blows against genuine Marxism-Leninism. As for Lu, this school principal, he was himself a "person in authority" and a "capitalist-roader" whom the teachers of Qinfeng Elementary were about to rebel against and who would soon "stand aside." Sun was a landlord's son, and if the Red Guards didn't believe it they could just go and look up his file. If his family weren't landlords, then he, Wang Zhiyuan, would willingly go to jail for rumor-mongering. Whether Hu Zhilin's husband in Taiwan was a special agent or not had yet to be clarified. She used to be a neighborhood cadre, but owing to the problem over her Taiwan husband she was stripped of that post by the Neighborhood Committee. Her in-laws were both from landlord families. Her daughter Fu Maodi's brain was filled with the exploitative thinking of the landlord class. Xia Shuimu was a Shanghai hoodlum who was protected by the Chinese traitor Wang Jingwei. The Red Guards were welcome to check through his files. Feng Shaoqing had originally been the boss of a sauce and pickle shop who had been criticized in the "Three Against" and "Five Against" campaigns of the early 1950's. He was a little insect who had wormed his way into the ranks of the workers' revolution, and even now he still wasn't a Party member, which showed he had a problematical history. No way should anyone be taken in by his false progress; the revolutionary masses were ready for the final reckoning with him.

One by one he attacked his opponents, pinning all kinds of serious accusations onto them followed by individual factual explanations. Regardless of whether these facts were genuine or false, were hearsay or concocted by himself, he poured them all out together in fiery language as if he only regretted not being able to burn his opponents at the stake.

"I, Wang Zhiyuan, come from a family of three generations of outstanding workers who have lived purely by their labor and never exploited anyone. My wife Wu Peizhen is currently a worker at the People's Life Pharmaceutical Works. My father-in-law Wu Jingan is an enlightened gentleman whose meritorious role in the 1953 "Three Against" and "Five Against" campaigns was praised by the city government and the Zhejiang Daily, as anyone can see by checking the newspapers of those times. My mother-in-law Chen Yueying is a food vendor who according to the Party class division is a member of the semi-proletariat—" On and on he boasted, blowing his own trumpet and promoting his revolutionary credentials. Then he raised his voice as if yelling "Charge, lads!" like a commander at the front, and excitedly bellowed to the crowd at the top of his voice, "Think about it, revolutionary comrades! Are we working people going to allow a pack of evil monsters led by Feng Shaoqing—landlords and capitalist-roaders with Taiwan "bandit clique" relatives who are joining forces against us, the prole-tariat class, and who dream of over-throwing the government—to make us working people suffer all over again? Or are we going to beat back these reactionaries' brazen assaults?..."

The seven or eight Hangzhou Number 3 Middle School students pressed into service for the occasion by Wu Yaozong immediately applauded and shouted, "No! No! Beat them back! Beat them back!"

Quick as fire, Wu Yaozong stood up and aimed a barrage directly at the above-mentioned neighbors in roughly similar terms to Wang. The two of them were simply electioneering, speaking in an incandescent fury which brought them to exploding point. They opened their mouths wide like frogs, flinging spittle in all directions, their reed-like tongues constantly on the go as they excoriated their opponents and wound up the crowd, firing off like a rocket barrage for almost two hours. The stream of invective didn't come to an end until a quarter past ten. Feng Shaoqing and Principal Lu wanted to speak, but a leader of the Red Guard squad looked at his watch and said it was getting late, so he would only allow Feng fifteen minutes to speak before disbanding the meeting. Superficially he seemed to be concerned that the crowd attending the meeting should go home early and get some sleep ready to continue grasping revolution and promoting production the next day; in fact, this little general had been up since seven o'clock that morning raiding people's homes here, there and everywhere. Any reactionary books, U.S. imperialist-style suits or women's clothes, leather footwear, high-heeled shoes, feudal porcelain and bronzes ... were carried away in seven or eight hempen sacks and twenty or so crates, sack after sack, crate after crate, all to be shipped far, far away to the relevant authorities. They had been shifting goods till their backs ached and their spines almost broken. They really were worn out. Neither did they eat a proper evening meal. Now he was starving and eager to fill his belly, go to bed and lie down as soon as possible, for tomorrow morning there would be another whole heap of mischief for them to get up to!

Although the charges and accusations made by Wu and Wang speaking for their two families were only one side's word against the other, their opponents were constrained by a shortage of time in which to speak. No matter how fiercely Feng Shaoqing raked his opponents with "machine-gun fire" or how telling his blows were during that quarter-hour, the effect of his firepower was limited. How could it compete with Wu and Wang's two-hour heavy artillery barrage?

The meeting was scarcely over before Chen Yueying, half running, half skipping like a grasshopper, dashed straight back to her own home wildly yelling.

"Long live the reddest, reddest red sun in our hearts! Long, long live Chairman Mao! Great Chairman Mao has spoken for our family! We, the Wu family, are victorious! Those evil monsters in the courtyard are defeated! Beginning tonight, let's see which landlord reactionaries still dare to lord it over the Wu and Wang families...."

Chen Yueying's crazy ardor overflowed in tears.

After this, the Wang and Wu families kept picking on Huang. If Wang didn't pile garbage at his door, he would take a big hammer and bang nails into the wall in the small hours of the night, hammering away so that Huang and his wife found it impossible to sleep. If the Huang's were on night shift, Wang Baoluo was urged to hammer nails at midday or even bang on the wall, compelling the Huang's to forgo their rest during the day. Or else Mrs. Wu and her children would pour out a torrent of abuse at the Huang's whenever they went out. If they swore back, they had ten mouths and the Huang's only two. If it came to blows, they had twenty fists and the Huang's only four. After holding out for two months, Huang finally decided that his best strategy was to get out.

Tonight Wang was lying in bed, still thinking: By tomorrow night old Mrs. Pu's cries would have weakened. He would then tell his parents-in-law of his wonderful plan. He would draw them aside and whisper into their ears, for he mustn't let the younger ones hear. They were all big-mouths who couldn't be trusted. They could wait until action was actually taken to be told. He had already worked out a master plan. He would say Grannie Pu had left him instructions that if she should die before Pu Ning was released from prison, or if he couldn't come home for her funeral, everything she left behind was to be entrusted to her next-door neighbors the Wu's, and that she had asked the Wu's to take care of her apartment and all her belongings until Pu Ning came back. To confirm these verbal instructions, in addition to her will, recorded by Wu Jingan at her request, there would also be her fingerprint as proof. If she breathed her last tonight, they could quietly lift her right thumb and take a fingerprint as easy as pie. As long as they had this piece of paper as proof, the Wu's would really be in business.

At this point in his deliberations, lying there in the dark, Wang smiled to himself as he genuinely savored his stroke of genius.

X

For two days since yesterday, no one in the entire courtyard had had a heavier heart than Sun Junlun's.

This morning, no sooner had those cries from the Pu's place entered his ears than he seemed to have stepped straight into that film of Shakespeare's "Hamlet" he'd once seen, in which Hamlet always felt his father's ghost upon him. Even without having set eyes on it, Grannie Pu's decrepit old face, almost horrifyingly pitiable, trailed him like a ghost. Breakfast had never been so gloomy. He cycled to work at the scissors factory where his accountancy work seemed to take more effort than normal, and he had dealt with things at a snail's pace. His mind was simply not on the job and the sound of those cries seemed to be constantly in his ears.

At lunchtime he had no appetite and ate a bowl less than usual. On the afternoon shift he felt more indolent than ever and just couldn't get going. The old lady's sobs, like a bowl of cold water, had partially extinguished his flame of life.

Arriving home from work in an unhappy frame of mind, he smoked non-stop and began to have a distinct feeling as if he himself were undergoing torture.

It really was unthinkable. Up to this moment, so it seemed, not a single person had yet pushed open her door, walked into the room and given that poor old woman a glass of water. Every twenty or thirty minutes she was still painfully begging and crying, although her voice was growing slightly weaker.

It occurred to him that in the whole span of human history there might never have been a case in peacetime of such shocking obscenity.

"Comrade Sun Junlun!... Old Comrade Sun!... Mrs. Sun!... Good Hong'er!... Good Qiuzhen!... Help!... Help!... I'm dying of thirst! I haven't eaten for two days and nights!... I haven't had a drink of water for two days and nights!... I'm dying of hunger!... Give me a glass of water!... For pity's sake!..."

Over the past twenty years the five syllables "Old Sun" and "Sun Junlun" had resounded countless times in people's mouths and in his ears, but never like this. Now they had become five steel needles, thick and long, stabbing straight into the depths of his heart. He really had no idea where to turn.

He wanted to say something, do something, demand something, and yet he was powerless to speak, act or demand. His voice, his actions, his desires were like people who were totally handicapped, blind, deaf and dumb, unheeding of any commands. So he too had become blind, deaf and dumb. And, most fatally, he felt the world to be more and more abnormal. The life he saw around him no longer resembled human beings, but a bunch of eating, drinking and talking stones; everywhere there were walking stones. His normal sense of himself as a man seemed some kind of mistake, even a crime.

By instinct he should have dashed into the Pu's home like a wild horse. And yet—

His personal tragedy was like his wife's and daughters' tragedy, and like the tragedy of many people all around, namely to be eternally playing a set role of being a demon's make-up man, prompting the demon its lines, banging a gong to clear its way, carving a huge bronze statue of it. In this historically unprecedented role-play there were times when he perhaps need not consider his own fate, but at the same time he had no right to lay his parents', wife's and three daughters' destiny on the line in a single terrifying gamble. To do so might be tantamount to murder. In this era, too much blood had already flowed from holes pierced by knife-points and bullets, and in such abundance that it could almost be described as a lake of blood wide enough to sail boats on. One day people might have to pay with fresh blood even to buy a pack of peanuts or a loaf of bread. How could he allow his own family to be further stained with blood?

In the early days when the red flag first flew over Hangzhou he had been noticed and taken up by revolutionary figures thanks to his business college diploma, his widely recognized abilities, his habitual generosity and kindness, his openness and sincerity toward people, plus his incomparable modesty and geniality. At one time he was a high-flying new cadre dealing with industry and commerce, and chalked up a number of achievements in the fulfillment of his duties. But in 1954 when the drives to eliminate counter-revolutionaries and examine cadres' personal histories began, it was found that his adoptive father was a landlord. Although his own family were middle-class peasants from Zhuji County and he had not been adopted by the Sun family until he was at elementary school, the fact that he had changed his surname to Sun meant that his family status was naturally considered to be that of a landlord. Yet with his outstanding achievements over the previous five years, the energy he had devoted to the Party and his excellent personal connections, his colleagues were not too hard on him. Even criticism and exposure of him went relatively smoothly and he easily passed those hurdles, merely being demoted from a minor leadership position to a worker on the workshop floor. After another decade of hard graft, during which he was frequently elected as a model worker and made a worthwhile contribution to the scissors factory, he had been assigned a few years before to the accounts department, eventually being promoted from accounting clerk to chief of the department.

In this extraordinary era, human existence was like climbing the Himalayas; one slip and you would be swallowed up for ever by the icy crevasses and snowy gullies all around. He couldn't afford to get all seven members of his family into trouble over a mere glass of water. And trouble of any kind could spell future catastrophe, including bloodshed.

And yet—

This second "and yet" was engaged in a constant trial of strength with the first "and yet." So many of those in the courtyard had already been cut short and overpowered by the first "and yet." At Grannie Pu's cries they had all turned into granite rocks of Mt. Tai. Should he follow their example?

"Comrade Sun Junlun!... Mrs. Sun!... Good Hong'er!... Good Qiuzhen!... Help!... I'm dying of thirst!... I'm dying of hunger!... For pity's sake!... Give me a glass of water!... Good old Sun! Surely you can't stand by and watch me die!..."

These last words were a brilliant stroke on her part, a cleaver that slashed through his heart.

"What? Sun! You're only having one bowl of rice?..."

At the sight of him eating two bowls less than usual, his wife Yang Ciyun couldn't help but ask. Beside the square table she turned her small, thin body toward him, a look of surprise breaking over her nun-like white face. Seeing that Sun remained silent, she quietly whispered, "Is it because of Grannie Pu?"

He heaved a long sigh. His eyes suddenly grew wet.

"Ciyun! A man's heart is not made of steel! I am a man, not a stone!" His voice choked with a sob.

With tears in his eyes he thought of old Pu. In the ten years they had known each other he had always been a good fellow, no matter what demands and criticisms were heaped on him. Who in the entire courtyard was as forbearing and tolerant as he? So able to endure what others could not? So able to accept what others could not? Even when old Mrs. Wu slandered and cursed him he simply smiled, for all the world like some Sakyamuni Buddha. There again, anyone of principle, any seeker after truth, could clearly see what the situation had been in China these past 20 years, and what kind of life people had led. Deep down he really secretly admired Pu's obstinacy, his lofty principles, his refusal to take a job or muck along with the rest. Old Pu had done what no one else had succeeded in doing. He at least understood more of Pu's inner thinking and spiritual state than most people, though not in its entirety.

Of course this was his personal secret, of which he would not normally dare breathe a word even to his wife.

"Grannie Pu is calling so pitiably!" Qiuzhen, their second daughter, the one at junior high school, said with a shudder.

"Dad, we ought to go over and see her!" quietly said their eldest daughter Hong'er, who was at senior high school.

Only their daughter Yingzhen, being of kindergarten age, ate her dinner in silence.

"It's so sad that Grannie Pu has been reduced to this!" Yang Ciyun said softly.

"And all because of the Wu's! No one dares to go in the Pu's door!" Sun could take no more and burst out in anger.

After a moment's thought he said excitedly, "It's absurd just to let her go on crying like this! It's too late tonight, but we must think of doing something in the morning." He paused for a while before saying poignantly, "Ciyun, a man's heart is made of flesh after all!" He turned over various emergency plans, but still came to no final decision.

It was the longest night of Sun Junlun's life, and the most restless. Lying on his big coir-strung bed, with his wife alongside him and three daughters on their beds already in the land of dreams, he tossed and turned, quite unable to get off to sleep. The cries from the other side of the courtyard sounded like lashing rain from the universe, piercing his ears with moans of agony. When eventually he did drop off to sleep he suffered from unremitting nightmares. In his dreams he saw Grannie Pu standing before him all disheveled and unkempt, shouting at the top of her voice, "Help! Help! Why are you just standing by and watching me die?" He woke up with a start, all covered in a cold sweat, and could not get back to sleep. A growing feeling of terror stole over him. It was as if the room were crawling with wild animals and venomous snakes, and the whole place had turned into an African jungle where hundreds and thousands of animal's eyes and snake's eyes were fixed on him. After twenty years he was already familiar enough with these fearsome eyes, but tonight he seemed to have cracked a little, and suddenly they frightened him.

The sky was lightening wanly at just past five o'clock when he climbed out of bed. First he opened the coal briquet stove which had been damped down overnight, stoked up the fire and brought a large aluminum pot of rice gruel to the boil. Then he damped down the fire again and simmered the rice gruel over the heat. At this hour none of the family had yet risen. After hurriedly washing he saw that the Lu's were stirring and went to knock on their door.

"Principal Lu, yesterday Grannie Pu cried out all day and all night begging for a glass of water, but of all the thirteen households in the courtyard not one person answered her call and took her a glass of water. It just will not do! Pu Ning has broken the law and is locked up in Little Cart Bridge prison under isolated examination. His old mother Grannie Pu has not broken any law, neither is she a counter-revolutionary, and now she is lying sick with no relative there with her, and for three whole days not one single person in the courtyard has visited her. Whether in the old society or the new society she has always been a simple housewife. She hasn't done anything wrong. She can't even read the simplest Chinese characters, and on top of that she is now 85 years of age. We just cannot stand by and watch her die. The Communist Party has always spoken of "revolutionary humanitarianism," and it is Party policy. According to this policy we should give a glass of water to Grannie Pu, shouldn't we? Surely we cannot just watch her die of sickness, thirst, or hunger?" Despite the extraordinary excitement in his heart, Sun Junlun's speech remained as peaceful and calm as could be.

"I think the same as you, but—" Lu pointed with one finger to the Wu's opposite. "You know perfectly well why no one will go to her aid with a glass of water. Who dares to approach her? I too have considered this question, and I have decided to speak to the organization first and ask them for instructions."

"Very well, let's go find the Neighborhood Committee chairman and see if we can ask his permission for us to give a glass of water to Grannie Pu."

"Shall we ask Mrs. Mao to go along too?"

"There may not be time. She isn't up yet. We still have to go to work once all this is over! Let's tell her afterwards!"

Along the way, Sun Junlun privately relished the fact that in the days when he had been in favor, Wang had been his subordinate, and relations between them had always been cordial. After he'd been dumped, Wang had still valued their friendship and had always kept in touch and shown him respect. If on this occasion he were to ask Wang to do him a favor, it might not be too difficult.

Wang Chuanfa, Chairman of the Baoqing Bridge Neighborhood Committee, started out as a small self-employed handicrafts entrepreneur making umbrellas. It was only after having joined the Party that he rose to chairman of the committee. A man of nearly sixties, he was tall and lanky, like an egret. Due to exhaustion from overwork his hair had turned white in recent years. His cheeks had shrunk to skin and bone and his eyes had the turbid blue tinge of perpetual sleeplessness. He looked seven or eight years older than his real age. He listened to Sun's report in silence.

"Chairman Wang, you have studied Marxism-Leninism and Mao Zedong Thought better than us, and you have a more accurate understanding of Chairman Mao's policy of "revolutionary humanitarianism" than we do. Based on this policy, Principal Lu and I are planning to give a glass of water to the invalid Grannie Pu. We have come specifically to request guidance from you, as we wish to ask for your approval." After setting out all the details about Grannie Pu falling sick and pleading for help, Sun finally raised his demand.

"I fully agree with Comrade Sun Junlun's views," chimed in Lu at his side.

Wang Chuanfa stroked the few white hairs on his chin and pondered in silence for a while before slowly saying.

"This man Pu Ning is indeed backward in his thinking, for despite the Party earnestly remonstrating with him and helping him again and again, he has never been willing to thoroughly reform his bourgeois view of the world. It is no injustice to him to have received this sentence of isolated examination." He gazed at Sun Junlun with warmth in his eyes. "Grannie Pu has in no way broken the law and retains her civil status, so we should treat her as one of the masses. At eighty-five she has after all attained a great age, and with no relative at hand, her neighbors ought to look after her to some degree."

After coughing twice and clearing his throat, he raised his voice in the manner of a judge solemnly delivering a verdict, "Lu! Sun! That's it then! Taking water to an 85-year-old woman so as to prevent her dying of thirst cannot be held to be against the law. As Chairman of the Neighborhood Committee, I authorize you to give a glass of water to Grannie Pu. If there is any responsibility, I, Wang Chuanfa, will take it. If there are any consequences, I, Wang Chuanfa, will bear them."

Sun Junlun rushed back home and without bothering to eat his breakfast dashed into the kitchen at double-quick speed, filled a large bowl with hot rice gruel, sprinkled it with savory pickles, and placed a white china spoon in it. Then he poured out a big enamel cup of hot boiled water from the vacuum flask. Afraid that it might be too hot, he poured it into a cold glass, added some cold boiled water and felt it to make sure it didn't burn his hand. Finally he took the bowl in one hand and the glass in the other and walked across the courtyard. Just as he did so he once more heard Grannie Pu's weakened cries.

"Old Sun!... Comrade Sun Junlun!... Mrs. Sun!... Help!... Give me a glass of water!... I'm dying of thirst!..."

"I'm coming! I'm coming! Grannie Pu, the Neighborhood Committee Chairman has authorized us to give you a glass of water!" Sun purposely yelled at the top of his voice as he passed the Wu's door.

The whole room was filled with a sour, rancid stench. The window and door had not been opened for three days, and on the square stool beside the bed stood a large enamel spittoon serving as a chamber pot. Full of murky yellow urine and feces, the spittoon emitted an overpowering foul odor. At the sound of someone coming, something stirred inside the cotton quilt on the five-foot coir-strung bed. On the blue cloth pillow a human head began to roll to and fro. The face on this head bore no resemblance to that of a living human being; it was like a skull with a layer of human skin stuck on, dry and sunken, withered and dark. If you insist on its being a face, then it was more like a hairy simian face; five or six days of hunger had left it all bones, bones adorned with a few freckles like the dots of color in a pointillist painting by Seurat. Her eyeballs were like those of a dead fish, set in her eye sockets as if they would never move again, giving her something of the look of a blind person.

As soon as she saw Sun close up she recognized him clearly, and her tears burst forth in a sudden rush of agony.

"Old Sun! Your kindness has truly saved my life! Kind savior! May the Bodhisattvas protect you and let you live a hundred years!..."

Sun Junlun couldn't help the tears welling up either. He swiftly wiped them away with his handkerchief and steeled himself not to weep as he felt her forehead. Her fever had indeed receded.

"Grannie Pu! You drink first! Eat a little!... Slow down a bit! Don't rush!" Sun said in a loud voice.

Not taking the slightest notice, the old woman forcibly pressed his hand down and madly gulped mouthful after mouthful.

In a little while she finished the entire large glass of water.

This glass of water was like an elixir. Sun was genuinely impressed by her burning will to live. Once she had drunk, she slid herself up on the pillow in a semi-recumbent posture, her head nearly stretched out straight against the wall. Then a sound came from her throat.

"Old Sun! Kind savior!... Just hold the rice bowl. I can eat by myself."

Like something out of the Biblical account of Egypt's "seven lean years," her right hand ceaselessly spooned rice gruel and savory pickles like a whirlwind until in a minute or two she had eaten the entire big bowl. It wasn't eating so much as swallowing whole. By this time Lu and his wife had walked over too. Mrs. Lu brought a small bowl of rice gruel and a glass of hot boiled water.

"Principal Lu! Mrs. Lu! You both do me a great kindness! As soon as my son Pu Ning returns, I'll ask him to kneel down three times and bow his head nine times to give you a resounding kowtow and thank you for your kindness!... Give me that rice gruel!" The final phrase was an order.

Dear God! After sixty-four hours without water and food, just getting a glass of water and a large bowl of rice gruel down into her stomach enabled her to sit up in bed and support herself against the wall. She snatched the small rice bowl out of Mrs.

Lu's hand and gobbled the food down so voraciously it vanished in a moment.

"My great benefactors! I'm going to live! I've got my life back! I'll drink this glass of water in a minute. Put it down on the stool...."

Once again the old lady shed streams of tears and wept bitterly. As she wept, she repeatedly gestured toward her three guests with clasped hands, thanking them.

"Don't worry, Grannie Pu, from now on we will come and see you. If there's anything you need, we will bring it for you," Sun spoke loudly into her ear.

"Grannie Pu! We'll help you! Don't worry about anything." Steeling herself against the smell, Mrs. Wu leant over too.

Sun quietly picked up the chamber pot, walked into the small bathroom at the back and emptied it into the latrine. Then he went to the big water tub at the main door, scooped up some water with a tin ladle and rinsed it clean before placing it back on the little bench alongside the bed.

"Thank you, thank you, you three kind saviors! By this afternoon I will be able to get down from my bed. Don't you worry, these old bones of mine are still hard and sturdy! I won't die! I'm going to stay alive!..." The old lady cried out with such spirited gusto that her voice cracked.

Epilogue

On the afternoon of September 9 that year, Pu Ning ended one year and three months of prison life, looking as thin as a hungry white stork. Following his release from Little Cart Bridge he learned all the details soon after coming in through the door of his home.

Around seven o'clock in the evening he entered the Sun's home, clasped both hands toward Sun and his wife in a gesture of thanks, then bowed three times from the waist.

"Old Sun! You are indeed our gracious benefactor, I really do not know how to thank you enough!"

With a kindly expression on his face, Sun Junlun stood in front of Pu Ning simply smiling, nodding and bowing repeatedly in reply. Instead of speaking, he held his right forefinger to his lips and went "shush" while all the time pointing with the left forefinger at the Wu's opposite.

Pu Ning understood and said not a word. Once again he gestured three times with clasped hands, bowed three times from the waist, and quietly withdrew.

(Written on Christmas Day 1979)

(Translated by Andrew Morton)

Flower Terror

It's been years since there were flowers in my room. I remember the last pot of flowers I bought, in the spring of 1958—a chrysanthemum, senecio cruentus—forty-odd huge purplish-red blooms which flowered for a full month or more on my teapoy. At the time I happened to have acquired a cream-colored radio, one with a modern Japanese casing. But somehow it didn't seem quite right listening to music without flowers, so I went into town to buy a pot of them.

These were no ordinary times, and besides, my status was somewhat irregular.[1] I had bought the radio set in Shanghai in secret, then carried it home on the train wrapped up with lots of clothing to disguise it as a big bundle of clothes. You could say it was an act of stealth. But it was only to counter the preternatural eyesight of reds, neighbors and people in general that I resorted to such subtle wiles, in the manner of some underground spy. Thereafter, whenever I secretly tuned into the Voice of America to listen to Chopin nocturnes, Lehar's "Merry Widow," or the international news, I was as tensed up as if I were committing a crime. I would turn the volume down as low as possible, just enough to set my eardrums vibrating, to prevent anyone outside from eavesdropping. In this way I might avoid the fate of certain young people who, for nothing more than a few minutes' enjoyment of Mozart, Schubert or real news, were spirited off to places like Cogongrass Ridge or Water Chestnut

---

[1] "No ordinary times" means the Communist rule. My "irregular status" refers to the fact that for many years I had not cooperated with the Communists, had not taken part in any work, and had not even taken part in study meetings. As a result I was constantly watched by the Communist police and residential community cadres.

Wilderness to dig mud, repair the earth or be underground
slaves for seven or eight years. [2]

As I listened to the music and admired the flowers, the
atmosphere of absolute secrecy made me think of a detective
with his ear to the wall listening to a conversation between
suspects.

Afterwards, I wrapped the radio up in a large white cloth and
hid it away under the bed. But I couldn't wrap up the pot of red
flowers on my teapoy, and that's what landed me in trouble.
Cadres from the residential community never failed to do a
double take when they walked into my room and caught sight of
it. A strange expression, as of astonishment, came into their
eyes.

"Do flowers still have a place in our life today?"

Sometimes they simply addressed me in a reproving tone,
"What, so you went into town just to buy this pot of flowers?"

God be my witness, anywhere outside the Asian mainland
such words of reproach would surely have been regarded as
utterly inconceivable as Martian language, or Eskimo lingo at
least; but in the land on which I stood it was only all too real,
and absolutely logical. For late that year, in this land of ours
shaped like a begonia with a petal missing, rural communities
were enforcing a system where men were grouped with men,
women with women, where husband and wife were completely
separated and only allowed to see one another twice a month to
sleep together for a single night, to mate like horses in a stud for
the sake of the next generation. Of course this strange
movement—the so-called "collectivization of life, militancy of
action"—was actually aimed at turning the whole country into a

---

[2] "Cogongrass Ridge" and "Water Chestnut Wilderness" are large-scale
labor reform camps with hundreds of thousands of inmates, the former on
the borders of Jiangsu and Anhui Provinces, and the latter in Jiangxi
Province. "Digging mud" means preparing water channels; "repairing the
earth" means opening up the wilderness and planting fields, and
"underground slaves" refers to workers who toil without pay. This slave
labor system is secret in mainland China. It is something underground
which is kept hidden from the West.

military camp and compelling men and women, old and young, to imitate Spartan warriors or ascetic monks and preserve their full vitality—"drain their last drop of blood"—for the sake of labor and production.[3]

To get back to the subject, these reproving looks and tones built up to the point where I felt a shock of flower terror. I considered throwing that pot of flowers straight out of the window. But something else proved even more persuasive— those forty sweet purple eyes amid the green foliage in that pot, those mysterious purple siren voices, gave me the strength to resist. So regardless of everything I kept them beside me for a while, until the last roseate eye, the last scented voice, had vanished from my sight and hearing and gone to its eternal rest within the depths of my soul.

At this time I was surrounded not only by flower terror, but by Mozart terror, Chopin terror.

But terror of this type was nothing compared to the cultural firestorm of eight years later, with its great struggle against Peony Garden, its bitter struggle against the flowers, trees of the West Hill Park, and its great criticism struggle against Mozart, Beethoven and Chopin. In those fierce storms, the little red warriors may not have trampled down peonies the way they beat up high officials in authority, but the flowers' protective green leaves endured a good deal of cursing and spitting—the gardeners and park cadres suffered for growing those flowers, and were subjected to stormy criticism struggles.[4] When the

---

[3] "Strange Movement" refers to the people's commune movement. This was a very complex thing, and only one or two features are mentioned here. "Draining the last drop of blood" for "production" was a slogan of the period.

[4] The rebel faction in the Cultural Revolution considered that the "Peony Pavilion" and "Peony Garden" at Hangzhou's West Hill Park, together with their exotic flowers and rare trees, were products of capitalist reactionary thinking. They pasted big-character posters all over the park criticizing the park's leaders and certain cadres, and even insulting the flowers and trees themselves. This took place in the autumn and winter, however, when the peony flowers had already gone over, so it was their protective green leaves which bore the brunt of the criticism.

battle against flowers reached its climax, the red guards almost wanted to throw them into prison as they did those so-called "traitors." Realizing the senselessness of jailing flowers, the red warriors instead shut up those gardeners who had been taking care of the flowers in the nursery when the struggle meeting was over. Said to be under isolated investigation, these poor workers were actually scapegoats of the shattered flowers.

In other big cities, a famous pianist who loved to play Mozart and Chopin had all her fingers chopped off, and great musicians who had slept peacefully under the soil of Europe a hundred years or more had their corpses bitterly fought over.[5]

Yet the flower terror that now enveloped me still held a bacteria-like threat.

It so happened that my wife Qing, who worked at the China Welfare Society's kindergarten in Shanghai, was hospitalized to have her tonsils removed. Visiting her gave me the opportunity to secretly take my new radio to Shanghai and sell it through an auctioneer. As time went on I had come to loathe listening to the great music of Mozart and Chopin in the manner of an eavesdropping detective. Better to spend ten years with my face to the wall, like Bodhidharma! Actually during these years the white walls around me could sometimes release a strange music that had the power to comfort me, and could sometimes even turn into a philosopher with thoughts, and hold discourse with me. But at this moment my tensed-up emotions were searing like oil burning in a pan, and the shadows of the mud-diggers at Water Chestnut Wilderness were bearing down upon me with a pressure that was too great. In the end, that cream-colored radio had become a huge hot potato that I just had to throw away.

My hunch was correct. People had probably received an intelligence report on my soul from that pot of chrysanthemums,

---

[5] During the Cultural Revolution, Shanghai Music Conservatory professor and eminent pianist Gu Shengying had all her fingers chopped off by the Red Guards. She committed suicide, followed by her entire family. Beethoven, Mozart, Chopin and other famous Western composers were subjected to fierce criticism, criticism struggle and unrestrained verbal abuse.

or caught my secret train of thought, perhaps, from a Mozart minuet or a Chopin nocturne. An even more likely reason, of course, was my long-term irregular status. Two months later, in the night of July 15 that year, eight men and women suddenly burst into my room like wild animals—public security personnel and resident community cadres. At daybreak, following a thorough four-hour search, some other "criminals" from various detention centers in Hangzhou and I were taken in a large yellow bus to a concentration camp on the shore of Hangzhou Bay. I don't intend to elaborate on life in the camp, which can be summed up in its entirety in three phrases: in the daytime we labored like cattle; at night we fought like wild beasts in criticism struggles; and for thirty-seven days I had nothing to drink but salty, brackish seawater.[6]

I thought I was never going to get out of there. To my surprise, though, I was eventually able to go back home again. And in my heart there began to germinate an insight into those gainsayers of my chrysanthemums. Those thirty-seven days of bitter, diarrhea-inducing seawater—among other experiences—brought home to me the meaning behind those reproachful looks of the past. But for now it was just a conceptual understanding.

My fondness for flowers didn't go away, though. Whenever I passed a flower shop I still lingered over the rows of chrysanthemums filling the window. I still went to the Yue Fei Temple, as in past years, to admire displays of spring flowers and autumn chrysanthemums. But I no longer ventured to bring them into my room.

Two years later, I was once again forced to leave my home alongside the famous Grand Canal. This time I really didn't think I would ever return to my cozy rectangle of living space. Despite myself, I even sold my beloved pale brown sakhu writing desk which I'd used for thirteen years. I was in the mood to burn all my bridges.

---

[6] This concentration camp is located in Xiasha (Lower Sand) district, near the shore of Hangzhou Bay. For a more detailed report of the hardships in detention there, see my "Punishment of the Sea."

I was to spend more than a year doing manual labor on a farm at Panban Bridge, 35 kilometers (22 miles) away.

Qing couldn't bear the separation and eventually came to the farm to visit me. Following our customary mode of "a marriage perpetually on the move," we spent yet another "traveling honeymoon" night together at a tiny chicken-basket of a guesthouse in Panban Bridge.[7] As we talked, I condensed an avalanche of words into depicting the following incidents.

Last year I formally began to turn out for manual work. Among the nearly 1,000 members of my first work brigade, I was considered virtually bottom of the list in terms of physical strength. Our detachment leader put me into a group with several women weaving fans of straw to use as roofing material. The others finished their task by three or four o'clock every afternoon and then quietly slipped away. Once I saw that I was alone, I would go and fetch more rice straw, dragging it back by getting down on the ground on all fours like a turtle and slowly crawling along, pausing every now and then. By the end my body was aching all over. I seemed suddenly to have turned into a person without bones—I could hardly stand up, let alone walk. When work finished for the day, I would have to do seven or eight minutes of gentle waist movements sitting down in order to be able to stand up straight, then another seven or eight

---

[7] I had been married for years to Qing, who worked as a teacher in the Chinese Welfare Society Kindergarten in Shanghai. Since the society was headed by Song Qingling, Vice President of People's Republic of China, their Shanghai kindergarten together with the North Sea Kindergarten in Beijing were the two most prestigious kindergartens in the country, and were attended by the children of many high-ranking cadres. I was in Hangzhou, and for many years had been unwilling to cooperate with the Communists. I refused to take an official job and was classified by the Communists as one of the "five black types." It was very difficult for Qing to be transferred to any work unit in Hangzhou, and she and I found it difficult to be allotted housing in Shanghai. Since the two of us got together only on holidays during the year, traveling constantly between the two places, we jokingly referred to our married life as a "marriage perpetually on the move" or a "traveling honeymoon.''

minutes of calisthenics before I felt normal enough to slowly trudge back home.

A good month or more of training allowed me to progress from a reptile to a true mammal.

In the depths of winter, when early morning temperatures reached minus five or six degrees Celsius (about 23 degrees Fahrenheit) and my hands were frozen stiff, I had to gather firewood wearing white napped cotton gloves. Sources of fuel were limited, and I was afraid to walk too far for fear of wasting time and energy, so I broke new ground by hacking down the most unlikely wild brambles, creepers and bushes in the immediate vicinity. With one hand I tightly grasped the thorny creepers or bushes, and wielding the long sickle knife in the other I blindly slashed away for a while. By the midday work break, of the three pairs of white gloves I wore out to work, the left-hand gloves had turned completely red-lacerated by thorns, they were stained with fresh blood, my hand having been pricked until it was drenched in dark red blood. During all that time, there was not a day when my left hand did not bleed.

On midsummer afternoons the mercury soared to over 40 degrees Celsius (104 degrees Fahrenheit) and the air outside was almost hot enough to boil an egg. Naked except for a pair of short underpants and a large broad-brimmed straw hat, I would manhandle a big heavy iron harrow to reclaim the wasteland—turning over the soil that had been loosened already. From hair to ankles, my sweat streamed down like rain—I turned into a "rain man." One afternoon I drank two big 10-pound hot-water flasks containing twenty cups of clear tea, and still felt thirsty.

For a year, our work tasks consisted of: planting and digging sweet potatoes, pulling up sweet potato vines, making sweet potato stores, opening up wasteland and reclaiming wasteland, scaling fish, digging deep holes, planting peaches and pears, trans-planting rice shoots, harvesting wheat, harvesting rice, scorching marl, growing vegetables, feeding chickens, ducks and geese, keeping pigs and goats, grazing cattle, mowing hay, gathering firewood, picking up roots, humping bundles of firewood, carrying bricks, carrying manure, picking tea, pulling planked carts, mowing grass, and building houses.

I personally performed the vast majority of these tasks.

Gathering firewood was particularly memorable.

I went off into the mountains armed with a sort of long-handled hooked sickle, which was the main tool for cutting firewood. After hacking the firewood down, you bundled it up tightly with string and carried it back to the farm on a shoulder pole. Anyone with strong arms who was used to this game could just cut down a few wild vines anywhere and tie the firewood tightly into two large bundles. But I lacked the strength to tie it up tightly, and lest it came loose on the way and scattered on the ground, causing an infinity of trouble, I made a point of taking several thick luggage ropes with me from home to tie the firewood with—these were easier to tie, as well as safer. I estimate that during the one year and three months I spent in the countryside, I must have gone through seven or eight luggage ropes. Taking along your own luggage ropes to tie firewood with was not only the talk of the farm, it was the talk of the village! No doubt I was the first person to set such a precedent since the beginning of the world, in all the villages from the dawn of history down to the present day, and of course it made me a general laughing-stock. Normally, a muscular and healthy person would spend three or four hours a day gathering firewood, and could easily manage to cut 200 or 300 catties (at a pinch, if you worked all day long, you might achieve 700 catties). As a tuberculosis sufferer, I spent twice as long yet only managed to gather 100 catties or so. For this I was once again roundly mocked. My way of walking carrying firewood was described by one woman familiar with Western literature as being akin to Don Quixote astride his bony nag preparing to attack a windmill. Also, the others cut firewood in a squatting position or bending over where they stood, but after one day working like that my back was ready to give out and the pain in my legs was unbearable. So I "created" a weird stance without precedent in history—cutting my firewood kneeling down. This spared my back and was easier on my legs, although it placed a heavier burden on my knees. Fortunately it was cold at the time so I was wearing sweat pants with thick trousers over.

Later I changed to cotton trousers, but by then I'd been kneeling for so long already that my knees had ceased to hurt. But as time went on, the knees of those old thick trousers and military-issue cotton trousers became completely worn through. As the weather warmed up with the coming of spring I had to change into lined or unlined trousers, and so to protect my trousers and make my knees more comfortable through the spring, summer and autumn, I bought a big gunnysack from the shop and folded it over and over to cushion my knees when I knelt down. My companions jocularly referred to this way of gathering firewood as "worshipping the Bodhisattva" or "setting up candles." One time my detachment leader—half joking, half serious—said to me, "I think when you cut firewood, you really should light a couple of candles on both sides of you to beseech the Bodhisattva for protection!"

Hearing my account of things, my wife could not help saying pityingly, "After coming here and seeing all this bleak countryside, I am really scared to hear what you've just said. But despite everything, you've made it through."

I knew she wanted to praise me, but I cut her short and quickly changed the subject. Dwelling on such painful thoughts in the nights to come would not only exact a heavy price from her, it would weigh considerably on my mind too, deep in the night.

I still remember how, in the spring, every time when I was all worked up cutting firewood and saw those red wild flowers making such a colorful show, I always felt like a criminal as I mercilessly raised the flashing sickle blade and hacked straight down. In my heart I silently addressed those flowers, "Please forgive my murderous act! I have to be savage with you for the sake of my own survival." But this was only the way I thought later when I sat down to rest and have a smoke, a kind of repentant afterthought. At the time, I felt every second like some Roman gladiator fighting a life-or-death struggle, and in a moment I had laid to waste all kinds of exotic blooms—how could they flash their subtle beauty upon my fiery eyes? Even less take root in my heart or leave a trace behind.

Later on, the work seemed to get a little easier at times. I would set off on my own with firewood knife, rope, carrying pole and gunnysack, and climb up Stone Pond Hill. The hilltop was all pine trees and lots of wild spring flowers—mostly wild azaleas, a ravishing sight. It was really a gorgeous hilltop garden, one great expanse of glittering, aching red. Often I would sit down and silently contemplate them—though not entirely for the beauty of the scene before me, because in my current life that pure innate "flower feeling" was almost banished from my senses. Now I tended rather to recall their past beauty in my sight, for I still remembered that they were, after all, a part of universal beauty. Amid these thoughts, I couldn't help gradually turning and silently gazing at the blue horizon far away. I needed to gaze into the distance. I lit a cigarette and lost myself in thought. I longed to think deeply, but this was just a superficial pondering, without content, without ideas, without fantasy. My only thought was: "How long can I stay here in the hilltop garden this time? Will I always live the way I do now?"

I am sure that even the pens of a hundred Shakespeares could not have recorded my feelings then. My reactions in those days were quite unlike human emotions, they were unrelated to any human mental condition—it was almost a kind of extinction of the soul. Little by little I became aware of the extreme pain of reality, but I couldn't transmit it even via my subtlest sensory organs. It was a strange spiritual state, to be deeply aware of pain yet without being able to feel pain—far beyond the power of Proust or Joyce to describe.

Sometimes I took a bunch of wild azaleas back to the dormitory and put them in our young work-brigade leader's soft drink bottle. He was in love, and often picked wild flowers outside to give to his girlfriend—a slightly cross-eyed young woman we called "the princess."

At night, lying in bed, my thoughts strayed from that hilltop park back to wartime Mount Wang, at the south bank of the river of Congqing, the verdant Wang Family Park on the hilltop, and me and my young girlfriend riding white horses up the hill to stroll beside the evergreen ilexes. My heart warmed slightly; but soon grew cold again.

Incredibly, after one year and three months, I did indeed return to my home—no more wielding the flashing sickle and laying waste beautiful wild flowers. It was utterly beyond all expectation. No, I just hadn't expected to go back so quickly. No, I had dreamed of it, but I looked upon it as a stroke of pure good luck—although one that I never anticipated would so soon fall to me.

I was home again, but my "flower feeling" still hadn't come back. This time it had strayed far, far away. I hadn't really noticed it, living in the countryside; but here at home it struck me. Back then, I'd thought that the reason I didn't have any "flower feeling" was: I don't have the time to cultivate it; I don't have the space to keep it; and I don't have the emotions to cherish it. Once I get back to "my room," this feeling will come straight back into my heart and mind at the same time as the rest of my old life.

But no! All kinds of concepts from my old life had drifted far away from me—far, far, far away. Now they were utterly unknown to me.

It was then that I realized I was now truly at one with those who had cast such reproachful glances at my chrysanthemums.

When I went into town, no matter what fine flowers or gorgeous blooms I saw, I didn't have the slightest feeling for them. No matter what lovely colors I discovered in a flower, there was not the least visual response. It was as if I'd gone color blind, so that red, green and yellow lost all meaning. Perhaps my case was even worse than color-blindness, for I had absolutely no sense of color, whereas someone who is color-blind is still aware of gray. My ability to distinguish red, green and yellow was more dependent on memory of the past than on my actual vision. As for the words "red," "yellow," "blue" and "white," the fact that I could still grasp their implications was also reliant upon my recall of an earlier vocabulary, not my

actual responses. Worse, even enchantingly beautiful West
Lake, the green-clad hills above the lake, the willow trees
swaying in the sunshine which used to move me so much, now
no longer evoked in me the faintest ghost of a reaction. I simply
did not understand what "beauty" was! But one thing I did
understand, and that was why those fifteenth-century French
troops could shoot a statue, a masterpiece of Leonardo da Vinci,
to pieces with bows and arrows. I felt now that that was a very
natural thing.

One time, an elderly epigrapher said to me, "There's a
marvelous exhibition of seasonal flowers on at the Yue Fei
Temple at the moment—the potted plants are quite outstanding.
You should pop along and have a look."

"I'm sorry, but my brain has turned to stone and I cannot
rouse any feelings for beautiful flowers of any kind. An
exquisite rose, to me, is just a lump of colorless stone. What's
the use of confronting one stone with another?"

At this he looked quite shocked. I knew he might think I was
a little strange. But to me it felt quite normal. After all, this was
the way of the world. Since the first day mankind began to be
active on the planet he has valued stones far higher than roses.
And to be frank, without those stones mankind might long ago
have been wiped off the face of the earth.

This was when I was spending all my time bathing in the
shadow of the great calligraphers Wang Xizhi, Wang Xianzhi,
Yan Zhenqing and Liu Zhongyuan. I thought: my safest course
is to seek survival in these left downstrokes, right downstrokes,
dots and straight strokes. You won't come across any volcanoes
in the "Tomb Inscription for Beauty Dong." And there are no
floods in the "Orchid Pavilion Inscription." For Heaven's sake,
a hard-pressed long-distance traveler must be able to rest awhile
on a tombstone, or inside a cool pavilion, and take a breather.

Why wrap myself up so long with forming these elegantly
rhythmic strokes, or following the eight-fold "yong"-character

method?[8] Because I had no idea how much longer I could give to it, and I hoped thereby to find a path toward a safer place— namely, my room. Quite simply, if I could manage always to stay in my room, nothing else would happen. On this planet, at that precise moment, I was sure there was nothing more precious than the word "me."

A year later things had changed a little. I didn't seem to be so preoccupied day and night with ancient calligraphic inscriptions, yet this didn't affect the tranquil way of life in my room. Gradually things became slightly more relaxed.

After two long years had passed, slowly—I don't know when—"flower sense" began to make a timid return to my feelings.

I can't remember which flower it began with. All I know is that I began to be able to distinguish red, yellow, blue and white once more, and in my sight these colors began to form beauty.

A minuscule speck of beauty—even tinier than a star to the naked eye. Yet slowly it expanded, multiplied, until it gradually formed into the starry firmament of the past.

A traveler on a journey through the "starry firmament," I decided one day to buy a pot of flowers.

This was a major event in my life of the past five years.

There were many reasons behind my wish to do so. Here are two of the most important.

Firstly, my room had gradually resumed its old "scenery." I had secretly sold off my cream-colored radio, and openly bought a grass-green one. ("openly" because time's bowstring had finally slackened a little—comparatively.) I had sold off my pale brown sakhu writing desk, and bought a dark brown beechwood desk. My worn blue cotton cloth curtains had been changed for new white plastic curtains with a floral pattern. And I had added some blue plastic tablecloths and purple plastic drapes. All this imparted to my domicile something of an air of "modernity." Of

---

[8] This calligraphic method is based on the eight strokes used to form the Chinese character "yong."

course this only refers to the "modernity" of my own little private space.

When neighbors from the courtyard walked in, there was a completely new feel.

"You should buy a pot of flowers for decoration," they said.

I liked the sound of this, for I had thought such words an absolute impossibility in my present life.

My wife urged me to buy a pot of flowers too, to go with the new furniture in my room—that semi-new beechwood writing desk.

By now she had forgotten that morning a few years ago when I had quietly set out for the countryside, when she and my elderly mother had wept and wailed. As for me, I had also forgotten those days when I attacked wild flowers wielding a sickle.

Secondly, it was almost Chinese New Year and Qing was about to come home. For Heaven's sake, in all these years it had never occurred to me to greet her with a bunch of flowers. Once, on Chinese New Year's Eve a few years ago, it was she who had come back first as a "guest" to welcome the "master"—myself, a farmhand.

The idea of buying flowers was already formed. But the mood to buy flowers arose by chance.

In mid January, my wife asked an adopted daughter of hers in Shanghai to bring me a parcel of things. One morning I went into town to collect it. I passed a flower shop, and there in the window stood row upon row of potted poinsettias of a very appealing shade. The desire to buy flowers suddenly welled up within me. Soon afterwards, while collecting my things from the upper floor of a department store, I saw a beautiful girl of pristine purity whose movements and voice put me in mind of dewdrops, which is just what her name describes.[9] I thought, if I had had a child, that is just the age my daughter would have been. Thinking along these lines, my desire to buy flowers grew

---

[9] Her name was Zhang Jie ("Purity" Zhang).

even stronger. Then I went to the "Great Hall of the People" to stand in line for a ticket to a performance by a foreign choir, and actually managed to obtain one. In my joy, I stepped straight into a flower shop—the only one of its kind in this whole world-famous city.

Times have changed; even the names of flowers have changed. In the shop they called poinsettias "a sweep of red," although to me they were still "Christmas Red."[10] They weren't expensive, 80 jiao (about 25 cents) for a pot of three blooms. I chose a pot with the longest stems and the most petals, one with four blooms, for just 1 yuan (about 33 cents).

I hadn't grown this type of flower, so I asked the shop assistant for some general tips on it.

"This sort of flower is highly susceptible to cold and it's more accustomed to living in a warm greenhouse. Best give it plenty of sunlight, and for goodness' sake keep it out of the wind. No need to apply fertilizer, just give it a little water every few days when you see the earth in the pot is nearly dry." The female shop assistant pointed to several pots of poinsettias in the corner. "Look, the pots in the corner aren't doing nearly so well as those in the window because they don't get any sunlight."

I took a look, and sure enough the poinsettias in the shade in the corner did seem rather dull, not so fresh and vital as the ones in the window. The shop assistant told me that even on a cloudy day, clear glass still lets light through from the sky.

---

[10] I once said to my wife: This flower has been renamed "a sweep of red," but I continue to call it "Christmas Red" because that is a far superior name. What does "a sweep of red" mean? It isn't specific; any red flower could be called "a sweep of red." And for me personally, "Christmas Red" has pleasant associations. The first time I saw a poinsettia was in the living room of a good friend, on an evening that was one of the happiest of my life. Thereafter, whenever I saw this flower I couldn't help thinking of that friend. Now he is overseas, and I had heard nothing from him for over ten years until recently. For me, keeping this poinsettia beside me functioned both as a memento and as a way of wishing him good luck.

This remark gave me an additional layer of insight into the word "sunlight." I realized that no matter how overcast it was, there was still sunlight.

Getting on a bus with a pot of flowers really is an awful bother—it's what people mean when they say "buying flowers is the easy part; just wait till you've got to carry them!" But luck was on my side, and the bus wasn't crowded enough for my flowers to get crushed. I managed to get a seat and even found a "standing place" for my flowers in a corner. From the moment the bus started, my eyes never left them. One or two passengers brushed against them, so I asked them kindly to be considerate enough not to damage my flowers.

It was probably quite unusual to find such flowers on a bus like this, and they attracted a lot of stares. Each one seemed to say admiringly, how lovely!

"What is it called?"

"Christmas Red," I explained. "It blooms around Christmas time."

"How much was it?"

"One yuan. "

"Not expensive then."

I looked with gratitude toward the passenger who had addressed me, while remaining inwardly on high alert to guard my flowers.

Another passenger chuckled, "You seem to treasure this pot of flowers more than anything else."

Several passengers laughed.

I didn't mind their passing remarks in the least. I knew that they might well never buy a pot of flowers—even a single flower—in their lives. Even to look at a flower might not necessarily genuinely interest them.

Five elementary school pupils got on at one stop. As soon as they caught sight of the poinsettias they were beside themselves with delight.

"Look at these flowers. How lovely they are!"

One child asked me, "Are they real?"

"Of course they are."

"But they look just like artificial paper flowers." Children's senses are so quick—they lit upon the flower's special feature at first glance. I'd had just the same feeling too when I first came across one, fifteen years before. And I'd even mentioned it somewhere in a book I'd written.

The child's remark struck a chord with one of the passengers.

"Why, when you look closely they do look rather like paper flowers."

"It's one of the nice things about these flowers that although they're real, the blooms come out like artificial paper flowers." There were a couple of other things I could have said, but I held them back. I wanted to say, "There are artificial paper flowers that look just like real flowers." And in another time and place I might have added, "No matter how real artificial flowers may look, they will always be artificial. Poinsettias may look artificial at first glance, but in the long run they're real."

Thank heaven, I saw my pot of flowers safely home from that crowd of folks. Not a stalk, not a leaf, not a petal was broken or scuffed. On the last stretch of the journey after getting off the bus, the northwest wind seemed to be on my side, for it did not come out to stroll or dance so that I safely surmounted the last hurdle.

At home, to my dismay, I ran straight into a heated row between two of my neighbors, husband and wife who had caused the whole family in an uproar. My mother had pulled the husband into my room to keep him out of harm's way, but the battle was not over yet. Soon quarrels broke out between wife and husband, elder sister and younger brother, elder sister and younger sister, mother and daughter—arguments developed into fights with people rolling on the floor, crying and squabbling together—it was as terrifying as if a nuclear world war had broken out. I was kept busy mediating among them for a good hour and a half before they calmed down.

I'd been looking forward to coming home and quietly drinking in the beauty of my flowers, but it turned out quite the reverse.

Never mind! At least the arrival of fresh flowers did not upset my neighbors. I was like a bridegroom softly leading the bridal palanquin through the doorway so as not to catch anyone's attention.

Where to place the pot of flowers?

It struck me in a flash, "Anywhere at all will be fine."

Indeed, wherever you place a pot of lovely flowers they will be beautiful—they'll touch the heart.

In the end, I placed them in the center of the room. That way, the whole room seemed to have flowers everywhere and the entire place was red. More importantly, this simple room now acquired a highly colorful centerpiece, like some lady of the house in all finery, gracefully standing in the middle of the reception room acknowledging her guests.

The undeclared war eventually came to an end. My neighbors forgot about their machine guns and hand grenades, and began to focus on my "lady of the house."

"What are they?"

"Poinsettias.''

"How gorgeous! With this, your room really seems like a new home."

"I know you bought this pot of flowers for Miss Pu," said one young woman.[11]

"I hope it will bloom until the day she returns."

But I was a little worried whether it would survive long enough for my wife to see it. It seemed so weak and frail, and it must have been uncomfortable to emerge from a clear glass greenhouse and suddenly find itself in my opaque, chilly brick room.

---

[11] Qing initially took my surname of Pu, but later reverted to her maiden name. Our neighbor was still used to calling her "Miss Pu."

All the same, it added a touch of fresh red life to the whole surroundings. By day, when I was writing, I would turn and gaze at her elegant crimson face. At night, by lamplight, I would sit on my old sofa and examine her closely. The more I looked, the more beautiful she seemed. It really was a little like gazing upon a beautiful woman beneath a lantern.

Her gentle, graceful stems stood there silently, her fronds of green leaves, so large and fresh—like green speech, green sounds—were a foil to the four red blooms, each petal like a red willow leaf, embodying an ineffable elegance and restraint. In the lamplight she possessed an infinitely sweet stillness. She surrounded me with a mysterious static beauty. I thought, even the most charming human beauty could never compare with a flower. Because even the most exquisite flesh-and-blood being can never possess the nobility, elegance and tranquillity of a plant. A plant exudes a magical, saintly quality which it lies beyond the power of humankind to show.

Sometimes, deep in the night, I would sit at a distance listening to music and gazing at her from afar. I felt as if I were living once again among Dante's "eternal roses."

Remarkably, the later the hour, the more beautiful she seemed. Once I found myself still staring at her at midnight, simply seduced by her infinite stillness and majesty. Perhaps it was because this lonely house of mine was now no longer lonely. Or perhaps this place seemed extra lonely—a loneliness not of the ordinary kind, so lonely I could touch with my hand the so-called flat "wall of the cosmos."

Soon things began to gather pace. Every day I looked at the thermometer. When the red mercury sank I worried she'd be too cold, so I dressed her in a cotton gown by wrapping her up in some cotton wool. Then I worried that old cotton wool didn't look good enough for her, so I used snow-white new cotton. As soon as the sun came out I rushed her outside and placed her in the sun. Then I worried she'd get knocked into by children, pecked by chickens or scratched by cats, so I begged and pleaded my neighbors to take more care. As soon as the wind picked up or the sun went down I quickly carried her back inside. Every few days I gave her some more water, and once I even fed her some home-made fertilizer.[12]

Despite all the care I took, disaster did eventually strike. One afternoon when she was sunbathing I walked over and saw that one bloom was missing. Peering more closely, I saw it had fallen down inside the pot. I felt torn apart inside, but I didn't fly into a rage. I had learned during all this time that people shouldn't get angry about things like this.

Asking around, it turned out that a five-year-old girl from the third floor had picked it and thrown it down. Despite myself, I dashed upstairs to complain to her grandfather. He apologized to me. That wasn't the point. I had only gone upstairs to make him understand that someone in his family had done something completely unacceptable. Lest this 72-year-old man still did not see, I put it to him in black and white.

"I went all the way into town to buy that pot of flowers and brought them home with great difficulty. The blooms flowered so well and what a pity your grand daughter picked one of them off!"

Not just me, even one of my "nuclear war" neighbors lamented over it. He said the one thing he had never been able to forgive was people damaging perfectly nice flowers.

I carried the flower pot indoors. Four heads had turned into three. As in the wake of a beheading, all that remained of the one empty stalk was a stiff torso with its head missing. The more I looked, the more devastated I felt. But the severed bloom was as fresh as ever. I couldn't bring myself to throw it away, so I filled a small wineglass with water and kept her in it all alone. How odd it looked from a distance! It exactly resembled a bloody human head floating on the water, like an oil painting a painter friend once gave me. Taking his theme from a romantic novel of mine, he had painted the heroine's head all red, floating

---

[12] Sometimes in this story the poinsettia is referred to as "she" as a sign of my fondness for the flower, treating it as a "woman." In referring to the flower as "it" I am thinking of it as a plant. This shows my changing emotions.

in a lake full of green water-lily leaves—a surrealistic modern painting in the manner of Dali. At the sight of it I felt grieved in the first place, but this later turned into surprise. I became reconciled to it as a painting with profound symbolic meaning.

But how many days could this floating woman's head survive? With only two small green leaves left, how long could respiration be maintained?

I grew uncomfortable looking at that "decapitated torso" in the flower pot, so in the end I broke it off. Now that the "four giant heads" had turned into "three giant heads," it looked a little more harmonious.

Day by day the weather grew colder, finally reaching below freezing point, and a few of the leaves below the flowers began to wither. I anxiously checked the calendar. It was only the end of January, another eight or nine days before Qing could come home. It was looking as if she would not be able to see my flower. In the next few days it was exceptionally cold outdoors and the sun rarely shone. After my lesson at the hands of that little vandal I no longer ventured to put the flower outside to get more sunlight. Occasionally I did so, but only when children weren't around, or with me standing alongside to keep watch. I preferred to let it have a glimpse of the sun indoors.

My sights weren't set very high: I just wanted Qing to come back in time to see her once. It was as if she were at her last gasp on a sickbed, hanging on to see some relative for the last time before she could pass away content. No, she wouldn't be content, it was I who would be content for her.

My desire for Qing to be able to see her stemmed from my not forgetting my wife's words. In her thoughtful devotion toward me at that time, Qing had hoped that a pot of flowers could keep me company through the lonely nights in place of her. For all my elderly mother's fondness, she needed flowers to be her heart's tender intermediary.

But more importantly, I owed an apology to Qing somehow. We had been surrounded on all sides by a raging red sea all these years, but to retain a minimum of human dignity, no matter how the breakers roared or what the cost, I had always maintained my irregular status. Meanwhile she, like the Linda of Greek legend, had braved the perilous waves and crossed the vast surging sea to clasp her lover in her arms. How was I to repay her? This was perhaps the greatest problem of my life. At the moment it was really impossible for me to strike a balance between those two determined opposites—"eternal" and "instantaneous."

Amid my agony of embarrassment, I thought a pot of flowers could help me out for a while. At least—perhaps reasonably enough, or even without any reason at all—it might express an apology on my behalf.

There again, I had never before arranged a pot of flowers to welcome Qing home for Chinese New Year. No, it was rather to welcome our traveling honeymoon. In all these years, like the mythical Herd Boy and Weaver Girl meeting across the bridge of magpies, our life had been virtually a traveling honeymoon—only we'd enjoyed more times and spent longer together than those two lovers in the sky.

Perhaps my emotions fed through to the flower! For strangely enough, although the green leaves one by one turned yellow, withered, wilted, and gradually curled up like huge silkworms, the flowers still bloomed as red, fresh and lovely as ever. It made me think of certain T.B. sufferers, who even with part of their lungs infected or cut away, remain full of vitality in their whole person.

The morning of February 8 was my happiest time. As I cast an eye over my three exquisite scarlet red flowers, I was glad that my wish had now really and truly been fulfilled. Unless Santa Claus had caught some sudden misfortune, my "Christmas Red" would certainly be red tonight. That evening it was raining as I fetched my beautiful Jina home from the station. ("Jina" was the pet name I had given my wife.) She was going to be here for the Chinese New Year holiday.

As we came in the door I proudly said, "Look, the wish I made has finally come true. When I bought this pot of flowers I silently said a prayer to Heaven that she might stay red and beautiful until the night she met you. Within a fortnight the leaves had begun to wither, and one bloom was broken off by a child. I thought it was all up, by the look of things she definitely would not live to meet you. I never imagined she would still be blooming so red and so beautiful tonight! Life is truly an inconceivable mystery!"

As she took it in, my wife was full of praise for its prettiness, gracefulness, and classical beauty.

"In my life, you are this poinsettia," I said to her with a smile.

That night was a real night of "eternal roses." No longer did I keep lonely vigil by the lamp, looking at my poinsettia in solitude.

The next day I didn't pay the same concentrated attention to my flower as before. After all, Jina had seen her now, even if only once—her mission was completed, the welcome I was aiming for had been attained. From now on, how many more days she managed to bloom would be her own business entirely!

Day by day the weather grew colder. It rained and snowed constantly, with not a glimpse of the sun for ten days or more, and it was often freezing outside. Strangely, not a single bloom of my poinsettia faded. While the leaves had almost completely withered and shriveled up like proper silkworms, that expanse of red remained as ravishing as ever. Even odder, the poinsettia in the glass with just its two little leaves hadn't faded either. Rather, it stayed in bloom for three more weeks. To me this was nothing short of a miracle, for not only had the flower stayed fresh, the leaves hadn't withered either. This "floating woman's head" was just fantastic!

I began to feel a pang of remorse. The flower seemed to be pitting itself against me: The more you neglect me and ignore me, the more I'll go on blooming just to show you!

A few days earlier—the day Jina left—I had been admiring the flower and said to her:

"Back then when I first bought this flower, the florist told me that with good care she could bloom for a month or more. I thought, in this cold winter weather I certainly wouldn't be able to look after her properly. I never imagined she would bloom from that day to now, a full one month and eight days. It still looks as if she could bloom a few more days. Just think this is the very coldest time of year. Since she was bred in a warm greenhouse, I thought she wouldn't be able to stand the weather. Now, she's inspired me with a deep philosophical idea."

She gazed at me, charming and gentle, without a sound. At times like these she always seemed like a little girl listening to my endless flow of talk.

Once again it was a chilly night. I saw Jina off on the train, and another page of our married life permanently on the move came to an end. A few days later I wrote to her in a letter.

"I really never thought the poinsettia would bloom so long; it far exceeded my expectation. What does this tell us? Does it symbolize its owner—me? Or does it symbolize something between us? Or is it an abstract interpretation of some cosmic phenomenon? Maybe all three possibilities are correct. At any rate, it has at least awakened something deep within my heart— for the moment let me call it "hope," or perhaps "a flame!" And this is no ordinary hope. It's the kind of hope meant to be impossible to hope for and a flame meant to be impossible to emit.

Now at last I see that in the universe, sometimes, there is a mysterious power which is strangely capable of enduring so long, so firmly.

As I gaze at the "floating woman's head" in the glass, I cannot help trembling—"

Today—the fifty-second day since my poinsettia arrived—it is still blooming, except for one flower that has fallen and another withered. According to my neighbor, once a poinsettia does begin to droop it fades away altogether. This one looks ready to fade away completely in a week at most, so the chances are slim that it will set a record of sixty days. But I'm already well satisfied.

But that "floating woman's head" in the glass is still radiating an aura of red. Perhaps it will bloom for sixty days.

Who can tell? This really is a genuine miracle! Yet no matter how unyielding or how much she struggles, she is still bound to wither away, I think. Fade she may, but to my mind she will always be an enduring existence.

It was with a feeling of immense happiness that I watched my pot of flowers gradually wither away, and finally I wrote this, my first formal piece of writing in three and a half years.[13]

March 5, 1964

Author's 1981 Note:

Between 1958 and 1960, my fondness for flowers and my buying flowers suddenly became a reason for people to discriminate against me and regard me with hostility. I didn't expect that simply growing a pot of chrysanthemums would mean exposing secrets of the soul that I had never formally revealed before. When I wrote this short story in 1964 the "flower terror" had receded for a while, but I still felt anxious and did not dare write directly. I felt compelled to use a more elliptical and hesitant approach, recording my feelings in an indirect, understated manner. At first reading, I'm afraid that this feeling will not be widely appreciated, but the sensitive reader will quickly put two and two together and gain an insight into my emotions at the time.

Now, in order to commemorate the temporary ending of that extraordinary period and my separation from my wife, one of the story's main characters, I have used the title of this story as the name for this entire collection.

---

[13] This story was initially called "The Story of a Poinsettia." Its title was changed to "The Poinsettia" for the first (Hong Kong) edition and the second (Taiwan) edition. For the third (Taiwan) edition it was re-titled "Flower Terror."

Author's 1987 Note:

Following the initial publication of this short story, I have taken advantage of the opportunity of this second edition to fill in more real background and add certain historic facts so as to further highlight its message. I have also amended some passages slightly. I should also explain that in the 2,000-year history of the Chinese short story there has never been one which had a flower as a principal character. The only exception is "The Old Gardener" from the collection "Wonders of the Present and the Past." But "The Old Gardener" is mythical story. This story of mine has a flower as its principal character, but it is no myth; it's a page of contemporary history.

(Translated by Andrew Morton)

Reunion

A Story of the Cultural Revolution

A heart-to-heart reunion with an old friend from the "outer part" you haven't seen in ten years is no trivial matter in these times.

Actually the "outer part" is just another expression for the Chinese hinterland. Ten years ago, the two of them had been colleagues at a certain printing works in Shanghai. Tang had relocated, along with the factory and its planographic printing machines, from the maritime port city of Shanghai to the inland city of Nanchang. Soon after, Yin had been transferred to Hangzhou. Tang, a seasoned local who could clearly remember every alley, lane, winding street, passage and even the location of every public convenience in Shanghai, had surely by now counted all the stones of the ruined Prince Teng's Pavilion and the pine needles in Nanchang's Sun Yat-sen Park. Meanwhile Yin had been a little luckier than Tang, for he had the green waters of the West Lake to gaze at and the Lake's sour fish and water-shield to dine on. From that point of view his life was a good deal more agreeable. The two of them first had been old colleagues, then friends "aiding the hinterland." Now one friend was coming from one hinterland area to visit a friend in another. As far as they were concerned, the "outer part" scenario mentioned earlier just didn't apply, for they were like two footballs in a regular game that had been kicked onto the field from outside.

The word "friendship" possesses many, many meanings. Way back in the age that we have now spurned it amounted almost to a miniature encyclopedia, encompassing a vast scope of subjects. It covered everything from a young lady's lock of black hair to an old man's cough; from carp in the Yellow River to autumn wind and rain by a small window. Every imaginable thing found a place there: the kites, spinning tops and crickets of childhood, the blues, whisky, serenades, scenic photographs and street demonstrations of youth.

In these times it represents new things quite unknown before. It doesn't represent a glass of new wine—new Fragrant Snow wine, or Green Bean Cake alcohol—nor is it simply a new moonlit night, the stillness of new leaves on a tree and the silence of the stars. It represents a vast new kind of abstraction—like the new Paris school of abstract painting, which, while highly abstract, means something, indicates something, and tells us something. There is a truly great concreteness residing within it. Before, people seemed to have grown so accustomed to the concrete that whenever they reached out they had to touch something, a stool or a table; whenever they looked up they had to see something, a plate or a green tree; whenever they lifted a foot they had to tread on something, a floorboard or a bitumen road. Now they have suddenly gone all abstract, and it is almost as if hands were not for touching nor sight for seeing. Those feet that once had to be treading on something do best now to rise briefly upon clouds and mist, or turn into miniature feet of the legendary Great Roc described by Zhuangzi, functioning virtually as wings.

At present, for Yin at least, friendship was a synthesis of all things abstract, a mysterious symbol. At least it could accommodate one's longing to soar aloft and drift away. Through this feeling, by means of lines and colors once considered as incomprehensible as an abstract picture, it could express a mystery of life which was an incredible combination of the extremely ancient and the extremely new. Again, it was like some mythical book whose message is all there for those who can read it, while for those who cannot it remains a volume of blank paper.

As Yin was sunk in thought, a slight figure slowly made its way up to him.

Who?

Yin hesitated a little, then suddenly almost shouted.

"Hey, Tang! It's you!"

Yes indeed, it was the friend he hadn't seen in ten years, Tang. He was carrying a black chamois leather case.

A warm handshake. Both hands seemed tense and trembled a little, and Yin's nearsighted spectacles slipped a centimeter down the bridge of his nose.

Yin laughed. Tang did not.

"This is my wife Chen—This is Tang, the old friend I've told you about so often—"

Looking toward Chen, who had come in at the sound of his voice, Yin made his introductions loudly and in a voice merry with laughter. Slim and petite, she wore a green plastic apron hung over her chest instead of an old-fashioned one tied around her waist, which made her look like a kitchen lady, and a little like a postman too. Having just come in from the kitchen, no doubt in a hurry, she was still holding an unpeeled bamboo-shoot in her right hand. This she transferred to her left hand.

Another handshake, but without the tension of a moment earlier.

"Please have a seat inside, Comrade Tang. Yin has been thinking about you for days. Once he knew you were coming today he went out before daybreak to get something nice for lunch, and bought half a basket of early bamboo-shoots. He selected the tender tips for he knows stir-fried bamboo-shoot is your favorite. Now Yin, you keep Tang company here."

After dropping into the room, Chen hastily darted off into the kitchen holding the bamboo-shoot and looking as if she were carrying a sheng (a Chinese instrument whose shape resembles a bamboo-shoot) to play in some Chinese orchestra.

"Tang, bet you'll love the stir-fried bamboo-shoot we're going to have today. I chose all tender tips, every one looking like sheng. I turned down all the ones that were too old, too thick or too long, and those with too many knots. When I got them home I didn't rinse them at all in case washing off the dirt might spoil their freshness. I waited till around the time you were expected to arrive before asking Chen to rinse and peel them. We'll have a dish of stir-fried bamboo-shoot for lunch today as a special treat for you."

The host was babbling away and laughing. But suddenly he halted in mid flow. His guest wasn't laughing. Maybe he was exhausted from the journey, Yin thought.

Yin poured a cup of jasmine tea and offered a West Lake brand cigarette. This jasmine tea and this luxury box of West Lake cigarettes had been bought especially for Tang; he normally only drank inexpensive green tea and smoked the cheap Xin'an River cigarettes.

"Come on, come on, sit down and have a cup of tea!"

Tang had not yet sat down; he was taking in the scene. His clear, charming eyes of ten years ago were bleary from exhaustion, but they still gleamed alertly as they swept over the furnishings inside the room. Pathetically, this modest room of thirteen square meters, which in the summer was exposed to the hot sun from both east and west, barely had space for a redwood coir-strung double bed, a light brown lacquered square table and four yellow lacquered low stools, while up against the window stood an oblong table of textured pine with a water flask and tea things on it. This set of tea things was a quarterly prize (bonus stuff such as utensils awarded to model employees on a quarterly basis). On a washstand in one corner alongside the table was a white enamel basin which was also a quarterly prize. In the other corner, on a shelf near the bed, stood two white wooden quilt chests, a camphor chest, and three red lacquered wooden boxes. There was no wardrobe in the room, neither was there a chest of drawers. Fortunately they didn't yet have any children, otherwise it really would have been like living in a cockleshell. This cramped room reminded him of those narrow passages which also serve as busy thoroughfares, where if two or more people pass through they are always rubbing shoulders or treading on each other's toes.

What drew Tang's attention, though, was not this cubbyhole or these furnishings. His Sherlock Holmes-like eyes were ceaselessly sweeping the walls. Looking every bit as gaudy as a temple fair at Spring Festival, these were hung all over with red and green strips of paper, mostly posters and slogans such as "Rebellion is Justified" or "Follow the Lead of—" or "Smash to Smithereens—" Most striking of all was an enormous portrait of the Great Leader with the "Four Greats" inscribed horizontally above it and new-style paired couplets down each side. There was also a new-style revolutionary New Year picture printed by some art publishing house. Yin guessed a little at Tang's astonishment. In the old days, when they had been colleagues at the printing plant in Shanghai, due no doubt to regular contact with books on top of his fundamental disposition, Yin had ended up becoming somewhat addicted to books and a keen reader of both Chinese and foreign literature. Not only had he loved books, he had also dabbled in calligraphy and used to keep a few hanging scrolls by minor calligraphers of the Republican period displayed around his home. How come this 180-degree turnaround now?

Maybe Tang had guessed that in order to fill in that mysterious hole that could never be filled, economically speaking, Yin had taken the sofa, the lauan writing desk and those redwood bookcases from his old home and sent them all off to the second-hand furniture shop when he left Shanghai. After arriving in Hangzhou this thirteen square-meter space had been far from easy to get hold of. It had been allocated to him only because he was getting married. It looked as though Chen had been very much in love with him, otherwise this furniture would scarcely have measured up to a new wife's basic expectations. (Though there were still newly married couples who had to stay in a hotel once a week to be together.) Still, it considerably outshone Tang's "one pair of overshoes and an umbrella" style wedding dowry. [1]

Actually the crux of the matter did not lie here, but rather in the atmosphere. No matter how plain a room is, a gentlemanly intellectual will use his ingenuity to arrange a little world of harmonious line and color, creating a studious or poetic

---

[1] At one time in Jiangxi province, it is said that a woman's wedding gift consisted simply of a pair of rubber boots and an umbrella.

atmosphere. But in this case, the way this room looked was evidently not the aimless blooming of a flower, but the intentional forming of a fruit. It was a portrait of one man's state of mind—for a room is the concrete expression of its occupant's inner being.

Tang's tired eyes fell on Yin. A blue Lenin suit, washed innumerable times until it had faded to a color that was neither quite blue nor quite gray. On his head a dark blue Lenin cap, creased and crumpled like a big dough pancake that had been left lying around for a month or more. To all appearances Yin looked even more travel-worn than Tang—and there was a certain style and quality of the experienced cadre about him (though in fact he wasn't one). This quality could be either genuine or false, for it was difficult to be sure at first sight.

The sound of a woman shouting suddenly burst from next door.

"Huh! Acting so creepy shutting yourself indoors in broad daylight and muttering away! Think I don't know!"

Yin thought it must be the woman from Nanjing next door scolding that Zhuji woman opposite who was as skinny as a little monkey, but her eyes were trained on his room.

Tang started to tremble slightly. The door was partially to but not closed, and now Tang ambled across and with a deliberately casual movement of his hand opened the door wide—now her field of vision was clear; everything could be taken in at a glance.

"So you're a cadre now?" Tang asked tentatively, a shadow passing over his thin face.

"What do you mean, a cadre! A few members of the revolutionary committee insisted on electing me to take charge of the workshop study group.... Why don't you sit down?"

Only now did Tan recall that in Shanghai, Yin had been head proofreader in the plant's typesetting department. With his superior cultural level it was only natural that he should now be in charge of a study group. He sat down facing those red and green paper strips on the wall and sank deep in thought. From the cup of jasmine tea on the table rose a sweet fragrance.

His host began to feel puzzled. Why had this old friend who used to be so free and easy suddenly turned Platonic? In the old days Tang had been in charge of disc chromatography, and he was highly cultured. He had studied at university for a year, and had only left off his studies and entered the factory because his family was so poor. They both liked Chinese and foreign literature and had always got on so well, but now.... Once embarked on this train of thought, after the rapturous enthusiasm he had given way to initially, he now found himself being infected by this classical platonic atmosphere and began to quiet down too. He looked his visitor steadily in the face. For the first time he became properly aware of an indefinable change in the face of this middle-aged man. That light-complexioned, plump round face of before had vanished, to be replaced by a skinny, hoary and dark triangular wedge. The darkness was not simply a color tone. It was more a gloom or shadow, like a long-established stain on some old clothes that could never be scrubbed away or washed out. His eyes, once clearer than spring water, had now turned into well-water after rain, ditch water even, all turbid and murky. They were the source of all the gloom on this face, which was like the profound darkness emitted by two black holes. He was no longer as he had been before, looking at you directly face to face. His eyes were hesitant, uncertain, and wandering. Tang used to be a plump fellow, but now a skinny one. It was as if he had been crushed by some compressor and his whole body had shrunk. His dark blue Lenin suit was neither new nor old, his moon-cake of a Lenin cap lay on the table. "Ah! His hair has turned gray, and he's only forty-five!"

Like Columbus discovering the New World, this came to him in a flash of inspiration at which he couldn't help suddenly breathing in a dark wind, a conceptual dark wind which often blew at this point in time. Who knows how many families had been blown over by this dark wind. With this mysterious dark wind, as if receiving an infection, he began to regret a little his own eagerness just now as too "open," too "unguarded."

Once this black wind blows, it brings down storms of thunder, lightning and violent rain. A huge flash of lightning once again illuminated his thoughts.

This old friend's body bore a clear sign, known in Shanghai as "desiccation." It could account for a person from either a positive or a negative angle. Whether he was a compressor or the one compressed, his form and spirit would always display a certain consequence of compression.

"Let me put your leather case on the table!"

Yin stepped across to take the black leather case from his lap.

"No, no, it's all right." Tang gestured with his right hand while his left hand remained firmly on the leather case.

"You're a cadre too, aren't you?"

"No, no, no...." Tang's gloomy eyes remained fixed on the door.

Eyeing Tang's black leather case, Yin came to a realization. Maybe he was a personnel cadre who had come to gather information? At least he was on an outside mission. But this sort of person was usually a Party member (although there were exceptions; this was a time full of "exceptions"). By the look of things Tang might have been one, and then again he might have not.

Not to speak of the last ten years, the upheavals of the past two years had spurred enough little reptiles to evolve into upright apes. "Perhaps he's chalked up some big achievement. It's hard to say."

Mulling over these ideas, Yin had an involuntary frisson.

Nowadays anything could happen.

"Perhaps he's come to find out about me." Another lightning flash.

Caution acts something like a humidometer in changing weather. Once rime, rain or snow appear, nothing can stem the mercury column's relentless rise. Yin's emotions at this point were practically drenching him in sweat. Again he heard the ticking of the alarm clock. So right now Tang was setting a trap for him; it was truly unbelievable. On what basis? Their historical connection? But no matter how far or how deep these tentacles extended, a mountain reared between them: ten years! Meanwhile on the street not far beyond the front door, gongs and drums were sounding. "Oh, these past two years!" He wanted to demolish this mountain peak with one phrase, with one word, or else use some inner chord as a rope ladder to scale its summit. But surely that was a little too naive. Or else seize the torch of their emotions of a decade or so ago and bum up the new "humanity" being stirred by the gongs and drums out on the street, but that also was too stupid, too ignorant of the times. His eyes suddenly fell on the visitor's pair of rubber shoes. With their grass-green uppers and tightly fastened laces, they looked as if they too were a quarterly prize. From these shoes right up to his graying short hair, the visitor seemed to exude a new atmosphere. This time he really sensed the other's ponderous reticence. "In the old days Tang was a completely different person!"

"Have some tea!" The host waved his hand, his voice somewhat quieter. Tang nodded, picked up the teacup, wetted his lips and put it down again as if it were a cup of poisoned tea.

Suddenly feeling he had nothing to say, Yin gazed at the visitor's long cigarette ash, which automatically dropped to the floor. Tang had in fact puffed no more than twice at his cigarette.

Yin offered another West Lake brand cigarette. "Have one more!"

"Thanks." There was a timid note in his voice, " I've just given up smoking."

"Mm. 'Given up smoking'?" Yin regarded Tang with puzzlement.

A strange silence settled over the room. The visitor felt no uneasiness at this. He seemed used to it. But the host felt uncomfortable and a little at a loss. It was embarrassing to be sitting with an old friend you haven't seen for over ten years and act out a dumb show.

"How have you been managing with the quarterly production goals at the factory?" With an effort, like squeezing toothpaste, he finally forced out a sentence.

"All right."

Yin almost felt like dashing across and giving Tang a good slap. What, after ten whole years, you won't even say a word to me?

In fact, the host might well have been too hard on his guest at that moment. The latter, suddenly making a point of dropping in today, had been longing for this reunion after ten years of separation. But as soon as he had set foot inside the door he too, like his host but one step ahead, had experienced Columbus's discovery of the New World, and perhaps more than so. It was this that had made him change his mind. In "these times" it was easy for a man to change his mind, even on a matter of great importance. It was of no concern to the one who had changed his mind no matter how offensive or disgusting that change might be.

Another burst of shouting came from the woman next door. It was just as if she were slapping the visitor across the face, although he hadn't reached any definite conclusion as to whether her shouts had anything to do with him or not.

"The hell with your political correctness! You just say one thing to my face and another behind my back, you two-faced swine!" The shouting grew louder and louder.

Tang looked a bit uneasy and shifted on his stool. His vigilant eyes were trained on the door as if some exotic creature or monster he was extremely interested in were hiding there. This monster was everywhere. He thrust out his right arm and glanced at his watch. Then he raised the glass teacup and took a proper drink.

"Well, so you have some rebels here in the building?" The visitor spoke low. It was the first formal utterance he had made since his arrival.

The host nodded. He rather appreciated the way he responded.

"You're a rebel too, of course!" Tang said alertly.

"Oh, no, no…. The host hastily shook his head and his face flushed red. "They dragged me along ... pinned a title on me ... really it's not so. I don't take part in any activities. How about you?"

"No, I am not." The visitor answered firmly.

The host immediately blamed himself for losing another move. His answer just then had once again been too "open," whereas his guest's response was precisely to the point. He was surely not being "open." "These days ... a person shouldn't.…"

For a moment he felt at a loss for words. Picking up the hot water flask, the host added some boiling water for his guest. Gradually the jasmine tea turned dark red as it truly exuded its color.

Sitting down, the host looked at the window glass flooded with sunlight and thought it really did seem like spring. Springtime in Hangzhou brought more clouds and rain than sunshine, and such a fine sunny day was rare indeed. He had intended to take Tang on a boat trip on the lake after lunch. But now he was wondering whether to stick to his original plan. It didn't matter much when the two of them acted out a dumb show here in the room, but it would seem a little grotesque if they were going to act like this on the lake and, worse yet, when they were eating the West Lake sour fish at the Louwailou (the restaurant he had thought of taking Tang to for dinner).

Just then the door opened with a creak and a household registration policeman appeared in his white uniform and cap.

"Comrade Yin, is Comrade Cheng, the subcommittee chair, at home?" He was asking after the next-door neighbor who for the past ten years had chaired the local alleyway subcommittee.

"Comrade Cheng has gone into town to see her daughter." Yin answered casually, without standing up. "Her only daughter is married to a junior doctor at the city hospital. Today is her day off, so she's gone to pay her a visit."

"Oh, you have a visitor?" The policeman cast a curious glance at Tang and eyed him up and down for a good half a minute before slowly going out. Next he stepped into the room of the woman from Nanjing who had been shouting a while before and stayed there for about fifteen minutes.

Yin's window faced directly across to the Nanjing woman's room, and today his chinz curtains were not drawn. Sitting facing south, his visitor could see the white uniform and cap perfectly clearly.

Before long, about five minutes after the white uniform and cap had disappeared, the woman from Nanjing started shouting loudly again.

"If you don't want people to know what you're doing, the only thing to do is not to do it! What good have you ever done? Call yourself an activist! To the masses it's crystal clear what you're up to!" Her shouting had only died away a few minutes when Tang suddenly stood up.

"I have something to attend to. I must go.... See you again on my next business trip.... I'll be sure to visit you another time.... Here's a small gift for your wife." Tang drew two square boxes from his black leather case. They were two boxes of fermented bean-curd, a famous local delicacy from Jiangxi province.

Yin jumped up as if a bomb shell had landed close by.

"Our lunch is ready! Don't leave without eating."

"I can't stay. My ticket is for the 12:20 train. I have to be in Shanghai by six for a business appointment."

What nonsense, Tang never mentioned any of this in his letter. Who knows what he had up his sleeve?

The host's genial manner took on a politely diplomatic tone.

"Well, have a bite to eat at least. It's only 10:45. If you eat fast, you can still catch your train. It's only half an hour to the station."

"Never mind. There will be ample opportunity another time. That's why I didn't specify in my letter how long I would be staying." He paused, then gave a chuckle. It was the first time he had smiled that day.

"You say I can make it to the station in thirty minutes, but I doubt it. There are swarms of 'little generals' around outside. The bus was packed with them. I had to wait a good forty-five minutes at the station before I could squeeze on a bus to get here. It's lucky I'm not old! Elderly people wouldn't stand a chance of catching a bus."

The memory of that scene surfaced involuntarily. Compared to the passengers on that bus, sardines in a can would have beamed with joy at the extreme comfort in which they lay. He shook hands with his host. "At least we have met. I'm glad you're doing fine and your wife's in good health. We're old friends, we can take the rough with the smooth, and time is on our side. When I come by this way on my next trip I'll definitely spend a couple of days with you. Well, goodbye then."

What a pity that just when Tang displayed his old free and easy manner for the first time, this was all he had to say. It was as if all his vital energies were being spent, not on reuniting with his friend after ten years and touring The West Lake with him, but on expressing a profound farewell.

By now Yin was no longer interested in expending undue energy on detaining his guest, or in using polite diplomatic language.

As they passed the kitchen, Chen, just like her husband, suddenly leapt out as if a shell had landed beside her.

"What, you're leaving? Lunch's all ready. Let's go ahead and eat. We've even bought wine...."

"Tang's in a hurry and must leave right away. It's no use trying to make him stay." Lying was the only way he could save the situation. Time did not permit him to explain the truth— there would be time later.

"Oh! I've just got the stir-fried bamboo-shoots done...."

"Thank you, thank you. I'll drop in again next time. Goodbye, goodbye."

"Goodbye. Goodbye. Be sure to come next time!" The host saw him to the front door.

At 12:20, Tang's slim figure was nowhere to be seen on any
train bound for Shanghai. Instead he was leaning against the
window of a lakeside restaurant, looking fixedly out over the
green waters of the lake waiting for the wine and food he had
ordered. He was sunk in thought. No doubt he had already spent
some while (including the time spent traveling) mulling over
whether he should have acted the way he had that morning.
Now, as he gazed at the lovely greenery by the lake, an answer
flashed in mariner's semaphore on the sea of his mind. It
consisted of just one word:

"Yes!"

He sighed. Anyway, he had at least escaped from a
nightmare, or a hypothetical nightmare, or perhaps not even a
nightmare at all.

(Translated by Andrew Morton)

The Turtle

For the thirty years preceding 1982, when I left China, a great many cities were overwhelmed by political changes unprecedented in the Chinese history. The absurdities that occurred stupefied visitors from outside the Bamboo Curtain. Even the events recounted in the *Tales of Arabian Nights* were far too unimaginative to convey the realities of that period.

Hangzhou's West Lake was praised for a thousand years as one of China's most beautiful spots. During those thirty years a high rostrum was often erected from which death sentences would be announced. Thousands of local citizens would be forced to stand for hours in the scorching sun and listen respectfully to some demon from hell. This was usually a high court prosecutor who would announce each of the crimes the condemned had committed and shrilly curse at all those who dared hold differing views from his lofty perch. This tourist attraction, adding the peppery spice of politics to the scenic beauty of The West Lake's colorful orchards and lush green willows, would leave the rare foreigners wondering whether or not they had left Mother Earth for some strange and evil world.

I also remember that in 1956 the emerald ripples of The West Lake, having played peacefully against the shore for over a millennium, suddenly ceded their place to the lifeless sands of a desert. The communist regime had drained the lake so its waters could be used to irrigate the surrounding fields. One day while I was walking in the still moist, black mud of the lake bed, I realized with a shudder that I was treading on a layer of tiny, dead fish.

All this was the conjuring of the divine sorcerer, Chairman Mao. He was always dressing himself up and showing off his skills. We people would have to follow suit, becoming simultaneously both actors and audience for countless tragicomedies that even a Chinese Shakespeare would have been hard pressed to plot.

I have already told the stories of many of these performances, but one remains untold. This is a story whose setting is a Chinese town with its public buses rumbling through the streets and its clack-clack railway trains.

Before I start the tale, it would be wise to recall the lines of the famous Tang Dynasty poet Li Po (701-762): "Oh, how steep! How high! How arduous is the Road to Shu! Even more so than the climb to the Heavens!"

I am not talking about the imaginary marvels of Aladdin and his magic lamp blocking the Chinese highway and railroad by placing in their way such barriers as Sword-Gate and Stronghold Passes, the Wine-Worshipping Ridge and the Qinling Mountain of Shanxi Province. I am telling harrowing tales of traveling or moving around in China.

During the horror of the Cultural Revolution, Mao Zedong called forth his youthful red guards eight times. Train after Beijing-bound train was packed full of these passengers. They were crammed in as tightly as tinned anchovies. One hundred passengers would normally fill a compartment. But during those times each compartment was packed to overflowing, swelling with up to three hundred passengers. People were everywhere, packed not only on seats and tea tables, in corridors and baggage racks, but also squeezed under the seats and lying prone on the floor between unfamiliar legs. More than thirty people were sitting, standing and gasping for breath in a space of four square meters. They reminded me of the monkeys that filled the trees of the E-Mei Mountains of Western China. Daredevils even packed the tops of the trains, braving certain death should they lose their footing.

One young female Red Guard sitting near the window appeared to be fidgeting uncontrollably, but there was no question of her getting through to the primitive facilities. As soon as the train stopped, she turned to her neighbors on both sides, asked for their understanding, and then, with a little assistance, climbed onto the tea table and peed out of the open window as if she were quite alone.

Seeing these things brought back to mind scenes from the Sino-Japanese War, when the Japanese Army conquered the Solitary Hill. The whole population of Guilin then swarmed toward Guiyang and it was nearly impossible to climb onto a bus. Whenever the bus screeched to a halt, everyone seemed to feel the desperate need to relieve himself and would press around the windows. Members of the "bottom holding" trade would then appear outside. They collected precious "night soil" for cultivation using one hand to hold out their shiny enamel potties toward the needy, and using their other hand to steady their customers lest they fall from their perches. Your imagination can probably finish the picture with far greater detail than I wish to provide.

That was during the time of the Sino-Japanese War. But things hardly changed on municipal buses and trains by the time of my tale.

Let Hangzhou, my hometown for many years, serve as an example.

Every time the bus stopped at one of the larger stations, like the Fish Market Bridge, Wulin Gate, Soaring Dragon Bridge, Xian-ning Road, or the Guan-xian intersection, the station instantly became a raging battlefield. The prospective passengers were the bloodthirsty warriors. They fought with a door-die desperation that fueled a killer's instincts. As soon as the doors parted, the first wave of battle-hardened veterans scrambled to get into the car. So great was their fear of being left behind that they would not make way for those trying to get off. Blinded by the rush forward, deaf to the cries of "I want to get off," they would charge on and finally wiggle their way, like earthworms, to the front of the bus. Once there, they would congeal into immobility. Only then could others finally struggle off the car, their nightmare over. It was not long however, before a second wave of pushing and elbowing occurred. The passengers were driven by a panic that recalled the mobs fleeing Genghis Khan.

The elderly, tripping and falling before the onslaught, were left crumpled on the ground.

Those whose herculean efforts got them into the car were the lucky ones. It was never easy. The "Little Generals" of Mao's Red Guards, who rode free during the Cultural Revolution, took up the sport of bus riding, using this mode of transport instead of stolen cars. Once they got into a bus, they would ride to the last stop, and then all the way back again, like a cat endlessly chasing its tail. Occasionally, a woman would make it to the bus door, surrounded by relatives and staggering and well into labor. She would kneel and plead with the Little Generals to let her in the bus so that she could make it to the hospital before her child arrived. The Red Guards would turn away their eyes, however, and ignore her.

Hot July afternoons made the passengers feel like they were surrounded by volcanoes spitting forth lava and poisonous gases. Temperatures often soared well above 40 degrees Centigrade, hot enough to boil an egg. The men and women standing back to back, side by side, were virtually stuck together, as if they were playing at being lovers, embracing and hugging each other. Their only relief was the sweat that rolled down their backs, like the Long-qiu Waterfalls in Zhejiang Province's Yan-dang Mountains.

Even the bus seemed to respond to Chairman Mao's urgings. They showed their revolutionary zeal by becoming elastic and expanding until they could accommodate more than twice their normal load of passengers. It seemed like the pressure inside the bus crushed each passenger by one or two centimeters until everybody was hardly able to take a breath.

Why am I going on and on at such length about buses? I want to set the scene for my tale, the tale of the Turtle, which took place on just such a bus.

It was in Shanghai in the 1960's that my tale took place. There were more buses and bus lines there, so the battles at the stations were not as fierce. But the density with which people were packed into the buses in Shanghai was certainly not unequal to that of Hangzhou buses.

It was a hot summer afternoon and the scorching sun made an oven of the Shanghai bus as it raced along its route with passengers piled on top of each other, nearly senseless from the heat and gasping for air. Suddenly, a shout was heard. "Ooh! Ow!" This was not just a cry of pain, but of dire agony, like a crashing plane sending out its last Mayday signal. A dozen or so passengers, pressed tightly against each other and numb from the heat, were jerked back to life and turned toward the direction of the sound.

A short, stout, middle-aged man was repeating the words "I'm sorry! I'm sorry!" as he shook his hand to and fro.

"Owh! Ow! Stop shaking your hand, you! I can't stand the pain!"

Only slowly did a few passengers realize that the short, stout man was holding a turtle high in the air with his right hand. At first he had been shaking this hand, but he had been stopped by the incessant cries of pain which came from the passenger at his side.

The scene began to unfold to other passengers. The short, stout man had bought a turtle, dropped it into a shopping net, tied a knot around its open end, and let it dangle from his right-hand. But as the heat became more and more unbearable, and the passengers were pressed closer and closer together, the man raised his hand and the bag out of fear that the turtle would die from suffocation. He had also, in the hopes that the reptile might survive until he got home, loosened the knot in the bag in order to give the newly bought turtle some air and a bit more room to sway around.

Who would have thought that the small creature, to whom greed was second nature, had found its way out into the steamy atmosphere of the bus, stretched out its little head and begun to nibble on the first piece of flesh it encountered. It was unclear whether it was a bit furious at its predicament, hungry, thirsty, or just yearning for a stretch. But it had opened its mouth wide and had bit hard and deep with its sharp teeth into the earlobe of a tall, thin passenger.

The short, stout man had to hold the turtle in the shopping net straight up over his head amidst the crush of the crowd. The turtle had then stretched its fig-shaped head out through the mesh and had found the tall man's tasty ear.

"You stupid fool! How could you bring a live turtle onto such a crowded bus? Oooh! It hurts! Ow! Ow! Ow!" The thin man shouted and swore in pain. He then cursed the unfortunate owner of the hungry reptile which, stubborn and unreasonable from its mistreatment, locked its jaws even more forcefully into the thin man's ear as its owner tried in vain to shake it loose.

Finally, the stout fellow stopped trying. But every time the bus stopped, shook, or swayed, the angry turtle would dig its jaws even deeper into the tall man's tender ear, thus provoking him to cry out in pain. Every few minutes, the stout man's arm would begin to tremble with fatigue. The shopping net would then start to sag in anticipation of a little relief until "Ooh! Owoo!" a stream of curses and howling shook the packed bus. "You stupid fool! Don't you dare move, I tell you!"

Then a savior, an army officer, appeared on the scene. "What are you two still doing on this bus, making all this racket? Get off at once!" he ordered.

"That's right! Get off! Get off!" The rest of the bus passengers shouted with one voice. Some of the younger passengers, wanting to see the turtle comedy with their own eyes, began to push their way through the tangle of people. Meanwhile the press of the crowd became even more unbearable and people sweated even more freely.

But getting off was easier said than done. Cutting a way through the mass of passengers seemed as hopeless an enterprise as trying to save Xiang Yu, the King of Chu, in his battle with the First Emperor of the Han Dynasty. Even if they had moved with the greatest of skill, they would not have moved faster than a snail. And the troublesome turtle, attached to the ear of the thin man and suspended from the hand of the stout man, hardly helped things. The two men, brought together by troublesome fate, were bound by this new "turtle-manacle," and could neither move too quickly nor too suddenly. At best they could only inch forward Indian-style, one after the other, the stout man leading the way and the thin man and the turtle bringing up the rear.

The thin man was indeed a sorry sight. His head was tilted toward the left to give the turtle as much leeway as possible. One wrong move, putting one of the men out of step with the other, would cause the vicious little reptile to renew its chewing and reward the crowd with another set of "Oohs!" and "Ows!"

"Oh, that's just so funny!" One onlooker would say without thinking. Another simple-minded one would follow with "I just can't believe it." Even those with an ounce of compassion and sympathy could barely constrain their laughter.

There were, thank heaven, a few helpful souls who slowly forced themselves back against their neighbors to make a small path through the thick human jungle. Gingerly, tortuously, accommodating the turtle as much as possible, the two, made their way to the bus door. Finally they got off, ever so carefully, at the Sichuan North Road stop.

They had hardly stepped onto the sidewalk before they were surrounded by a crowd of excited and laughing spectators, giving the impression of ants in a hot pot. Imagine the unlikely pair! One tall and thin, the other short and fat, both linked by a turtle. They were walking slowly and carefully down the side of the road, their movements meticulously synchronized like soldiers on a drill. One man held his arm high in the air, the other cocked his head to the side that had a large turtle earring dangling from his earlobe! It beat anything you might see in movies or on television. And this was real!

"One, two, three, four!" loudly chanted one group of onlookers. "One, two, three, four!" echoed another with great delight. And then the whole crowd laughed and shouted, "Ha, ha, ha, ha! This is great! It's so funny!"

Only heaven could imagine the deep embarrassment of the pair of men.

They had no choice but to walk that way. The little turtle's teeth were sharp. To be bitten was bad enough, but it was so much worse to have the beast keep chewing in the same place.

The turtle seemed to be completely enjoying itself as the two struggled down the street. Its four short legs were treading the air and its little stump of a tail was wagging with ferocious energy as if to keep time with the forced march of the two men. Soon, however, the turtle began to feel the heat of the blazing Shanghai sun. The gray and black shell and the pale belly underneath slowly began to heat up and place the turtle in acute discomfort. It started to chew again at the earlobe, causing our tall friend to screw up his face in agony. The odd pair, denied the ability to don their straw hats, also began to suffer from the sun. Beads of sweat rolled from their purple-red foreheads and soaked their shirts. It dripped from their ears and chins like the spray from a steaming hot shower.

The thin man was a Shanghai local and had a square face with bushy eyebrows and narrow eyes. His eyes, however, were half closed from pain. They had virtually become two straight lines etched into his face. It was almost as though he had no eyes at all. The stout fellow was from Anhui Province. His face was round and his eyebrows thin. You could read his anguish and exhaustion in his large eyes. The two men looked like two stragglers from a party, warily making their way along the street on a moonless night, expecting catastrophe to strike at each step. Their antics were reminiscent of the famous Hollywood duo, Laurel and Hardy.

Only the turtle, oblivious to all the trouble it was causing, continued to tread the air, wag its tail and hold on to the delicious piece of meat that it grasped in its mouth. Being a connoisseur of fine meats and used to feeding on live fish and insects, it probably felt a bit surprised that its prey was not trying to escape, and that it was not able to bite off a morsel. In any case, the juices of the meat in the turtle's mouth tasted good, so it decided that it was worth the effort to just hang on.

Blood was now beginning to trickle out of the thin man's wound. This made it hurt even more. Hiring a pedicab was out of the question, for the bumps, jolts and resulting bites would be more than he could bear.

Finally, thank goodness, they found a small clinic. It was Sunday, however, so they had to register for emergency treatment.

"Doctor, I beg you," the stout man pleaded, "please operate at once!"

The physician stood there in a white smock with a white cap perched neatly on his head. He smiled while he stroked his bristle-brush beard. "And just what exactly do you propose that I do?" He inquired. His smile broadened and he appeared to be stifling a chuckle. "How am I supposed to operate?" Then with one eye on the turtle and the other on the stout man, he asked, "You are not suggesting that I behead the thing, are you? Comrade, surely you realize that these turtles are like their cousins, the tortoises. The head of this little fellow could not remain outside of the shell long enough for me to get a hold of it, let alone "operate" as you demand. It would be far easier to try a more creative form of execution. And have you forgotten your friend's ear? I'm afraid there might not be much left of it by the time we finish. Turtles are renowned for their hot tempers!"

Just then, the thin man began to wail. "Ooooh dear! So what can be done?" His head was still cocked to one side. "This has gone on for an hour now. I don't know how much more I can stand! This damned creature! There must be some way to help me get rid of him! Ooh! Ooow!"

While speaking, he had let his head move slightly. The turtle, thinking that its prey was trying to escape, had sunk its teeth in deeper. It did not want to loose its gourmet meal after all the suffering it had endured.

The thin man was obviously in great pain. So, the doctor thought for a while and then relented. "I guess the best thing to do is give the thing a dose of anesthetic. That will probably do the trick. But—He glanced sternly at the thin man as he stroked his beard. "I must warn you that nor matter how much it hurts, you'll just have to sit still and bear the pain."

The thin man's face was filled with woe, as if he was about to place his head on a guillotine. He hesitated for a moment and then gave in. "I guess I really have no choice." He sighed as he looked warily at his executioner, the doctor.

The stout man was not so easily convinced. "Doctor, please give the thing a strong dose then, so you'll only have to do it once!" He feared that if a second shot was needed, the turtle might move at a critical moment—perhaps even biting off the thin man's earlobe. If that happened, the visit to the clinic would be a waste of time and money.

The doctor, though no longer able to hide his amusement, offered his profuse assurances in the success of his treatment. "No need to worry! The amount of anaesthetic that I'm going to use would not only fix this turtle, it would flatten a grown man within minutes!" Then, glancing at the turtle, he added, "But while I'm giving it the injection, please hold the creature very tightly!"

The words were hardly out of his mouth when he grasped the glass syringe filled with anaesthetic and pushed it through the tough skin and into the soft body of the turtle. The thin man let out another loud wail. It was as if he could feel the guillotine's blade teasing the back of his neck. The turtle, provoked by the pain from the needle, had bitten the man one last time before its jaws released the ear they had clamped for the past hour. The wound, about a third of a centimeter deep, was bleeding profusely.

"There we are! There we are! You're free! You're free! You're ear is free! Congratulations!" The doctor said as he laughed. "But don't go yet. I want to put some iodine into that wound, and some ointment, and then I want to bandage it up properly so that it won't get infected." With that the battle ended. The thin man's ear had suffered grievous indignities, but the war between man and turtle was over.

Now that the combat had finished, the negotiations began.

"What do you think should be done?" the thin man asked the doctor as he began to rail at the stout man. The thin man was obviously a veteran of many "Three-Against" and "Five-Against" struggle meetings, during which workers would vent their suppressed hatred at those guilty of harboring "capitalist thoughts." He was one of those workers who would saunter onto the platform constructed for these meetings and shout out accusations and complaints.

"It's all this damned creature's fault. I didn't do it on purpose!" The short fellow from Anhui bleated as he hit the turtle viciously with his right hand. But the attack did not bother the turtle. It had long since retracted its head and was sleeping deeply in profound and ignorant peace, completely oblivious of the rights and wrongs, the luck and misfortune, of the human world.

After much haggling and bartering, and with the doctor acting as mediator, the turtle's owner finally took out seven new green bills from his pocket and gave them to the turtle's victim to reimburse him for the medicine and compensate him for his pain. The bout with the turtle had cost the man about four days' wages.

"Confound it! You bloody turtle! I'll be damned if I don't kill you and make you into a tasty soup!" The stout man cried as he started on his way home. When he got there, he hurled the turtle onto the ground and railed, spit and cursed at it in front of his wife and two sons. He sounded as though he was reading out a list of crimes committed by a hardened criminal. "Damn it! I spent two yuans buying you to make a nourishing meal for us all. Great! Now I'll really need the meal with everything that I've gone through today because of you! Even ten turtles wouldn't be enough to get all of my strength back! Why the hell did you have to bite that idiot's ear and then hold on with all your might?!! You didn't think of me for one measly minute! I have to work like a dog for only fifty-four yuans a month, and then I have to waste seven of them on you!"

For the most part, all that the stout man said was nonsense, but the last part, about the money, was true. He had spent almost a seventh of his month's income on the turtle.

The stout man was about forty years old. He was employed in a state-run department store and was married to a woman (also originally from Anhui) who worked in a Shanghai textile mill. She was five years his junior. Both followed the policies of the Communist Party by getting married late. They had two sons, one nine years old and the other eight. Both sons were in primary school at the time of the turtle incident. A few years earlier, when a series of natural disasters had struck Anhui, the starving peasants in rural Anhui villages were surviving by eating grass and gnawing tree bark. A Voice of America report at that time estimated that ten million people had starved to death. The local papers, however, carried not a word about the famine. All of this occurred around 1962. The famine caused refugees to flood into Hong Kong. Thousands tramped across the Luohu Bridge from Shenzhen, just north of Hong Kong, and thousands more packed the streets which led to it. All of the famine reports circulating at that time were probably accurate. People visiting Hangzhou's West Lake during the famine told of countless Anhui beggars swarming Hangzhou's streets.

Not all of the stout man's family back in Anhui died from the famine. Many had fled the catastrophe and come to Shanghai. They spoke of people being so hungry that they ate the bodies of the dead—and dying. It was gruesome beyond belief. The stout man and his wife did not want to hear more. They were afraid of being reported and charged with helping these reactionaries. "How could people starve in the New Socialist China?" the authorities would ask. "It's impossible!" they would say. But still, the Anhui refugees were relatives. Not helping them was out of the question. Since food was rationed at that time, they could, at best, save a little from their meager meals. Some of this they wrapped up in a few banknotes and sent back to Anhui.

And so the stout man and his wife also went hungry until the three years of natural calamities finally came to an end. The stout man, normally quite fat, lost well over twelve pounds. His appearance changed considerably. His wife also lost weight, so much so that she had almost been reduced to a skeleton. The children, of course, suffered the most. Deprived as they were of important nutrients during their growing years, they grew thinner by the day. Their sickly yellow faces were covered with parched skin drawn tightly over their protruding bones.

In spite of all the suffering, this couple still managed to remain in fairly good spirits and praised Buddha for keeping them alive and in Shanghai. Had they returned to Anhui, they would have been just a pile of bleached, white bones.

By the time of the turtle incident, the situation had improved somewhat. The refugees had, one by one, gone back to Anhui. The stout man had only recently got back into the habit of buying eels or other meats traditionally thought to be nutritious. Such delicacies would allow his family members' bodies to fill out and grow stronger. He was particularly angry because he had taken great care to choose this particular turtle. He had been told that a big one would be poisonous and a small one of no use. Thus, he had thought for a long time before choosing this one, whose two-pound size was apparently perfect for a family of four. Who would have thought that....

The more he ruminated, the angrier he got. By the time dinner was served, he really didn't feel like tasting the delicious meat of the turtle. He drank a mere two spoonfuls of the thick white soup and barely touched the two slivers of meat in his bowl. But as he watched his wide-eyed sons down the soup with great pleasure, and his wife chew the meat and crack the bones to get at every morsel of tasty turtle meat, he felt a bit better. At least they were helping him get his revenge on the troublesome thing.

He sat there feeling completely relaxed, and smoked a cigarette when dinner was over. After a while, he threw the butt onto the floor and ground out the embers with his shoe. Then he noticed that the atmosphere in the room was a bit strange. He looked at his wife and his two sons. Their complexion seemed to have taken on a greenish tinge. Just a moment earlier they had been eating happily, ravenously, like Pigsy, the legendary character from *The Journey to the West*. Now, one after the other, they put down their rice bowls, closed their eyes and sat there like wooden puppets. His younger son could not hold himself upright, and slumped over onto the floor. Soon, his older son's head drooped forward until it rested on his arms, which were folded on the table top. His wife, somewhat more stably balanced, let her head fall forward until her chin rested on her chest. All three were soon unconscious.

He glanced again at the earthenware pot used to cook the turtle. The bottom of the pot could now be seen through the bit of soup that remained. Of the round, fat turtle, only the gray and yellow back and belly shells remained. The meat had all been eaten up.

"Food poisoning!!" The stout fellow cried out loud as he leaped to his feet. The turtle had probably suffered a heat stroke and gone bad, he suspected. Or was it the anaesthetic the doctor had injected? He held his hand in front of the mouths of his sons and his wife and felt their chests. "Thank goodness!" he thought. They were still breathing.

He dashed out of the house and hailed a pedicab, loading the bodies of the three sleepers into it. It was barely seven o'clock in the evening. With luck, the bristle-beard doctor would still be on duty.

"Doctor! A catastrophe!" We ate the damned turtle and now we've all been poisoned! The three of them have all fainted. I only ate a little because I was so mad. So I didn't pass out. But they all ate a lot and they've all collapsed. Please! Please! You've got to help us!"

"No, no comrade," the doctor said as he stroked his beard and chuckled in spite of himself, "It isn't food poisoning. A fresh, live turtle could never cause that. When you demanded that I give the turtle an injection this afternoon, I used three times the normal amount of anaesthetic. It's no wonder the turtle went out like a light, and those who ate it did too. It never occurred to me that you'd rush off to eat it without waiting a while for the effect of the medicine to wear off."

He looked at his watch and measured the pulses and temperatures of the stout man's family.

"Don't worry," he said. "I'll give them a heart stimulant and they'll be fine. But you'll have to wait for two or three hours before it will take effect. But it might act a little faster. It will depend on their physical conditions."

Bristle beard then gave each of them an injection as he chuckled silently to himself. He didn't dare say what he was thinking. It would be a waste of words and only cause another concern. The stout man wouldn't believe him anyway. With or without the stimulant, the stout man's wife and sons would wake up in a couple of hours. There was no doubt about it.

The stout man had been home for over an hour when, one by one, his family members began to come to. Our stalwart hero began crying and praising Buddha with one breath, and cursing the turtle with the next. You confounded beast! Hell-spawn! What misfortune will you bring us next?!"

He continued ranting and swearing for a long time before the day's exertions finally took their toll and he drifted off to sleep.

Epilogue

The story isn't quite over yet.

The stout man's mother, having died a few year's earlier, had asked that her bones be brought back to Anhui for a decent burial. A Chinese proverb goes "No matter how tall the tree, its leaves will always fall on the ground." Since she had died during the Anhui famine, there was no way to comply with her wishes until the calamities had passed. Consequently, the urn housing her remains had been left in the crematorium at the nearby Temple of Peace and Quietude.

The evening before the turtle incident, the stout man had brought the urn to his house. He was planning to finally take a day or two off around the end of the month so that he could honor his mother's wish and take her remains back to Anhui. As he had been terribly busy, however, he had only mentioned this plan once to his wife and had completely forgotten to tell his two sons. With all of the commotion caused by the turtle the next day, he just wasn't thinking straight.

The day after the turtle incident, at around six in the evening, he walked into the living room and noticed something amiss.

The black lacquer and gold urn had somehow been moved from the household alter onto the table. He couldn't ask his wife what had happened since she had not yet returned home, so he walked over to investigate. The urn was strangely light. He opened it gingerly and recoiled in horror. It was completely empty!

"Elder son!" he shouted in shocked rage as he pointed to the empty urn.

"What is going on here?!"

The boy, seeing that his father was red with rage, knew at once that he was in for trouble. He couldn't even get his words out straight. "Today, after school," he stammered, "brother and I were so hungry that we opened the urn to see what was inside. We saw what looked like a delicious dish of hard rice noodles. They smelled so good, and were so crispy and sweet, we couldn't help eating them. Please don't be so angry!"

"Damn it!" the father screamed, but he was too angry and overcome with disbelief to say anything else.

I myself would likely have added, "You good-for-nothings! You've invented a new kind of burial: burial by eating."

(Translated by Richard J. Ferris Jr.)

A Type

Foreword

The true meaning of my short story can easily be ascertained by those readers who hail from mainland China, Hong Kong and Taiwan. I am reminded of an article published in a certain Hong Kong newspaper shortly after the story's printing. The newspaper's editor wrote in the article of how "A Type" was the best description of a member of the Communist Party that he had ever come across.

For those readers who cannot avail themselves of a wealth of mainland China communist experiences however, I add the following information for clarification:

Communist China of the 1950's was characterized by a voracious need to keep secrets. This need originated with the members of the Chinese Communist Party and was soon contracted by the rest of the country. I remember that, in 1956, sources in the media discovered that the Shanghai Zoo was importing a lion from Africa. A reporter from one Shanghai paper scooped the rest of the media agencies and printed the story in his paper. As a result, he was severely reprimanded by the government authorities. It appeared that the release of the "zoo news" was not authorized.

It is easy to assume that if news about the importation of a zoo animal is considered sensitive information, then military matters would be secrets to be guarded with one's life.

The main character of the following story, Feng Zhongji, is an officer in the air force. You could say that every cell in his body was a military secret. It would be odd, therefore, if he were not extremely cautious as to his actions and words. In "A Type" the reader should realize that when Zhongji visits his family, he has been especially sensitized to the secretive nature of the society in which he lived. Naturally, he is suspicious of direct, or indirect, contact with agents of the enemy. Even those at his dinner table might be seeking ways to glean air force secrets from him.

In a sort of "hair-trigger" tense atmosphere as this, Zhongji's only method of protection was to act the mute. Anyone attempting to pry telltale speech from his mouth would therefore find his efforts in vain. In this way Zhongji found security. In this way he could rest at night.

At that time in mainland China Zhongji was not unique. I would like my readers to understand that those playing the role of mute numbered in the tens of thousands. Through just one speechless person, however, I hope to impart to my readers the atmosphere of an era.

May, 1991

The events in this story occurred in 1956.

A character in a legend is like a figure in a dream, seemingly as close as an arm's span, but actually far beyond reckoning.

The words of others, even if they amount to only two or three terse sentences, like sparse droplets of water, can sometimes hold a magical essence much like that felt at the dissipation of a reverie. These "droplets of water" can sanctify and beautify the person in a legend or dream, transmuting the unsavory into the attractive.

This is perhaps true for women in their view of a legendary man, possibly even more true, drawing from my own experience, for men in their view of a legendary woman.

The focus of this short story, however, is just one ordinary man as seen by another ordinary man. This second ordinary man was me, and the first, the younger brother of my former landlady's husband. I say "former" because all the land over which she once lorded so effectively is no longer in her family's possession.

I got along extremely well with my landlady, Mrs. Feng. This feeling of neighborly friendliness spread quite freely from myself to her daughters, parents-in-law and even those brothers-in-law, etc., whom I hadn't previously had the pleasure of meeting. Taking on the role of a contractor, I found that my close friendship with Mrs. Feng required that an amount of friendship be carefully and equally dealt out to each member of the Feng clan.

Mrs. Feng was middle-aged and big-hearted. Her husband had gone overseas leaving her with the responsibility of raising four school-age daughters. This quasi-widow of more than ten years had long ago earned the respect of all her neighbors.

People of the same age find it easier to understand each other's feelings. I was also middle-aged and I felt for this lonely hen who was single-handedly bringing up four chicks. It made my contracting work all the more important.

I hope, here, that my interest in the family isn't misinterpreted. I was just a busybody shouldering the concerns of others. That's all. This was the result of the prolonged reclusion I had enforced upon myself to recover from an illness. I felt I was in danger of growing moldy from this hermitlike existence, however, or at least invisible to all those except my wife who taught in a Shanghai kindergarten. It was natural, therefore, that Mrs. Feng's household, only a few steps from my own, became the focus of my friendly concerns.

I had too much time on my hands—the whole compound seemed to exist within my irritatingly slowed time frame. Whenever a visitor of any kind approached the house of one of my neighbors, the sound of their echoing footsteps would draw my head from my sanatorium to listen for what could be heard. Sometimes, I would shake myself free of my convalescent surroundings and shamelessly walk over and strike up a conversation with the compound's latest visitor—as well as the objects of the visit. If no footsteps were to be heard, I could easily kill a sultry evening listening to Mrs. Feng telling story after story about her impressive family.

One of Mr. Feng's younger brothers named Zhongji was often the main character in these stories. Since Zhongji numbered six among his brothers, by the Chinese custom, Mrs. Feng called him the Sixth Uncle. You could say that she was just being fashionable in her being particularly interested in her Sixth Uncle.

In those chaotic days, everywhere the eye could see—heaven and earth, from the Yellow Sea to the South China Sea—all seemed to be churning in a giant cauldron of boiling water, which was resting in an even more impressive oven. At all times, the sound of the angry water could be heard. Under the cauldron's lid, the steam rising from this water whirled into patterns and spread into lines. In the theater of the imagination, these lines simply joined into one and struck down with a force sufficient to cleave mind, as well as body. The steam was an irresistibly attractive force, mysterious and primeval in its raw energy, and it had covered the heart of Asia.

At that time, certain people belonged to the burgeoning class of "Party members."[1] They were truly a "type of steam," or at least made up the cauldron from which it rose. Even from afar, the vapor of these individuals could be seen, smelled—and enjoyed by many.

Zhongji was a Party member of the steaming variety. I say this because any Party member, at any time and under any conditions, made it a personal goal to release the potential energy from elements within their influence, much like James Watt's revolutionary steam engine.

Of all the members of Mrs. Feng's extensive family, the densest steam rose from wherever Zhongji stood.

It appears that he was once an admirer of literature. He actually studied the subject in college for two years before an official order resulted in the redirecting of his studies to something more practical—mechanics. After graduating, he was

---

[1] Members of the C.C.P. or Chinese Communist Party.

allocated work in the aviation field. Only a few years later, he not only became a member of the Communist Party, but also a commander of a logistics station in the Air Force. Because of the particularly intense "red" color of the water which buoyed him up to these new levels of achievement, he himself was naturally indelibly stained the same hue—through to the heart, so to speak.

In conversation, Mrs. Feng's parents-in-law often spoke of how, of all the children, he was the most obstinate. Apparently, he had argued with his mother and father—and stormed off to join the military. Because he showed promise, the Government sent him directly to college, eventually to become their intentionally educated apprentice.

Mrs. Feng's family was great in almost every sense of the word. This was due primarily to the "hard work" of her father-in-law, Feng Boju, which was often the subject of private jokes between that energetic individual and myself.

Feng Boju had two wives. His first wife gave birth to five sons and one daughter. The eldest of her sons sired eleven children—not including the two who were stillborn. These grandchildren, in turn, had become the parents of Feng Boju's great grandchildren. His second wife gave birth to three sons and three daughters. Mrs. Feng was the wife of the eldest of the sons. An estimate would number the Feng clan at about sixty-three at that time. This sum left me a staunch believer in the theories of Robert Malthus.

One day, the fair-skinned and somewhat plump Mrs. Feng appeared before my house with the news that, after eight years of separation, Zhongji was finally returning home to visit his family. During those eight years, he rarely wrote home—and appeared to prefer that his family didn't write him. He kept his address secret, using only a post office box. No one was sure as to his exact whereabouts.

Feng Boju was the head of his family in the traditional Chinese sense. To his credit in those times of upheaval, he was able to maintain and enjoy the customary household of a rapidly disappearing China. His first wife lived in the old Western-style front house while his second wife lived on the top floor of the green brick, Western-style rear house. Though both wives were over sixty years of age at that time, they were no strangers to jealousy. Feng Boju had only to stay overnight in the rear household—to pass some time alone with his second wife—and the first wife would wreak destruction upon bowls and chopsticks. Her anger would be evident for about two days. She didn't dare make too much of the situation, however, because no one would commiserate with her, and she would risk airing too much of the family's dirty laundry, much to her discredit.

The front and rear houses were separated by several old-style houses which were rented out to an area department store as warehouses. The store had these houses locked and thereby forcing the Feng's to make a large detour to get from the front to the rear house. The walk between the houses took seven or eight minutes and required crossing two streets.

I had heard of Zhongji's arrival, and had been very tempted to see this person of "story and legend." I had previously, however, never managed to get out and navigate my way around to the house of his family to see him.

Who would have thought, (actually, I would have thought) that one afternoon I was actually provided with this chance.

I heard the chatter of voices burst out from upstairs at Mrs. Feng's house. My curiosity wouldn't allow me to be left out of what seemed to be a happy event, so I put all politeness aside and walked over with a mind to at least vicariously participate in what sounded like a joyous reunion.

I had not walked far when I saw him—the person who had been so much talked about. I was in the habit of introducing myself to Mrs. Feng's relatives, so I didn't see any reason why he should be any different.

The contents of my self-introduction, or at least my opening words, merely constituted an explanation of the fact that I was a long-time neighbor of Mrs. Feng and how, over the past eight or nine years, this gentle landlady had been very kind to me, her old tenant, for which I was eternally grateful, etc., etc. Actually, these words should have been spoken to her husband, newly returned from abroad—who would have warranted an explanation of my special concern for the Feng family—had he, in truth, returned. In the husband's absence, however, I had no choice but to make my self-introductory "announcement" to any and all Feng relatives and Feng friends.

This announcement was not long in becoming formulaic—a sort of script which was kept handy for the next introductory encounter. Each time I repeated the familiar words, Mrs. Feng would corroborate my recount of the history of our friendship, attempting to counter my embarrassing praise with equally embarrassing admiration of her own, replete with examples of good deeds that I had performed, all-in-all reinforcing the effect of my script.

We acted no different on the occasion of Zhongji's arrival.

The peculiar thing was, that usually after Mrs. Feng and I had completed our well-rehearsed prologue, the guest or guests would reply with polite remarks and small talk, quickly dropping all defenses and beginning to converse like old friends. This time the effect was different.

I took a careful look at the guest whose appearance reminded me of Napoleon Bonaparte.

Napoleon boasted of the adroitness of his soul. He spoke of how, upon arriving in Rome, he embraced Catholicism; how, when reaching England, he adopted Protestantism; how, after entering Egypt, he practiced the Muslim faith. Where he to have reached India, he probably would have taken up Buddhism; and where he to have traveled in ancient Persia, he most likely would have accepted the principles of Zoroastrianism. This ability to continually exchange one set of beliefs for another is somewhat like the ability of a diva who is able, without effort, to leap from the highest to the lowest octave while singing.

Sometimes a man's physical appearance can achieve the same mysterious and impressive changes. Although the physical self cannot manifest lightening changes which can be likened to a drop from the highest to the lowest octave, the body can gradually make what is comparable to the steps from the highest, or eighth, to the fifth—or even the fourth octave. I am not talking about changes associated with aging or disease, but other sorts of bewildering changes, manifested in the countenance.

Napoleonic souls were in abundance in China at that time. The most evident of these were the young riders of the political tide. These Party members were able to easily make the leap through the full range of octaves—to perform a metaphorical one-hundred-and-eighty degree turn—sometimes in the most subtle and imperceptible way.

The features of the young guest that sat a whisper away from me had undergone just such a chameleon-like change as to put Napoleon to shame. He had short, bristly hair and thick, black eyebrows. Large, raven eyes commanded one's attention from their posts in his swarthy, square face, set high above a pair of thick and expressionless lips.

This kind of young face was in vogue. You could see such a face on screen, stage, street and page, in class and especially in certain political organizations. This face had also made an appearance in Mrs. Feng's "boudoir," where we all sat reciting our introductions.

Based on what I know of the Feng family's household, history and education, coupled with my own interactions, the facial features of the young man of twenty-eight or so that sat close by should have been pleasant to the eye. Perhaps it was a coincidence, some sort of pressure, a kind of inner change, or simply a fashionable response to societal trends that effected the countenance next to me. The dark, conditioned features on this face led me to believe that they were the more likely result of being fired in society's mold, as were the spirit, attitude and emotions of the young man himself.

After Mrs. Feng had finished her courtesies, that young, square face turned inconspicuously above a white poplin collar, giving the appearance of a judge seated stiffly in his lofty chair assessing the criminal below with a glance from the corners of his eyes. In my imagination, those two enormous coal-black eyes became two great rubber balls which, in the space of a gasp, had been rolled over my entire body.

A judgement was already written on the square face which expressed only silence and a seriousness which belied the youthful age of its master.

This entire action took place in the span of a few seconds. It seemed that, before another thought could pass, the face had returned to its former position and was directed at Mrs. Feng's daughters. This was the expression it had held before any notice had been taken of me—an expression dominated by a smile which was both simple and complicated, and which, when coldly reflecting the mirth of the daughters, sometimes appeared ready to give birth to a laugh—but was in the end frustrated in its labor.

'Sixth Uncle, Grandma already has someone picked out for you. We're going to be treated to some candy soon! Hee hee hee!—[2] Mrs. Feng's fifteen-year-old daughter, Meixue, giggled as she pointed a skinny finger at his nose. Her voice was weak and muffled, like an insect's chirp heard from without a bed of tender green reeds.

"Oh! A girlfriend! A girlfriend! Fair-skinned, clean, plump and healthy, with bright, beautiful hair—like, like licorice! Ha ha ha ha!" The smartest and naughtiest of Mrs. Feng's daughters, thirteen-year-old Meisi, cried out in glee. She was all at once the audience and the performer, dancing here and clapping there—her bubbling laughter striking through to the heart of her uncle.

"Nonsense! Women's hair doesn't look much like licorice!" chuckled the second youngest sister, Meili, as she stared nearsightedly at the others.

"Right! We're in the midst of the Great Socialist Revolution! Women's hair is cut just as short as men's. Not much licorice left on anyone's head!" Meisi laughed.

"Okay! Comrade licorice sticks! Licorice ladies young and old! Sixth Uncle is going out to buy us some candy. Some

---

[2] In China, to invite friends and relatives "to eat candy" is to announce that an engagement for marriage is to take place. Candy here symbolizes sweet wishes for the happy couple to see them through to old age.

licorice candy! Ha ha ha ha ha!" Meixue laughed in a thin screaming voice.

At this, all four girls burst out in laughter—the more boisterous of the four drowning out the others. The obvious joy of the youngest daughter, eleven-year-old Meida, seemed to also have some success in breaching the uncle's cold exterior.

He was laughing with the girls. But it was a silent laugh. Sometimes, there seemed to be some sort of sound—but so small as to be inaudible. After completing this mime, he continued his incessant caressing of Meida's bangs.

Mrs. Feng had lingered long enough to share in some of the laughter, but then went downstairs on some urgent errand.

I found that I had been struck speechless. I searched for something to say as I awkwardly joined in the merriment.

"Meixue! Don't talk foolishness! You're being very rude to your uncle." I had at last come up with a sentence or two. Looking directly at the object of my simple discourse, I then said, "Comrade Zhongji, they are just children, naughty by habit, please don't take it personally."

He glared at me with those sloe-black orbs, seeming to voice the reply, "Is that so?" And perhaps also asking "Are we comrades?" No actual sound escaped his lips, however, which were still frozen into that smile.

That glare of his shook my soul. It also caused me to remember the fact that I did not belong to this family and that, eight years after Liberation,[3] I was still a jobless nomad. But still—

"Comrade Zhongji, how many days do you plan to stay?"

The glare struck me again. This time his pupils seemed to have grown larger—and blacker! They were like two lead balls speeding toward my face.

I thought he didn't hear what I had said, and so repeated myself.

"Comrade Zhongji, how long do you plan to stay?"

---

[3] "Liberation" here refers to the Communist liberation of China in 1949.

My continual questioning didn't seem to make him at all nervous. He finally lifted his head, moved his thick lips and appeared to be clearing his throat—preparing to speak.

I was eager to listen.

But no words were forthcoming. He just grunted a bit. Perhaps he was really just clearing his throat. Maybe he had let out a low grumble, or it might have been that he made no sound at all. I had seen his neck move slightly. I was probably oversensitive.

The trademark smile soon returned to his square face. This not only seemed to be his answer to my question, but also his only method of communication with the children.

"Sixth Uncle! Mr. Pu asked you how many days you would be staying!" Meisi was really the naughtiest of the girls. As she repeated my question she sat there, shaking her uncle's arm.

"Uhmm—hmmm—" This time I was positive that the thick-browed, square-faced human statue which posed before us emitted a couple of low, throaty sounds. Someone hard of hearing might have thought he was about to cough and, failing that, only let out a couple of guttural sighs.

Suddenly, he lifted up Meida, whom he had been holding in his lap, clapped his hands and started to play patty-cake with her. It was not long before all four girls were taking turns playing this game with their uncle. The question mentioned a short time earlier was left unanswered.

Under these circumstances my remaining seated where I was required a little Eastern discipline, not unlike that attained by the fifth century Indian monk, Dharma, who had stared continuously at a wall for nine years. Paradoxically, these conditions excited my curiosity. I decided to be thick-skinned and remain seated there. I wanted to see how long the mute play would continue.

"Sixth Uncle! Sixth Uncle! Teach us a dance song!" Meida cried out, pulling on his hand.

"Sixth Uncle! Sixth Uncle! Teach us an air force song!" pleaded Meisi, shaking his arm.

"Sixth Uncle! Tell us a story! How about one by Hans Christian Andersen?" suggested Meili.

"Tell us a joke, Sixth Uncle!" chirped Meixue.

He shook his head four times in answer to the girls requests—that smile never leaving his face.

At this point, many different emotions flashed across the two dark cheeks which appeared to be supporting the smile held between them—only to be crushed and scattered, like the petals of a flower.

"Have you ever been to Beijing?" Meixue suddenly asked her uncle.

"Have you ever been to Nanjing?" added the naughty and giggling Meisi. "Ah! Are there any other place names with the word "jing" in them?" Meisi bubbled.

"Yes! Yes! I heard Fifth Uncle say that Xi'an was once known as Xijing!" exclaimed Meili who went on to ask, "Sixth Uncle! Have you been to Xijing before? Your planes travel everywhere, don't they?"

"When you fly in a plane are you scared?" asked Meisi.

This time he not only produced his characteristic smile for us, but also pulled a silly face at the girls, causing them to break out in laughter. He then drew both Meida and Meisi toward him and held them close, caressing their hair. Children seemed to hold a special place in his heart.

Occasionally, he would glance over at me. At these times, the smile on his face would disappear, overcome by an expression of deep thoughtfulness. The judge's seriousness—the judge's verdict—returned, combining to effect a look of warning. The moment the face turned toward the children, however, the smile re-emerged.

If it weren't for the children's inconceivable mischief (actually very conceivable), there would be no telling how long that mute play would continue. In any case, I was preparing to leave without a word. I had decided that it would be impossible for myself, or any other person—even Li Kui, the so-called "Black Tornado" from the Chinese classic *Outlaws of the Marsh* with his horrible, slashing axe—to break loose his two lips, which were like two nailed-fast planks on a coffin lid, so as to release even the slightest fragment of true speech.

Five minutes before I surrendered to hopelessness, patted my hindquarters and went downstairs, one of the girls, I don't know which, screeched out.

"Dummy! Big dummy! Big dummy! Ha ha ha!"

"Big dummy! Big dummy! Sixth Uncle is a big dummy! Ha ha ha ha!"

"Uncle Dummy! Dum-dum! We're not going to play with you! We don't play with dummies!"

After one of the girls had shouted out these taunts to her silent uncle, the others joined in. Soon, laughing and tripping over each other, they all fled downstairs. The sound of my own parting footsteps was, needless to say, drowned in the overall cacophony.

Before descending the stairs I stole a last look at him. He no longer sported the smile. His square, dark face revealed a hint of sadness. Those different emotions, which he had so recently crushed and scattered like the petals of flower, bloomed anew. His big, black eyes were staring at the four walls of the room. Slowly, he stood up. The sounds that ensued from this action were louder than any noise he had made that day—though these were more intense perhaps, only in contrast with the loneliness which then hung like a pall over the room. At last glance, the sides of his expressionless, thick lips were raised ever so slightly in a bitter smile.

Such was the afternoon time! Such was the young man who had reportedly in times past been sharp-tongued and sharp-witted—and who had returned home for the first time after an eight-year absence for what was probably the last time—just to kill one-and-a-half hours with four innocent children. He saw, heard, laughed and acted during his visit, but never spoke one intelligible word.

Later, Mrs. Feng told me that she and her daughters had sat with him for half an hour before I ascended the stairs, and even during that time, he had not spoken a full sentence. Eight years earlier, he often came to the house to see the girls. He would hug them, play games and jest with them. He was well-spoken and loved to crack jokes and tell stories. His recent visit to the compound was expressly for the purpose of seeing the girls (little thinking that Mrs. Feng's eldest two daughters were away at school), and not to visit Mrs. Feng. In order to avoid talking with Mrs. Feng, upon his arrival, he immediately lured the girls upstairs and laughed with them for quite some time—though from beginning to end, he voiced not a word.

Two days after I had taken my parting view, the living statue took leave of the compound. Mrs. Feng laughingly said to me, "This time when Zhongji returned home, his father was not too happy. He said, 'What? After eight years' separation my son has become a mute—not even one sentence for his father! For shame!" Mrs. Feng then added, "He lived with us for seven days and not even ten sentences passed between him and his father. He spoke in secret with his mother, but even this didn't amount to much. Just one-word answers to every three of his mother's questions—which mostly concerned marriage. (It was the only topic he was willing to respond to.) In Shanghai, his younger brother invited both him and his older brother out to dinner. At the table, he said very little and created a lot of silence. After dinner, all three left together. His two brothers had thought to take a stroll with him, but he excused himself saying that he had some business to take care of elsewhere. His brothers believed him and wanted to see him to his destination, but he refused their company. They had no way of knowing that, after parting with him, he went to a large old building to hold a "meeting"— on Jianguo Street, only about one hundred meters from his younger brother's home! His brother saw him going there. Isn't that interesting?"

I listened, but made no reply. When confronted with a situation like this, I thought it would be best to learn from him— to play the part of the impenetrable, or wisely silent, golden man from the temple in historic China.[4] This would be much safer and more appropriate than playing the part of a modern-day living, speaking man.

Recently, everywhere the eye could see, all seemed to be churning in a giant cauldron of boiling water—overflowing with steam.

After thinking hard, I found I could commiserate with him, though there were some things about him which I still could not understand. My thoughts on this subject, however, were not necessarily one hundred percent correct.

Nearly a year later, Mrs. Feng gave me a bit of news concerning him.

The modern-day golden man had received severe criticism during the Anti-Revolutionary Suppression Movement, reportedly because of his "black background." His elder brother was none other than Mrs. Feng's husband. Though the two men shared the same father, they were each born of a different mother. Mrs. Feng's husband left mainland China for Hong Kong after the Sino-Japanese War. After ten years in the British colony, her husband left for Taiwan because his business had failed. When in Taiwan he gained employment as a company clerk. At that time, Zhongji was only eight years old and rarely saw his brother—especially since this brother (Mrs. Feng's husband) had only returned to the mainland twice during his ten years in Hong Kong, by which time Zhongji had already left home.

Apparently due to his family background, Zhongji soon found that he had been transferred out of the air force unit to which he had been assigned, into a common trade unit as an

---

[4] In ancient China statues of metal were called "golden men" though they were actually made of bronze. The story is told of how Confucius, when passing through the state of Zhou, visited a temple. At the front of the stairway in the temple stood a "golden man," the mouth of which was carved with the lips pressed tightly together. On the back of the statue were carved characters telling how the statue-person was famous for being particularly careful in speech.

even more common worker. His career change had been sudden and unwelcome.

I was not able to find out whether, after he began his new life as a tradesman, he continued the mute play. And I will probably never find out, because in this life—on this planet—I'll probably never see him again. Nor do I have any interest in hearing any more taciturn anecdotes.

(Translated by Richard J. Ferris Jr.)

Silken Veil

My luck changed in the summer of 1951. I was chased from my home like a magpie flushed from its nest by turtle dove. I found myself forced to move from my home by the side of the West Lake in Hangzhou to the residential district lying along the Great Canal in the outskirts of the city.

The experience of that move was unique among those of my life. When the caravan of vehicles, laden with our worldly possessions, sidled past the West Lake, the brilliant surface of the Lake's serene water appeared blood red. Maybe this was a temporary hallucination. Yet this hallucination pulsed with the reality of the reddened plant at the Lake's edge.

I took this as an ill omen appearing on the heels of my recent misfortune. I soon started my own subtle and secret preparations to resist the unrelenting pursuit of the "turtle dove." It was not long before I took to my brown canvas cot and embraced the cloak of sickness, the feigned beginnings of tuberculosis.

From the viewpoint of those who commissioned the building of the Lady Liberty, who had probably watched the waters of the Hudson flow freely by, my actions had sentenced me to life imprisonment within self-drawn boundaries, with the articles inside my new living quarters serving as my fetters. And all this to escape the incessant threat of my oppressors.

Even under these circumstances, with my self-imposed isolation, it was natural that I treasured the sight and sound of the river that flowed past my neighborhood. After a day or two, I decided that I needed an airing and allowed myself a period of exercise in the "yard." As I strolled to the water's edge in front of my lodgings, the light which sparkled randomly on the water surface was reflected eagerly by my eyes, as eagerly as the feet of a truant schoolboy romped through a field of dry, fragrant grass. And oh! The boats! More than my eyes could take in!

Large and small and made of brightly painted wood, they bobbed in the water, sporting sails which seemed enormous in comparison with the vessels underneath. The sails were motley with patches so that it seemed as if huge butterflies were drifting slowly over the river. That scene, for a time, refilled my soul with the serenity and leisure of past pages, to the point that time appeared to come to an abrupt halt.

On the same day that I was enjoying these visions, at a little past ten o'clock in the morning, two plain-clothes officers appeared where the lane adjacent to the cosmetic powder factory in our neighborhood opened into the main street. They seemed to be scrutinizing all that fell within their vision along the riverside. Upon seeing them, I was both startled and filled with apprehension.

The existence, or life, of a person or thing is actually only manifested by that person's or things' distinctive characteristics. Nothing can be said to exist without these characteristics.

No matter how carefully they were camouflaged, the faces and behavior of the plain-clothes officers could not but reveal some peculiar qualities. These alerted, almost painfully, the sensitivities I had developed as a writer. The officers could not conceal their overly serious manners and their piercing glances! They were somewhat like the Tibetan god, Yenmo, who has a third eye in the middle of his forehead, making people feel nervous about their stares. The mysterious air they conveyed was intensified by the fact that they seemed to be in constant communion, though not a word was spoken between them.

Every so often, someone would come along and turn into the small lane where these officers had posted themselves. The officers immediately intercepted the unfortunate and interrogated him or her before ordering that person away with a hand gesture.

"What are you doing here?"

I had fallen within the sights of one of the officers.

"Airing myself," I replied, trying to appear calm.

"There's nothing to keep you here. GO HOME!"

These last two words were barked at me.

Though I was bewildered and confused, I quietly obeyed and turned back toward my quarters.

I had come to understand that this was a time when capital punishment was the reward of logic. For protection, it was necessary to be skilled in the art of dealing with surprise.

But what a puzzle!

When I returned to the compound where my lodgings were located, I could not resist the lure of the mystery that the arrival and actions of the plain-clothes policemen presented. I decided to ask my landlady, Mrs. Fu, what she knew of the day's events.

Mrs. Fu was a middle-aged woman with delicate manners and fair, shiny skin. She was our neighborhood's committee head and therefore had access to much information which was hard to come by.

Odd! I had spoken only three short sentences when her face fell and her eyes seemed to flash with anger! She then silenced me with a motion of her finger against her lips and left without a word, like an Egyptian in ages past who had heard someone invoking the Pharaoh's curse.

I could not help myself at this point. I was swept up in a whirlwind of curiosity and persisted in my search for the solution of the mystery.

I directed my steps toward my neighbor Mrs. Wu, a thin and frail little woman. Usually she was as chatty as a magpie, stopping to gossip whenever she had the chance. A few minutes earlier, I would never have guessed that, after overhearing my brief questions directed at Mrs. Fu, she would shake her lean and tiny hand and turn away, ignoring me.

"Why all this avoidance? Am I someone to spread the plague?" I thought to myself.

I stepped back a few paces. The atmosphere seemed to be flooded with dizzying pigments and white noise. It was as if a gaping hole was rent in the ozone layer miles above the compound, making the air in the place both visible and audible, and exposing those that breathed it to a bast of sickening heat.

What was the true source of this abnormality?

Yenmo's three eyes were omnipresent. Everyone felt their oppressive glare.

It had apparently been predicted that the pressure brought to bear on my neighborhood would create revealing cracks in the lives of its inhabitants. It was hoped that these would be large cracks—large enough to hold Western cathedrals. Today two women had presented me with frosty silence, but this was only a hairline crack and nothing to worry about. As an author, I felt that I was fated to leap into these cracks, figuring out when and where I could find them—or at least get some handle of them.

I had learned long ago that the amount of safety existent is in direct proportion to the amount of time that has passed. The answer to the mystery in my neighborhood appeared to be well-hidden. The revealing of the answers I sought was a slow and seemingly interminable process, like the measuring of a snail's pace.

About twenty days after I had become aware of the strange in my neighborhood, Mrs. Fu was still observing her personal vow of silence. That Pharaoh's curse was still ringing in her ears. The magpie's mouth, however, had begun to move again though no sounds were being formed. The silence appeared to be grating against her loquacious nature and she was showing signs of rebellion.

One by one she let drop the pieces of the puzzle that made up the neighborhood mystery. Her information, added to the various tidbits gleaned from two other neighbors, finally enabled me to put together the events which led up to the peculiar atmosphere of that day I walked to the water's edge.

It seemed that sometime during the night, afternoon, or early morning before I took my long-contemplated airing, Mr. Lu, the boss of the nearby cosmetic powder factory, had committed suicide. His family, to their horror, discovered the body the following morning and immediately informed the factory's security guards. The guards swiftly reported the news to their superiors at the Tea Pavilion Temple Police Station.[1] The station personnel reacted violently, as if they had been informed that war had been declared. Apparently, a large group of officers appeared at the scene with uncanny speed. The group included the director and assistant director of the station, police from our residential district and the cadre in charge of political security. The lane outside was then placed under the scrutiny of the two plain-clothes officers. It was their decision that no person who was not a cadre of the Party or a resident of the same compound in which the Lu household was located, would be allowed entrance.

The atmosphere of the place must have mimicked that of the time when the German Chancellor, Adolph Hitler announced that he was placing the country under martial law. The station director used the most serious of tones and assumed the most fierce of manners when he announced the seven rules to the family and neighbors of the deceased.

"Under no circumstances will anyone reveal the news that Old Lu committed suicide. If anyone is to ask the cause for his death, say that it was result of a serious illness. (He had a history of lung disease.)"

"No funeral services of any kind will be conducted by the family."

"No one will wear funerary gowns, or attach black bands or memorial swatches of cloth to their clothing."

"No family member will cry or show any other signs of mourning."

"No family member will invite monks or nuns to read scriptures over the deceased."

"No family member will worship the deceased's ancestral tablets (including lighting candies and/or incense)."

---

[1] Once a tea house where free and life-sustaining drink was provided to travelers. Later, as a result of the place's life-saving reputation, the tea house was converted into a temple, only to be turned into a police station after the Communist takeover.

"No family member will invite any friend or relative to pay their respects."

After the director had announced the last of the rules, the voice of one of the residential district's officers could be heard reverberating throughout the compound, as he tried to enforce the new and already transgressed "Rules."

"Your husband did not wish to conform to our wishes. He was stubborn, reclusive and would not accept the aid and nurturing of the Party. He was an Anti-Revolutionary! You had better cut your ties completely with the deceased now! Can you guarantee that you will comply with the director's seven restrictions?"

The officer's voice seemed to have the effect of manhandling the deceased's widow, Mrs. Lu. Her face had turned ashen. This was the first time in her whole life that she had faced such unthinkable horrors and demands.

"Yes," the widow replied in a voice that was close to a whisper.

"Good! Your family must adhere to these rules. And listen, you must also not move your husband's body. We have people who will come this evening and see to its disposal. Remember, you must not allow your neighbors to snoop about and ask questions."

After this lecture, the assistant director reiterated several of the director's instructions. Then, the director himself and several cadres from our residential district split up and interrogated the Lu family's neighbors.

"Do you know what happened at the factory?" the assistant director asked one of the compound's inhabitants.

"Boss Lu killed himself " was the reply.

"Bastard! Under the leadership of the Communist Party all are enjoying the fruits of a new socialist China. No one would commit suicide in such a prosperous society. You're spreading slanderous rumors!"

"Uh—Uhm—I didn't mean that—I think—" he stammered.

Luckily, the neighbor was quick to react and did an about-face after a second or two of indecision.

"I think he died of illness. He had been suffering tuberculosis, you know."

"Right! Now these are the words of a revolutionary! Who in the new socialist society does not wish to live a full life, to enjoy yet another day? You learn very quickly!" The assistant director squeezed a smile, but for only a fraction of a second. Then his face quickly resumed its standard stern expression.

"Listen!" the assistant director announced to all others standing in the yard of the compound. "None of you will mention anything regarding Old Lu's death, no matter how it occurred. If any of you dare speak of this event, the most severe of consequences will be yours to bear."

One plain-clothes officer was left behind. He immediately began scrutinizing every movement.

Yenmo's presence filled the compound. The provisional martial law was in effect.

At midnight, under the watchful gaze of the plain-clothes policeman, a black hearse parked in the lane leading to the compound where the Lu's lived. No light shone in either lane or house. In the inky darkness, several hands grasped the casket and loaded it into the awaiting hearse. After the hearse sped away, the Lu family got into a pedicab and followed it to Mr. Lu's final resting place.

The family and the accompanying officers spent the whole night at the crematorium. Mr. Lu's ashes were left there temporarily.

I heard that the officers, after arriving at the Lu household, used no lights when seeing to the proper disposal of Mr. Lu's body. Only once, for a second or two, did a flashlight beam slash the darkness. Not a word was spoken by these men who worked with practiced hands. No sound could be heard even as they loaded the coffin.

I am afraid it appeared as if this were not the first time they had performed this miniature drama, nor the last. After the family had followed the remains of Mr. Lu to the crematorium, the compound was left in utter darkness and complete silence, unbroken by the slightest flicker or movement.

For many days following this event, no one living in the compound—or elsewhere—dared speak to any member of the Lu family, or even approach their house.

This atmosphere was maintained for so long that I do not think that anyone really took note of what time the martial law was actually lifted from our neighborhood. I myself was unaware of the exact time that the police left their heavily trodden posts. I think that this numbing of our senses was due to everyone's having struggled at the edge of both humanity and fear for such a long time.

The magpie's courageous—if not instinctive—vocal act in direct defiance of official orders, was probably what precipitated the thawing of the frigid martial law atmosphere which hung over the compounds in my neighborhood. The Lu compound, which was just a thirty or forty seconds' walk from my dwelling, very likely saw this change in the atmosphere at the same time as the others.

I only remember seeing Mr. Lu two or three times as he passed by during one of my "airings." He was short, emaciated and swarthy. His pupils were coal-black and he appeared to be in his early forties. He had the look of someone who was slowly succumbing to the trials of lung disease—and the burdens common to the new society.

It was this sickly man who had borne the brunt of many movements for the suppression of anti-revolutionaries, which were organized by the neighborhood's communist cadres. During these movements, Mr. Lu was subjected to the factory worker's scathing criticisms which targeted him as an exploitative boss.

His brother was a leader of the outlawed Yikuandao[2] religious society and as a result had been arrested and sent to an

---

[2] The Yikuandao was labeled a reactionary religious organization whose members reportedly held meetings in the nude.

outlying labor camp. Even though Mr. Lu was not a member of any such infamous societies, it goes without saying that this blood tie added venom to the attacks of his enemies. With his weakened state of health he could hardly repel the constant physical and mental blows which he was being dealt at the time. Added to all this were the financial problems in the factory and problems with the workers. He had no way of handling the whole situation and chose to leave everything behind by going to the extremes.

The dark and work-ravaged complexion that sharpened Mr. Lu's features had been carved into my memory during the few passing glances that I had of him before his death. His face looked like it had been forged in hellfire and still bore the marks reminiscent of some demonic smithy's furnace.

The black of his features contrasted almost too sharply with the white associated with his cosmetic powder factory.[3] In my mind's eye, the atmosphere of his factory was made indistinct and surreal from the great amount of white dust which was constantly being stirred up into little cloudlets. The factory as a whole appeared "clean" and "innocent" in its whiteness. I realized, however, that Mr. Lu's soul had been swallowed up by this very atmosphere. I benefited from this new awareness which had been enriched by my singular experiences of that time. It served as a precious lesson that would be of great value to me in coping with—or even thwarting—the actions of the "turtle dove" that had previously caught me unaware and flushed me from my resting place. I had at least pierced a hole in their

---

[3] The powder which Mr. Lu's factory produced was made from a certain white stone brought in from outlying areas. This so-called 'goose-egg powder' was used by many women in traditional China, and is still used in the rural areas of modern China, to whiten their faces for cosmetic purposes. In the factory, the rocks are first ground into a fine powder. Then the powder is mixed with clean water and allowed to soak for close to one year. The resulting mud is passed through a filter to ensure that the final product is an exceedingly fine powder. After the filtered mud is dried, it is mixed with herbs and scented oil and the mixture is placed into duck's-egg shaped molds. After being removed from the molds, the "duck eggs" are sold in the local market.

camouflaged defense to demystify the illusory and attractive atmosphere which, like layer upon layer of thick silken veils, screened the harsh and cruel reality.

Mr. Lu's suicide occurred only one hundred meters away, but it took me close to a month to learn the truth behind what was taking place in my tiny neighborhood and to see the true "face" of death. Silken veils like these obscured the image of the country as perceived by the outside world. From 1951, when the events in this story took place, to 1955, few if any of those in the Free World could have penetrated the heavy opaque veils which masked the China within.[4]

I am sure someday these veils will fall as the result of the increasing rents and tears which they have suffered in recent years.

It will be worth the wait.

Author's Note:

In the second paragraph of this story, I mentioned how "the brilliant surface of the West Lake's serene water appeared blood red." My imagination hints at the horrible violence of the "Counter-Revolutionary Suppression Movement" which lasted from the winter of 1950 until the end of 1951.

According to statistics issued by sources abroad, those who died directly or indirectly as a result of the "Movement" neared nine million. In 1956, Mao said, during his lecture on "How to Deal With Contradictions Among the Masses," that the oversea allegations that the Suppression Movement had caused the deaths of several million people were exaggerated—the actual number was close to several hundred thousand!

When his speech, recorded by those present, was officially published, the last part about the "actual number" was left out. I, however, did see one set of original lecture notes.

---

[4] The year 1956 saw the start of the "Hundred Flowers Movement" in China, characterized by a relative tolerance for freedom of expression.

My 1951 move from the old home was at the height of the
Counter-Revolutionary Suppression Movement. I therefore was
in a state of unspeakable terror as I passed the beautiful West
Lake and my eyes could only register signs of violence.

(Translated by Richard J. Ferris Jr.)

Duck's Tongue Cap

The Events in this story occurred in 1951.

A duck's tongue cap. A passing deep thought. Each time I grasped it in my hand and put it on my head, I felt I had donned a small but perplexing problem, like rapping on a tiny and mysterious door.

The duck's tongue cap itself was actually anything but mysterious. It was made of soft, light-gray nylon cloth with a smaller-than-usual peak. I bought it in Shanghai in 1946.

The cap's becoming a problem, however, was a little mysterious. During the last half of 1949, as most people know by this time, China, the country that Chinese people say looks like a begonia leaf with a petal missing, had already come under new management.

My so-called "problem"—"mysterious door," was actually a very active sense of self-protection. New events require that people be sensitive.

That year saw the start of a "new historical era" during which it seemed like we were experiencing another biblical Genesis. It was as if there were no universe, no earth, no society before 1949. But suddenly, upon the commencement of the "new era," there appeared one or more god-like spirits who created the sun, moon and stars, the flowers, grass and trees—the very shape of the land, for the Chinese people.

I didn't really go along with the situations represented by this analogy, so I had no choice but to be like an octopus among a school of sharks, nervous and ever-ready to release my supply of ink.

The success of the human race in having survived on this planet and having lived and enjoyed life for so long, is due for the most part to the ability of its members to recall the past. If the whole of my memory resembled a modern department store, and suddenly, by some magical means, all the fashionable goods arranged on its shelves and in its glass display cases were made worthless so that its patrons would not even condescend to look at them, like a scene from *Strange Tales From the East*, what a horrible nightmare that would make! But it was not a nightmare. I was living it!

I remember the time that I wrote a letter to thank the principal of the Fish Market Bridge Elementary School for her introduction which secured my renting a unit in the new housing complex by the canal. I addressed the envelope to "Miss Lu," not at all expecting that the word "Miss" would incite an uproar among the school faculty, who for several days joked about how I had become an antique and had forgotten to throw this word out with the rest of the terminology of the old feudal society.

There was much more to this new era than can be gleaned from the above anecdote. At that time, even the color, pattern, design and material of clothing was standardized to stifle personal likes and desires—a reflection of the country's new ideology and the result of a long and deliberated decision-making process.

It was the decision-makers, the Marxists of every size and shape, who seemed to be ever waiting in ambush behind camouflaged screens in the cortexes of our brains, spying on even the most casual of thoughts.

And it was in the midst of the beginning of such a turbulent era that the duck's tongue cap became a true "problem."

On the streets at that time, Western-style nylon caps and Panama straw hats and the like had long ago joined the ranks of pre-historical artifacts.

Both the Lenin-style and longer-peaked worker's caps were made with indigo or dark blue cloth. The only exception to these standard designs and colors was the green-cloth, octagonal Liberation Army cap which, of the three, differed the most from my own.

From the last part of 1950 to the present day, I have not seen another person wearing anything quite like that duck's tongue cap.

In that social climate where tens of thousands of lives were being choreographed so that they were, in a sense, performing the same march in the same costumes. Anyone who entertained the idea of mixing colors or sought to stand out in any way was seeking disaster himself.

The curious might then ask: why did you have to wear that cap? Answer: my vision is poor. In the scorching sun I had to wear dark glasses. They, however, were the mark of the American or Taiwanese "Spy-Bandit" in Communist China's motion pictures. In wearing my duck's tongue cap, which could also shield me from the sun, I was just picking the lesser of two evils, choosing to stand out, but not as a bandit. Furthermore, my cap was basically of the same family as the sanctioned Lenin and Liberation Army caps, underlining the wisdom and sagacity of choosing my cap over a pair of sunglasses.

As a matter of course, my latent rebellious nature was aroused in the contemplation of the above, pushing me to engage the status quo in a silent struggle—to use my cap as a solitary boat with which I would navigate the waters of that new society and see at what time, place and under what conditions I would run aground.

One afternoon, I slowly picked up the duck's tongue cap as if I were bearing a great weight, which had been strapped to me for some time and which gave me an air of severity on that morning that showed in the expression on my face. I had decided to take an "exploratory stroll." In the past, whenever I went outside and walked along the side of the road, wearing the cap always attracted the attention of others and caused the raising of no few eyebrows. My audience was probably just curious and meant no ill will. The People's Republic of China had yet to promulgate a law forbidding the wearing of caps like mine!

The street that knew my measured steps so well was thronged with people. Perhaps, I thought, the crowd would act as my bodyguard.

"Today," I said to myself, "I want to explore."

The other side of the canal was always a temptation to me. I couldn't help thinking that the vegetation growing there was a mass of extraordinary green flames, full of meaning and summoning my limbs to further liberation.

Ever since the winter of the previous year, in order to defend against the endless pressure which the society "outside" brought to bear on me, I had excused myself from the world at large on the pretense that I was convalescing from a serious respiratory illness. It was as if I had sentenced myself to imprisonment within the confines of my little domicile, only airing myself every so often with a ten or twenty minute walk by the riverbank outside my door. Even though the lure of the external world's precious spaciousness and verdancy was powerful, I dared not linger too long.

I was only separated from the neighboring village, the lush and whispering bamboo forest and a broad, emerald carpet of grass by a single ribbon of a river. These things, however, were to be gazed at but not approached. Despite this realization, each time I puttered about the area outside my living quarters, the dense fields of grass across the river presented too great a temptation. It was as if those blades of grass were the forbidden fruits of my Eden.

That day was the day I was going to pick those fruits.

Finally, I stepped upon the imposing stone bridge which arched the river.

This bridge was a relic of the Ming Dynasty and was built in the architectural style attributed to that dynasty's founding emperor, Zhu Yuanzhang. It formed an acute bow and gave the bridge the look of a small mountain. When I was climbing up the bridge along the steps, thoughts occurred to me that if I were wearing traditional Chinese clothing, resembling the cassock, of a Buddhist monk, and fang chin or hood worn by intellectuals during the Ming Dynasty, what a fine, classic painting the bridge and I would make!

It was too bad my heart was devoid of classic thoughts at the moment. After crossing the bridge, my mind was clouded with modern worries. The further I penetrated into the grassy landscape, the more sensitive I became to my surroundings. I had the newfound eyesight of an eagle—sharp, searching, and seemingly limitless. In my subconscious mind, any human creature I perceived set off a violent nervous reaction.

For the greater part of the three years that had passed since 1949, too many things had occurred to instill the feeling in me that the fresh jujube groves that surrounded me after I stepped off the bridge, as well as the luxuriant date trees and densely packed shrubbery, were just so many splendid paintings. Once I found myself within these natural masterpieces, however, the feeling was much different. Some mysterious blast of intimidation had distorted my appreciation of the illusory world I had fixed in my mind after so long.

At this point I realized that the village I was approaching was perilous territory considering all the "great changes" that had occurred of late.[1] That afternoon, I was like Columbus as he approached the new continent. I was entering, for the first time, the young world which had been born after 1949.

"Who are you?"

The New World finally uttered a sound, though its tone was far from friendly.

I halted my forward course as the sudden appearance of a man caught me off guard.

---

[1] "Great changes" refers to the Chinese Communist Party's rigorously enforced "Counter-Revolutionary Suppression Movement" which lasted from the winter of 1950 to that of 1951. According to statistics which came out soon thereafter, those who lost their lives either directly or indirectly as a result of this movement amounted to close to nine million including village landlords, wealthy peasants, etc., most of whom could not escape capture.

"No one in particular," I said with a hint of nervousness in my voice.

"And what are you doing here?" he added in the common dialect.

"Taking a stroll," I replied.

"A stroll?"

It appeared that I had stumped my conversational partner. I had already concluded that he was a local peasant.

"What do you mean *a stroll?*" he continued.

The expression on his face made me think of the look Copernicus probably had the first time someone asked him whether the earth revolves around the sun.

I started to take in the appearance of my inquisitor. He had large, dark and sallow eyes, was at least thirty years of age and wore unkempt, tattered clothing.

"A stroll means to take a walk," I said to him.

"All of this walking about ... who are you looking for?" he continued with his interrogation.

"No one," I answered.

"No one? Then why are you here?"

I suddenly awoke to the fact that, in this person's dictionary, no reference is made to the word stroll. Trying to get him to understand my concept of aesthetics would be like inviting him to a lecture on nuclear physics. He was also in the midst of acting out the role of a secret agent—against which his simple peasant self seemed to rebel. I was at a loss as to how to react to this odd drama.

"I've been bed-ridden with a respiratory illness" I explained. "My doctor told me that I should attempt to get up and around, to take frequent strolls, in order to improve my blood circulation and speed up my recovery."

"Let me see your employee's card," he replied all the same.

"Do you need an employee's card to take a walk?" my voice was gathering unfamiliar strength.

"Stop jabbering and give me your employee's card," his true colors were revealed. He should have been a criminal prosecutor.

I found it exasperatingly hard to hold any respect for this simple peasant with an affected sense of power. It was as if a turbo-charged motor which drew limitless power from the Central Government were working somewhere deep within his soul, activating his proud and forceful air.

I quickly remembered that this was perilous territory. Under no circumstances could I win an emotionally charged fight in this place.

"I'm sorry. I'm still convalescing, so I have no employment," I explained. "I live just on the other side of the river, at number fifteen, in the Hua Guang Bridge housing complex."

After I had spoken these words, and thought deeply for a moment, I got up the courage to add one question.

"And who are you?"

"I'm the cadre here," he said.

He didn't appear too happy at my question. His two eyes gnawed eagerly at me, seemingly rending every thread of my clothing from me, denying me even that minor protection.

"Come with me," he commanded in a firm voice.

"Where?" I asked naturally.

"To the Tea Pavilion Temple Police Station."

"Why?"

"We want to find out more about you."

"Why?" I asked again.

"It's none of your business. Come with me."

At this point, I felt that I was taking part in a Spanish bullfight and my opponent was a madly rushing bull, while I was a matador who was somehow ignorant of the arts of his profession. I didn't even have a square piece of red cloth with which to distract my adversary. As a frail scholar, I was no match for a bull and could only raise the white flag with stealth.

During the years leading up to that event, I had often played this role, though my part was more often one of a small field mouse, hiding under the cover of the earth's darker places. Even if necessity required that I venture forth in the light of day, the surface of the land acted as my protector, allowing me to become a kind of invisible creature.

I had developed this character very well, but at that specific point in time, I had to be extremely careful in order to thwart any attempts at exposure.

Ten minutes after I had agreed to accompany the cadre, we entered a narrow lane, huddled with shops.

Just as we emerged from the lane onto the Hua Guang Bridge, I heard a woman's voice.

"Mr. Pu! You're out for a walk?"

My savior had arrived. I sighed inwardly and called out. "Mrs. Fu!"

Mrs. Fu was my landlady and the wife of my former teacher. She was also the committee head of the neighborhood in which I lived.

It was as if I were a complainant who had the fortune of having his case heard by the righteous Judge Pao of old.[2] I quickly summed up my situation for her and asked if she could speak to the custodian at my side and vouch for my character.

She quickly told him in the local dialect that her father, Fu Ruihe, was formerly a powerful merchant in the village, and that her eldest son, Fu Zhongqi, was formerly the area's District Chief. She went on to say that she had seven sons and over twenty grandsons many of whom, when the Communist Party liberated China, immediately joined the armed forces and have since achieved positions of influence.

Even though Mrs. Fu was herself but a minor neighborhood committee head, she was also the matriarch of a large family, the members of which had acquired power and influence which

---

[2] Pao Zheng, 999-1063, an honest and just official known for his stressing the dignity of law.

spanned both generations and governments. Therefore, any words which she spoke on my behalf carried much weight with the peasant cadre who had taken so great an interest in me.

"Comrade Fu, since you'll vouch for this person, then I guess there'll be no need to go to the Tea Pavilion Temple. You can take him back with you."

I'll never forget the look in his eyes as he left us. It was a look which reminded me of the expression of someone who was watching a magic show. His sights were fixed on my head, as if I were balancing an Indian magic pot thereon: one minute erupting with flowers, the next bearing a multitude of fruits. He gazed at my head for nearly a minute before finally turning and walking away.

Mrs. Fu wrinkled her eyebrows and also looked at me, as if she were trying to read my thoughts. She didn't seem surprised at my "magic pot," but rather looked shocked, as if I wore an unexplainable and malicious object, a Polynesian taboo on my head.

"Mr. Pu, why are you wearing that cap?" she asked, her tone full of curiosity. Then she added gravely, "Next time you go out for a walk, leave it behind."

I chuckled, embarrassed, slowly lifted the duck's tongue cap from my head and silently followed her home.

(Translated by Richard J. Ferris Jr.)

Onto the Bridge

The words are so simple in themselves—no more than nineteen strokes in the modern script that has evolved from the pictographs devised by Cang Jie, goddess of words. But for over a decade, they seemed almost as weighty as the 10,000-ton cables of San Francisco's Golden Gate Bridge. Occasionally they still glimmer in the deep recesses of my memory, displaying their unique weightiness. As time passes and things change, they at last seem to have become divorced from their original sense and just symbolize a kind of pressure, a mountain peak that is very difficult to cross, or riddles that are none too easy to solve.

In human history there was a period, at least for me personally, when going "onto the bridge" really was one of the records which interpreted that "immortal age."

But first, a word about the pagoda at the foot of which the bridge stands.

Hangzhou is well-known for its three pagodas. Baochu Pagoda on Mt. Precious Stone is solid in the center and cannot be climbed; Leifeng Pagoda on Mt. South Screen, which fell into ruin in the early Republican period, was hollow in the center and could not be climbed either; the only one you can climb and admire the view from is Six-Harmony Pagoda.

Standing alongside Full Moon Peak, which rears up like a large full moon on the southern slope of Mt. South, Six-Harmony Pagoda was built in A.D. 970—during the Northern Song dynasty, and thus is about a thousand years old. The pagoda rises sheer up from the ground, sturdy and rough. With all the wisps of Sutra chanting and rhythmic beating on the red-lacquered wooden-fish from a large temple nearby, the pagoda's conical red walls and dark gray upturned eaves struck me first as anything but the tranquillity of Zen consciousness. The bustle of visitors was part of the reason, but the crude form of the pagoda itself also seemed to detract from the noble Buddhist ideal.

Structurally the pagoda consists of 13 floors, but only seven flights of stairs can be climbed. Ascending from the first floor with its inscription "First Stage Is Firm" to the seventh floor "Seven Treasures Are Glorious," I felt that each flight of stone steps was so quiet, unyielding and gloomy that it was like entering a tunnel. Yet as I passed through the sixth story "Borne by Six Turtles," arrived at the topmost floor, leaned on the red lacquered window frame and looked out—

I couldn't help uttering a sigh of amazement.

And this is why I, having lived in Hangzhou for over a third of a century, often felt pity for those people who would often tour the West Lake but forget to climb to the top of Six-Harmony Pagoda and enjoy the view over the Flushing Springtime River. It was like "buying the box and handing back the pearls."

I don't really want to enlist the support of Wu Jun's famous poem, written 1,400 years ago in the Liang dynasty, to describe this river:

> Wind and mist alike are pristine,
> Sky and mountains share one color.
> I drift as the current wills,
> East or west, whither it pleases....
> This extraordinary scene of mountain and river
> Is matchless in beauty the world over.
> The water is all a pale blue-green,
> A thousand fathoms clear to the bottom.
> Swimming fishes, tiny pebbles,
> Are directly visible without hindrance....[1]

---

[1] After the change of government on the mainland, a hydroelectric power plant was built on the Flushing Springtime River. Together with pollution from factories along the banks, the river has long ceased to be "all a pale blue-green/A thousand fathoms clear to the bottom."

I simply trust my own vision: the Flushing Springtime River converges with the Qiantang River, bending in its course to form a spectacular L-shape.

How do I compare this with the West Lake?

I must admit to the loveliness of The West Lake, which really does call to mind a stunning woman's body wrapped in silvery cicada-wing silk gauze. I've dwelt beside her for three and half years, and her incomparable beauty has wafted time and again through the long glass window of my study. Gazing upon her from morning to night, I've lost count how many thousands of times I must have appraised her verdant features. Best of all, though, is to stand atop Northern High Peak and see the West Lake divided by Su Causeway and Bai Causeway into a triptych of mirrors, lending it an even more enchantingly lovely aspect, as if carved and worked like jade into some exquisite filigree, resembling nothing so much as a series of jadeite-green crystal pools in an imperial park, set around with bank upon bank of slender green willows. And yet this stretch of porcelain-green beauty has been constrained by its conspicuous boundary lines into a modest Cinderella. Boldly breaking through these boundary lines, the Flushing Springtime River exudes a yet deeper beauty. After all, the West Lake is but a lake, and no vast inland sea such as Lake Tai, whereas the Flushing Springtime River actually is somewhat like the sea, generating a sense of boundless freedom, spreading endlessly far and wide, and gathering to the power of a myriad lightning bolts, its changing scene dazzling the mind, its ranked clouds and rising mists epitomizing mighty grandeur. There are times when this stretch of river hardly seems to be water at all, its flow not so much that of moving water as of smoke, haze, cloud, or mountain mists. The river surface seems more metallic, glittering, sparkling, sequined, a fantasy of colors enveloped in mystery. In the background, on the further shore, lies the delta with all its serried ranks of paddy fields, and in springtime the land is covered with golden yellow rape, forming a gorgeous foil to the green of the river.

For me, the West Lake symbolizes the finite while the Flushing Springtime River embodies the infinite. This contrast alone explains everything.

As eye-catching as the grandeur of the Flushing Springtime River is the Great Qiantang River Bridge opposite the Six-Harmony Pagoda.

A gigantic rainbow of steel and concrete spans the yawning void. High overhead it reaches across the sky in one smooth expanse. No matter what clouds swirl or gather about it, and no matter what moaning of wind and water rises and falls at its side, this gigantic rainbow always stands tall and firm, as if some Great Wall-like tearing swathe of cosmic time had come to a screeching halt. Its intimidating air as of a fighting bull at full charge goes straight to the onlooker's guts, making him involuntarily bristle all over with pride and courage.

Great is that 1,453-meter double-tiered main span, with its 280-meter southern approach bridge and its 93-meter northern approach bridge. With its all-conquering length, that dead straight line of one single mighty calligraphic stroke resembling "number one" in Chinese character plunges right into the inner recesses of one's soul. Its cross girders of steel-chromium alloy, those four tall square piers that descend straight into the rock on the river bed,[2] all pulse splendidly with the incisive vigor and genius of human life. Afterwards I heard that the documentary film about the bridge's construction reached 2,500 meters in length. What with the "water-shooting method" of pile-driving, the "floating transportation method" used for the surrounding barrage and steel girders, the "suspended transportation method" and "cement spraying method" used for the caissons, each caisson weighing 600 tons, plus 14 boxes of documents and records on the building of the bridge. . . .

The vertiginous and magnificent visual thrill experienced by me as an onlooker, and the sight enjoyed by passengers crossing

---

[2] The main span of the Great Qiantang River Bridge is supported on 15 piers, of which only six are built directly on the riverbed rock. The remaining nine rest on 38-meter long wooden piles, 160 piles to each pier, which reach down to the rock.

this bridge by train or by bus, owe everything to the peerless creativity of "man," the "featherless animal." Two vivid sentences from those days still seem to shake the oval windows of my aural membranes. They were addressed by the deputy chief of the Nanjing Railway Board to the outstanding scientist responsible for building the bridge.

"If the bridge cannot be completed, you must leap into the Qiantang River! . . . and I will jump in after you!"

This bridge is truly a "pride of the twentieth century" for the descendants of the Yellow Emperor.

Strange to say, ever since taking up my modest residence in Hangzhou in 1946 I had held back from venturing onto the bridge to show my reverence and affection. For two years I'd lived in seclusion as a "male nun" at Wisdom Heart Convent, jumping the fiery pit of literary wizardry, almost neglecting to sleep and forgetting to eat. Later I moved out to the foothills of Mt. Geling and on the shores of the West Lake, where from dawn to dusk through every season of the year my sight was saturated with scenes of beauty, which somehow made me forget giving due obeisance to the great bridge.

On occasion, accompanying visiting friends and relatives up the Six-Harmony Pagoda, I would make a point of showing them the long scroll-painting of the Flushing Springtime River, together with the magnificent sight of the great bridge, but I never took them onto the bridge.

Time slipped by, and suddenly red flags appeared on every side. With the change of dynasty I quickly realized what an idiot I'd been to have spent five or six years in the blessed purlieus of the West Lake without ever having gone "onto the bridge."

And this was no minor oversight. For now, in the wake of the gory bloodshed of 1951, heaven and earth had changed and the universe had assumed an altered aspect. Within a circumference of 11 million square kilometers all cats and dogs were wiped out. The sky was virtually devoid of birds, even the squeaking of rats was greatly diminished.[3]

At this time, my physical movements were of necessity coordinated with the political barometer and meteorology. The tidal waves of the 1952 "Three Against" and "Five Against" campaigns were followed by a brief interlude for people to catch their breath, and in my poor state of health I used the excuse of going to hospital to sneak along to the Crane Releasing Pavilion area of the West Lake for a walk. Several years later I again took advantage of a similar period of calm to occasionally climb up the Six-Harmony Pagoda, look out over the sweep of the Flushing Springtime River, and gaze upon the great bridge. . . .

Yet still I did not venture onto the bridge.

While the political skies might clear up briefly from time to time, the faces of the bridge's two PLA guards couldn't be relied upon to be sunny. Counting on my fingers, I could reckon up at least five traps that might be waiting for me. I did not dare go onto the bridge.

The first trap: By this time the majority of people on the mainland, men and women, young and old, whatever their intellectual level, had undergone years of "thought-bathing" which had "touched the depths of their soul." Traces of this bathing couldn't help showing through: their faces betrayed something akin to what the Greek philosopher Plato called a "universal aspect." These were weird times, for just as "property" had to be "held in common," so did people's moods and feelings. This "universal aspect" could also be termed a "common condition." Its characteristic features were: silence, expressionlessness, a touch of dumbness, blankness, and rather

---

[3] During the 1950s Mainland China promoted a campaign of "eliminating the four pests," aimed at catching flies, mosquitoes, sparrows and rats. Along with sparrows, other species of birds were also caught because they affected farm output by stealing crops and cereals. At that time one rarely saw a bird flying in the sky. Meanwhile people scarcely had enough food to feed their own families, so how could they spare any to keep cats and dogs? These were also thoroughly eliminated. The communists killed all the stray dogs and stray cats.

disciplined reactions. I, on the other hand, was altogether lacking in this "universal aspect" or "common condition." Pretend as I might, I just couldn't keep my face blank or expressionless; it always bore some trace of sensitivity or liveliness. As soon as I opened my mouth I betrayed some "individuality" or "peculiarity" which was at a certain remove from the "universal aspect." Thanks to the "olfactory super-sensitivity," with which they were widely infected, the PLA soldiers on the bridge only needed to give a gentle sniff to sense someone who was "not one of us."

The second trap: In the past few years a vogue for "togetherness" had swept the mainland, and whenever you went traveling it was naturally also "together"—if you didn't organize a "sightseeing group" or a "visiting mission" then you would at least travel in a body of three or four people. I dare say no private individual had ever gone onto the Great Qiantang River Bridge to sightsee or to take a stroll completely on his own. If I went all alone, as soon as I turned up the soldiers would notice me and there would immediately be trouble. After all, in those days even elementary schoolchildren's math problems, as well as many of their games, involved stories, episodes or characters based on the struggle against class enemies and the capture of secret agents. Preventing the enemy from sabotaging the great bridge was beyond all question the guards' foremost task.

The third trap: Should a guard challenge me, I was not only an unemployed person of no fixed abode, without a work permit, but also had a problematic personal history. It would only take a few questions for me to be hauled off to the police station for interrogation. As the popular concept of those days put it "unemployed wanderers are tantamount to criminal elements in waiting."

The fourth trap: If the soldiers were to ask, "What are you doing here on the bridge all on your own?" and the answer came, "I'm taking a stroll," on the cerebral level the soldiers would already have determined your guilt. "What! The Chinese people are occupied day and night working at production, working at class struggle, working at political campaigns, yet you have the leisure to take a solitary stroll on this bridge?!"

The fifth trap: If the military guards inquired further, "What is your purpose in strolling on the bridge?" and the answer was, "To appreciate the beautiful scenery." That word "beautiful" would instantly make their "thought" do a big flip, so they would have to call me to account....

As for the other traps, I don't even want to enumerate them.

But it is a shame anyhow that, having lived in Hangzhou for over a decade, I had never been onto that great bridge.

My desire to go "onto the bridge" grew and it was akin to sexual desire in that the more unattainable it became, the more I wanted to satisfy it.

Perhaps this is one of the forces that drives history; mankind always wants to transform the "nothing" on his empty hand into "something."

In 1964, the political barometer really did turn to "fine." While there was wind, it was only a grade one on the Beaufort scale,[4] a soft breeze, the kind which often makes fishing boats feel a slight motion on the sea, or allows smoke on land to indicate the wind direction, but which is incapable of turning a weather vane. At most it was a grade two wind, a light breeze, which makes fishing boats hoist sail and travel with the wind at one or two kilometers per hour.

After ten years of blustery thunderstorms and typhoons, the earth lay still amid a rare climate of calm winds and fine sunshine.

I didn't know how long this stillness would last, so I drummed up my courage and decided to go onto the bridge.

After carefully thinking things out, I chose a Sunday and asked my old friend Yu Shuwen[5] and his family to be my

---

[4] This scale was devised by the British admiral Sir F. Beaufort. (d. 1857)

[5] Yu Shuwen writes under the sobriquet "Hui Ma" (Gray Horse) and his modern poem "The Kiss" has been published in the literary supplement of Taiwan's United Daily News.

bodyguards and escort me. Yu, a designer at the Hangzhou Printing and Dyeing Works, counted as working class. His wife was a child-care worker at a civilian-run kindergarten and their son Jianjian was attending school. All three of them were at that time completely free from political taint and could pass any questioning by the military guards. Sandwiched between the three of them, I figured that I could probably get through all right. If by any chance I were to be questioned, at least they could confirm that I was a good citizen and had not so far worn any kind of "hat."

Needless to say, while I had no work permit I did have a voting certificate on me, which certified that I was a "citizen" and not one of the "Five Bad Elements."

Look at this group of four progressing onto the bridge in literary terms! As we went over the approach bridge at Zhakou on the northern shore, Yu leading the way made up the "phoenix's head;" I myself right behind him constituted the middle section or "hog's belly;" and mother and son trailing behind me passed for the "leopard's tail."[6] Two PLA soldiers in green uniforms were patrolling with rifles over their shoulders, wearing solemn expressions. I intentionally avoided meeting their gaze as you would with a wild animal, and turned to look at the main bridge instead, assuming an air of blissful innocence and naturalness. Even so, as we passed not far in front of them, I still felt a degree of tension. Though I was well aware they weren't likely to stir up a fuss and question a group of passersby, my heart still quickened its beat as in the old days, like the morning of July 16, 1958, when I was transferred from a detention center to the concentration camp at Lower Sand. According to Pavlov's theory of psychology, this was my "conditioned reflex" toward the PLA, a chain reaction of

---

[6] In his discussion of short drama, Qiao Mengfu of the Yuan dynasty termed the opening section the "phoenix's head," the middle section the "hog's belly" and the closing section the "leopard's tail." This formula was followed in later times when analyzing the structure of ancient composition.

pressures built up over the course of a decade and more. I wanted to overcome it, but I could not.

We walked onto the main bridge in silence, and slowly trailed along across the center of the bridge. We didn't dare walk quickly for fear of stirring the guards' suspicions, even though we knew well enough that any such suspicions would have been a trifle excessive.

Keeping straight ahead, I strolled right to the end of the approach bridge on the southern shore, a total of 1,826 meters. It was this experience of slowly treading on the long dragon-like body of the great bridge that gave me a glimmer of insight into a decade of thinking, and over ten years of waiting. It is impossible for me to give any accurate picture of my emotional state as I walked along. Was it love? Was it hatred? Was it hope? Or disappointment? As I lingered in the center of the bridge I was still a little tense, as if enjoying a happiness to which I really had no right. And because of this, half of my attention to the view on the bridge and my interest in appreciating it was displaced by this twisted emotional state. Yet as I made my way back from the far end, gradually, my toes and heels finally took in the hardness of the rebars and alloy steel of the bridge's arched and cross girders. It dawned upon me that any pair of human eyes, seeing those immense sturdy bridge piers like huge monsters amid the coursing current of the Qiantang River, would instinctively brim with pride for the genius and vision of the Sons of the Yellow Emperor. At that particular moment it was for me myself to savor this pride.

Walking along, I began to feel that my own individual life had burst into flower, as if filled with thrilling excitement. Although my heart was seething with vast emotions, I did not want, and did not dare, to reveal it to my companions. I had the impression that those two guards were nearby. Or maybe they would have some secret remote-control listening device on the bridge with which to record our conversation.

It was late autumn. The sky was overcast, the wind strong, and sleety rain seemed in the offing. This was hardly the weather to enjoy the river views—the Qiantang River was concealing its charms, even the sweeping scroll of the Flushing Springtime River was shorn of its customary striking beauty. All that was visible was an immense body of water raging tempestuously, churning, boiling, flailing, foaming, jetting spray—an extraordinarily intimidating sight. This watery scene seemed to symbolize the perilous state of the world all around in the past ten years and more. Needless to say, the grand panorama of river scenery I had originally hoped to take away with me went up in smoke. But far from being disappointed, I was very contented. At last, in my eighteenth year of residence in Hangzhou, I had finally been onto the bridge.

We paused for ten minutes or so in the center of the bridge without saying much. Perhaps we were all reduced to silence by certain strange thoughts. Eventually, just as we were about to leave, as if I'd finally decided to lift a heavy stone from my heart, I went ahead and uttered to Yu in a quiet and painful voice.

"At this moment, I'm aware of only one thing. Having lived to the age of 47, at least I really understand the meaning of the word 'freedom'!"

His only response was to give a bitter smile.

(Translated by Andrew Morton)

Flower Play

Three modern females of 1950

Meeting

A gloomy blanket of clouds dominated the sky above. A thick, wet feeling in the air made the blanket all the more oppressive. It would not require a stretch of the imagination to foretell my emotional response to the sudden appearance on this scene of three gray uniforms.

These uniforms were a contradiction. They appeared to have been newly tailored, but also worn for many years, washed and hung to dry times beyond count, so that the only special characteristics of the original gray cloth—the texture and sheen—had been long resigned to memory.

I felt that the uniforms were in reality three gray animals. No, three dark-gray marine animals. And not freshly caught mackerel or carp either, but old, stale fish that had been left in an overlooked basket at the marketplace for too many days, still permeated with the atmosphere of some Stygian depths and perfectly in tune with the mood of the day.

The wearers of the three uniforms were soon right next door, keeping company with my cousin, Qing.

Although the vibrations from the sounds they were making shook me where I sat, and although I had seen them all once before, I was very hard pressed to recall even the faintest image. My impression was that their faces were like the thin, whitewashed wall that then separated us. Its surface revealed no features—eyebrows, eyes, noses, mouths.

The awesome times we were living in cultivated this sort of perception. Very like an experienced magician who is able to turn a box stuffed with pigeons into an empty carton, the atmosphere of the time was able to turn the faces of populace brimming with expressions into so many unreadable pieces of paper.

Later the sound of my wall-mates' laughter increased gradually until it seemed to have absorbed all other noises. This laughter, however, was not merely a sound. It brought with it a hint of the personalities of its creators, though it was still divorced from the physical world and offered no clear picture to the listener.

Then, an idea rose from the depths of my mind to overcome my thoughts: "The sounds of unknown women are among the most deceitful."

After a brief tap sounded on my door, Qing accompanied the girls into my room and took over the formal introductions.

"These are my colleagues, Comrade Lin and Comrade Zhou. They're from Suzhou City. This is Comrade Wang from Ningbo City. This is their first visit to Hangzhou. They would like to know if you'll be their guide."

After a few cups of Dragon Well tea and some small talk, I began to feel that the wall which separated us had diminished a few inches. This is not to say that the distance between us was actually reduced, but that in the few moments of our meeting, I had taken in the appearances of these twenty-year-old girls and found nothing surprising. Further study would not have brought any insights.

Soon, probably because of our gradually increasing familiarity, they acted a little more relaxed and even made some attempts at friendliness. It was very much like holding a piece of ice in your hand in the winter. At first the ice is numbingly cold, but then, slowly, your fingers regain their warmth.

Time can play havoc with a first impression. A startlingly beautiful first impression of a flower can sometimes turn repulsive with the passage of time. In turn, time can sometimes improve upon an unattractive first impression of a flower. No matter how commonplace a woman is, she will in some way reveal a little floral essence.

Under the sway of my thoughts, the girls' faces began to form features.

At first glance, Zhou would probably stand out. Her face looked fresh-scrubbed and was slightly plump but well-formed. She exuded a learned poise and had a lively speaking manner. Her perfect Beijing accent was sufficient to give her the air of an opera actress.

I quickly found, however, that Lin had a much more lively manner than did Zhou. Skinny but athletic, Lin had a head of hair that could be described as "artistically styled." Her eyes had a dull look, and were constantly unfocused, as if she were lost in a daydream. Her complexion was dark, but the potentially serious air that this gave her was mellowed by the sweetness of her expression—a temperament peculiar to Suzhou girls.

Lin was wearing a dark green, poplin shirt, decorated with white polka-dots. She had intentionally worn the collar of the shirt on the outside of the uniform, in an attempt to dilute the oppressiveness of the gray shell. The effect was a little like the corner of a bright, soft cloud framed by a prison window. The coarse faded cream pants which she wore had been stylishly tailored. They reflected the originality of their Shanghai creator who proved that even one of the great proletariat could preserve a little "nobility." On her feet were a pair of modern flats. It was evident that she had struggled with the dull atmosphere that her uniform embodied.

Lin's features were delicate, and replete with the characteristics of a typical young Suzhou woman—hinting at many years of experience in a Shanghai parochial school.

Zhou's deportment, her every move, seemed to mark her as a stranger to Suzhou. One would mistake her for a Hefei or a Nanjing woman who could speak Mandarin Chinese with the best of them. Even the yellow wool collar which she wore on the outside of her uniform failed to add a hint of elegance to her appearance. She had the look of a wealthy housewife, one used to several comfortable years of married life, though she was actually still single. It would be easy to imagine that she had already had ten or so years of experience managing a household and possessed an unfailing knowledge of the amount of bottles of oil, canisters of vinegar and boxes of salt in her compound's kitchen. She had a speaking manner which could easily, if brought to extremes, land her the lead part in Shakespeare's *The Taming of the Shrew*, as Katharine, that vociferous, vinegar-spitting lady of the house who spent much of her time cursing and railing at her husband.

Of the three girls, Wang was the most unattractive. No light shone from her face. Of the three, her face most retained its resemblance to the featureless wall which had separated us so short a time ago. If you were only introduced to the other two girls, it would have been the same as meeting all three. This girl's face truly lacked any trace of femininity. At first glance, you would probably wish to differ. But then, you would conduct a more careful assessment. Before you was the dark, sallow, aged and weathered face of a woman who had spent her life in the African bush! Rough with promontories and vales, that face had no area that could be called smooth. It was fear-inspiring topography. Frankly speaking—she simply let me, her beholder, feel as if I were in the presence of one of my prehistoric Javan ancestors.

My cousin, Qing, said Wang was from Ningbo and I truly believed her. She had the complexion of those hailing from that city. Her skin was particularly dark, dark enough to give her the appearance of a lively black squid which had jumped from the waters which washed upon Ningbo's shore.

Curiosity was the main factor behind my careful examination and description of these girls. I sought to perceive exactly what appearance these girls portrayed through the heavy camouflage which was standard issue in that era. The next day would supply ample opportunities to continue my thoughts.

On the Lake

We decided to go boating.

As soon as we exposed ourselves to the heavy atmosphere outside of my abode—and stepped out onto the street—Lin and Zhou began to immediately prove true what the Chinese have long attributed to the dwellers of Suzhou, a peculiar propensity for snack foods. More important than the hiring of a boat was the search for the sweetmeats shop and the fruit stand.

Like two emaciated ghosts that had seen seven years of classic Egyptian famines, they purchased—all at once—great quantities of candies, persimmons, diminutive walnuts, preserved plums and yew nuts (a favorite of the region looking much like enlarged macadamia nuts). The two locusts searched the stores and stands for more potential fodder, but in the end, decided that they had bought all that was worth their gastronomic attention.

"You'll find that around here, the most famous stores are Caizhi Hut and Rice Fragrance Spring," I commented. These were two famous Suzhou sweetmeat and snack stores which had branches outside of the province in which they had originated. "I'm afraid that if you two Suzhou ladies choose some of our Hangzhou sweets stores, you'll definitely be disappointed!" I chuckled as I made this observation. People from Suzhou were also very particular about the quality of their snacks.

They laughed with me, but I found myself wondering whether or not this was just an act of courtesy.

Our next errand was to purchase some film to take advantage of the camera conspicuously dangling from one of the girls' arms.

"Do you have 620 film?" Zhou asked the shopkeeper in a stentorian voice.

"Nope. I only have number 612 film," replied the shopkeeper in an equally sonorous voice.

"Doomed!" cried out Zhou.

"Doomed!" parroted Lin.

These two knells of "Doom" had a magical effect on the Javan ancestor, who soon also followed with a special shout of "Doomed!"

I had to fight back an urge to make the same dour exclamation, if only to ensure that I was not remiss in my manners as the girls' host. I only contemplated this urge for a short time, however, letting the thought stroll about my mind for a few moments before I allowed it to pass on into oblivion. Truly, the sounds of the three prophetic expletives spun within my brain and stirred up some other thoughts in their travels. I had concluded that all three girls exuded a strength or force which seemed very masculine expressed in the atmosphere of a China that had yet to shake off the perceptions of the "old society."

The boats were rented on an hourly basis. I rented one for four hours, or about half a day.

"It is now 9:30 AM!" Lin shouted out as she looked at her wristwatch.

"Hurry up! Hurry! Get on the boat! We can't lose a minute!" prodded Zhou, in a tone reminiscent of shouting "Doomed" a short while ago.

I ordered our boatsman to find somewhere nearby where we could buy some boiled water for a pot of tea. This search took about thirty minutes to complete, which precipitated no few doom-like expressions to appear on the faces of my companions.

As soon as we got back into the boat, a succession—no, a parade—of velvety persimmons, dusty brown yew nuts, fragrant walnuts, red and slightly sour preserved plums and a rainbow of colored candies was directed toward the three girls' tireless mouths.

The snacks were being devoured at an alarming rate. Although there seemed to be more than enough to sate their appetites, the dainties were being dropped into their mouths in a fashion very much resembling an unending and furious bombing raid. The girl's gray shells were quickly stained with a variety of indelible vibrant colors, which would long recall the pleasure of the feast.

When the bombing raids increased in their ferocity, the girls' bodies seemed to have been charged with renewed energy.

The girls were busiest then—and possibly happiest.

As for the spellbindingly beautiful West Lake, our boat was at that moment continuing in its lonely progress over the water's surface.

"There's nothing so great about the West Lake. I don't see anything beautiful." Zhou made this gutsy statement and then immediately continued her gastronomic bombing raid.

"Before we came to Hangzhou we heard nothing but talk of the wonders of the West Lake. The real thing leaves a lot to be desired." After Lin gave her opinion, she fired another yew nut into her mouth.

"What a disappointment!" said Wang, her face expressing all the dignity of man's fifty thousand year-old predecessors.

These "literati" frequently announced their bold conclusions with the finality of the last echo of a gallows door.

I finally sat up and commenced my *pro bono* work in the defense of the West Lake.

"Taking in the sights of the West Lake under clouds and mist is like attempting to appreciate the features of a beauty's face in the obscuring twilight. Only in the honest light of a thrilling sunny day can one comprehend the Lake's unforgettable characteristics."

Even with that emotional defense, the great counselor lost his case.

"I don't like it! I just don't like it!" said Zhou, in between bites of a small walnut.

"Mmhmm! Mmhmm! I agree," spat out Wang while busy adding to the numbers of persimmon peels and pits scattered around her.

In the end it was our daydreaming Lin who proved the most astute.

"In any event, it's all behind us now, and we are better off than never having seen it." She seemed to be consoling herself as she sat eating preserved plums.

Soon, the boat was again pointed in the direction of a candy shop. The judgment of the three noblewomen had been passed down: the yew nuts were bland, the persimmons flavorless, and the candies weren't worth mentioning. Only the walnuts were worth a little consideration.

Nevertheless, the boat was decorated with candy wrappers, persimmon skins and pits, and the shells of yew nuts. Eventually, even the flavorless preserved plums had one-by-one been introduced into the girls' formidable digestive systems. A few tiny, brown walnuts, resembling miniature tanned pates of Buddhist monks, were left untouched on the round table that was the scene of the repast. Though they were also the girls' temptations, the walnuts were a little hard to crack. Suzhou ladies were notorious for their avoidance of such inconveniences. The myriad of snacks and sweets found in Suzhou markets proffered only shelled walnuts, or walnut candy, to the customer. Whole walnuts were unheard-of crudities.

Qing and I reclined to one side of this spectacle watching and chuckling. Mostly out of a desire to make my guests feel at ease, I occasionally reached over and claimed a few yew nuts for myself. I spent the rest of the time, however, silently puffing on my pipe and enjoying the lake's scenery.

As soon as the boat reached the Su Causeway of the Lake, Zhou again voiced her judgement.

"There's nothing on the Su Causeway. Nothing at all worth looking at."

I laughed and said, "On overcast days a view of the Su Causeway from afar is very pleasing. On a clear day, a morning stroll on the Causeway, or perhaps a Causeway bicycle ride, is also very refreshing. But if you approach the Causeway from afar—then stand upon it and bend over to stare into the mud—there's naturally nothing much worth your attention. In truth, the mud that makes up this causeway is not much different from any other mud."

They listened to me, laughing. As dusk was approaching, in order to make up for the miserable failure of the Hangzhou snacks, I decided that I would direct our boat to one of West Lake's most scenic attractions, a place where the moon left three separate images in the water, and treat my guests to some of Hangzhou's famous lotus root soup.

The girls sat reclining in rattan chairs, devouring on the lotus root soup I offered them. After they had finished, they licked their lips expressing great satisfaction. At long last, Hangzhou had offered me the means to win a match.

Gradually, the girls were gaining some interest in what we were doing. When we arrived at a white stone bridge arching the waters at a place called "Liu Guesthouse," they were suddenly and unusually attracted to the slender willow branches which cascaded over the bridge's railing. All three girls stopped in their tracks.

"Oooh. This would be a great place to take a picture of." Lin sighed.

"If only it weren't for that 620 film!" The wealthy housewife almost cursed.

"Damn it!" Wang shouted and just continued to stare off at the overcast sky.

They all took a bit of this anger with them as we turned and walked toward the river bank to get back into our boat. Just as we arrived at the shore, three pairs of eyes riveted on a target like an equal number of snipers. All three girls' heads had snapped in the direction of a nearby spicy dried tofu stand. With somewhat conflicting looks of desire and asserted self control, the three of them circled the stand a few times, finally stopping and passing sentence with a concerted shake of their heads.

"No way. Not going to buy any."

"It's dirty. Unhealthy!"

"Not worth eating. Not going to buy it!"

They released these words in rapid-fire procession. The effect was like the passing of a death sentence on the vendor.

Qing and I had been sitting in the boat for quite some time when the girls finally made their leisurely way back. Walking and laughing, they munched at large brown squares of dried tofu while carrying a handful of such spicy and fragrant pieces which were quickly disappearing into their mouths.

Those expressions—that scene—would be truly worth the effort of the ill-fated 620 film camera.

Liu Guesthouse was the ultimate goal of our boat trip, and it appeared to be everyone else's as well. It was Sunday and the place was filled with a lot of traveling groups. In the background, a phonograph was playing a Soviet song which went on about the "vastness of our motherland...." These sounds were joined with the more fluid notes of a bamboo flute and an er-hu[1] issuing from a nearby teahouse.

In the park, groups were playing badminton. A few were even playing basketball. At one corner there were some people screaming (it really wasn't what you could call singing) Beijing opera. Everyone truly seemed to be competing for ground and airwaves. Even in the midst of this general roar, however, some guests of the tea house could be seen sleeping in large rattan chairs, snoring like thunder. There were also some guests who had spread out their red sleeping mats on the mahogany smoking chairs in the front pavilion of the tea house (a place said to be used for entertaining opium smoking guests in the older days), and fallen asleep. These tourists hadn't come to sight-see; they'd come to sleep—to drift through a multitude of evanescent dreams. They were the truly fortunate.

Probably due to the very infectious nature of the "lucky ones" at the park, after finishing their tour in the Liu Guesthouse, all three of the girls were sleeping soundly in the boat. Both Zhou and Wang had taken off their shoes, arranged the white cushions from the boat sofa on the floor, and flopped down thereon. They looked like two wounded soldiers just brought back from the furor of some battlefield. One of Zhou's legs was stretched out on the sofa, creating her own "gray stocking exhibit" for all to see.

When the boat floated slowly underneath a pavilion at the center of the Lake, the two girls, who had been diligently snoring shot up from where they were like flying fish, pulling on Lin and Qing to follow and hopped up into the pavilion's temple. Once inside, they picked from a bunch of bamboo

---

[1] An "er-hu" is a two-string Chinese instrument.

sticks, engraved with divinatory characters, seeking answers to what the future held. I didn't get out. The things that the sticks told them were secrets to be respected. I didn't dare intrude. Probably nothing more than marital affairs. No wonder that they were so interested in the Lei Feng Pagoda[2] which had collapsed many years earlier. They had probably heard that there used to have a renowned matchmaking temple.

Just as we approached the shore, Zhou looked at her wrist watch.

"It's only one-fifteen. We still have nineteen minutes! We can't waste it! We've paid for it!"

She suggested we row along the shore for the remaining time. Everyone agreed.

Though we shouldn't have taken advantage of our oarsman's labor—I suppose he shouldn't take advantage of our money either!

Evening Mist

I left for home first, as it was getting late and I wanted to prepare meal for our guests. Qing remained with the girls and joined in their game of hide and seek. It was some time before they finally returned to my room.

The overcast day outside had been darkening rapidly. At dusk, it was already as black as night and the clouds had finally released their rain. The sound of rain and the dark of night have always seemed to bridge the distances between people. The rainy night was like an enormous umbrella, and we sat protected under its shelter, jointly gripping its handle. We were all experiencing a kind of awkward, new closeness.

Underneath my motley, parasol-shaped floor lamp, the three girls left their gray outer shells behind and revealed the brightly colored clothing that was their true youthful selves underneath.

---

[2] The reputed site of the Chinese legend in which a white-snake fairy fell in love with and married a mortal man.

After a day of sightseeing, happiness was mixing well with fatigue, diluting my guests' forceful moods and dulling their sharp tongues.

At that time, the deafening noise of the day's judgements and disappointments had died out. A bountiful meal followed by fruit and snacks offered my guests some further joy. This was really the best time of the day, that warm lull just before you recline on your bed in search of some sympathetic dreams—the time when you're most relaxed.

At last, now, my guests were more or less presenting their purest inner selves—no longer bearing any resemblance to the forceful, "new society" personalities which had been in command during the day.

Even the Ningbo squid began to reveal some effervescence, some glints of the goldfish within.

"You're a novelist. Tell us a reeeeealy loooong story, okay?" asked Zhou after the meal.

"Well, I'll tell you a reeealy short story," I said chuckling.

As a rule, I usually told guests "the story of the stingy host" to entertain them if it was their first visit. So I related the story for the girls. It went something like this:

"There once was a man who was a notorious miser. He never fed his guests. One day, his brother-in-law rode over on his mule for a visit. At the noon hour, the miser said 'I'm sorry, I've nothing to eat so I can't ask you to stay for lunch.' His brother-in-law replied by saying, 'Nothing to eat? Then we'd best kill my mule and roast the meat!' This placed the miser in a very awkward situation. No one had ever called his bluff before. He reluctantly invited his brother-in-law for lunch and got out some wine glasses. The miser's wine glasses were very small. You could say they were doll's glasses.

"The brother-in-law picked up one of the glasses and was about to take a drink when he started to cry. The miser asked what was the matter. His brother-in-law replied, 'My father was very stingy. He loved to use this kind of tiny wine glass. One day he was drinking some wine and accidentally swallowed his glass. He died soon thereafter. So when I saw your wine glasses I couldn't help thinking of my father and started crying.'

"The miser was speechless. He switched the wine glasses for a pair of somewhat larger ones. After lunch, when the brother-in-law was taking his leave, he suddenly said to the miser 'Brother! Please box my ears three times!' The miser was shocked. He asked why. The brother-in-law replied, 'When I return home, everyone will know that I had lunch at your house but my face won't be flushed—it will be obvious that I haven't drunken my fill and everyone will call you stingy. That would be too awkward, so please box my ears a few times. With the appearance of a drunken flush upon my face, you'll be able to kill two birds with one stone. Your wine will not have been wasted and your miserly reputation will be cleared.' "

Sometime after the ladies' laughter had died down, our conversation drifted to foreign religions. My guess proved correct: Lin had recently graduated from a parochial school run by the Catholic Church in Shanghai.

"Those matrons at the school were so feudalistic. They ruled the female students with iron hands!" Lin laughed as she spoke.

"In our middle school, males and females were separated. Females in one school, males in another. On Sundays, when we all attended Mass, males and females couldn't even sit together. We weren't even allowed to glance at each other! You would get a demerit for even appearing like you wanted to look at someone of the other sex. But naturally, the more people are forbidden from doing something, the more they want to do it. Even though they knew they'd get demerits, some of the boys would seem to struggle to peek at the girls. There were some boys who even tied love notes to soccer balls and kicked them onto the girls campus! The whole blockading system was ineffective!"

Everyone chuckled after Lin finished. I also told a first-hand anecdote of my own.

"There was a particular professor who taught at a Catholic college in Shanghai. He held classes on both the men's and women's campuses. He had two wives. One was his 'true' wife and the other his concubine. When a social function was held on the men's campus, he would bring his true wife. When he attended meetings on the women's campus, his concubine would accompany him. This continued for several years without discovery. The reason for this was that the students and professors of each school never crossed boundaries. It was said that, except for the professor—'not even a male fly was allowed on the women's campus!'

"The oddest thing was that his true wife didn't even have any inkling of the existence of his concubine. The true wife lived in the faculty dormitory on the men's campus. She never had reason to go to the women's campus.

"All the more ridiculous was that this professor had advertised his marriage with the concubine in a local newspaper. His true wife was really cast in the same mold as Robinson Crusoe, for she rarely, if ever, had contact with society."[3]

Later, my guests' conversation switched to one of their primary school classmates, a girl who was unequivocally a devout Catholic. Zhou told the following story.

"She was obsessed! During our first athletic meet, she suddenly began preaching a sermon to us! Without anyone's permission, she just started talking—to herself—on the stage. She said, 'I hope the Lord above helps the lost sheep among you find the path to salvation.' Everyone tried to stop her from continuing by pulling her down from the stage, but she struggled away saying, 'I haven't finished. I still have something to say!' There was nothing we could do!"

Zhou continued, "When we were studying, others would be looking at documents and listening to comrades lecture. She, however, would be secretly reading her bible. Later on, they

---

[3] After the telling of this story, both wife and concubine happened to exercise their visiting rights on the same day, while our professor was enduring a sentence in a Communist labor camp. I'll leave the awkward results of this reunion to the able imaginations of my readers. This was the same professor who had been heard calling his wives "love nests."

didn't allow her to continue her religious reading. She couldn't stand it. All she would do was sigh. I think ... that even though she held Party documents in her hands, she was silently reciting the words of her lord above, long ago committed to heart. Aaah. She was addicted. She'd preach to everyone, gospel here gospel there. She couldn't forget the Bible even when going to the bathroom—let alone when she was eating or resting in bed. What a hopeless case!"

"Was she an old woman?" I asked.

"No. She was only twenty-two years old," Zhou replied.

I was surprised.

Written in 1950

Trailing Thoughts

I chose to end my vignette here. To continue would perhaps cause me to exacerbate my trespass of the rules of courtesy. This would be unbecoming of my role as host in the story. I wrote the chapter "Evening Mist" primarily for the purpose of making amends for the first chapter's more discourteous illustration of my guests. I would still like to add some information, however, which will hopefully impart a little more understanding of the fragments of life portrayed in this tale.

Owing to the overall anti-climactic impression of the West Lake that my guests had created for themselves, they returned to Shanghai a day earlier than planned. They did this without waiting for Qing to accompany them. This sudden change of heart had taken form on the second day of their visit absent any knowledge on my part. Even though they stayed only next door and we shared one thin wall, when I awoke on the second day of their stay, they were not there.

Qing told me that they'd gone back.

I didn't know what to ask of my cousin. I guessed it was probably an unhappy topic, and pursued it no further. At the time, I was laboring under the regrets of having carefully made preparations for their lunch and supper that day. I had asked my neighbor to buy some vegetables for me at the market to add a little festiveness to our repasts....

Several years later, I heard that all three women had blossomed into true revolutionaries. Lin was the deputy head of a primary school. She ruled the school with the authority of a post-liberation Charles de Gaulle. Zhou, during a political struggle meeting directed at an old female boss, jumped up onto the stage, and started to pull at the boss' hair until she drew blood. Wang's acts overshadowed Lin's. She had long ceased to recall visions of a lively black squid. She had become more reminiscent of something dark and carnivorous in purpose. She followed Zhou in her flight onto the stage. While Lin continued her frontal assault on the victim's hair, Zhou dealt blows to the right and left. "Bang! Bang! Buh! Buh!" She boxed the ears of the old boss five or six times. Bone-crunching sounds filled the room. Witnesses were later reported to say that the echoes from the sounds of those blows reverberated until another I.in's bones were shattered in Outer Mongolia.[4]

Written in 1971

(Translated by Richard J. Ferris Jr.)

---

[4] Another "Lin" refers to Lin Biao, once a general and statesman of' the Chinese Communist Party. He was also one of Mao's closest advisors. He was said to have fallen from grace and died when the plane carrying him to sanctuary in Russia crashed, allegedly by accident, in the Mongolian People's Republic in 1971.

The Secret on the Pamirs

The Pamirs are a mountain system and high tableland on the border of Tadzhik in the U.S.S.R. and Xinjiang Province in China. The area is called "the Roof of the World" because of its height above sea-level. Some people believe it is the place where human beings first came into existence. I know of a Swedish geographer who once made an investigative tour of the Plateau and came back with an extensive knowledge of it, which he turned into a book. I have read this Swedish geographer's book, but I have forgotten most of its description of the Pamirs. For me the high tableland was a mysterious place which I thought I could only reach by imagination.

However, in the summer of 1969, I met a man from the Pamirs who told me all he knew of the mysterious place and disclosed thereby a secret which I think should be of great interest to people of the Free World.

That summer I was imprisoned at Little Cart Bridge Jail in Hangzhou for being "anti-government." One day I saw a young man with a face like a goat's pushed into a neighboring cell. When the jailer who sent him in was leaving, the young man cried out abruptly, "Why did you arrest me?" Hearing this, an old prisoner nearby was amused. He replied humorously, "Well, we certainly never arrested anybody. The jailer has already left."

Then another jailbird commented, "You're a thief. You deserved it, didn't you?"

"No," the goat-faced man replied. "We live by our special skills. We're are just craftsmen like you. We don't deserve to be arrested, or confined, or treated below our dignity." Seeing us all amused, he added, "If you have no skill, you can steal nothing."

That was the first time I ever heard a thief define his calling so proudly. This conversation indeed aroused my interest in this newcomer. From then on, whenever the opportunity arose, I would talk with him.

He was somewhat talkative. After I learned he was from Aksu, a place near Tsungling belonging to the Pamirs, I was even more interested in talking with him.

He told me that the Pamirs were a great expanse of wilderness. People living there had to import all their daily necessaries from outside, especially from Wulumuqi, the capital of Xinjiang. He said he was born in Shanghai and lived there for a time until the Red government implemented the "sending down"[1] policy and he was sent accordingly to Aksu to exploit the Pamirs as a pioneer. He was naturally not accustomed to life in the desert. Therefore he took advantage of the chaotic situation during the Great Cultural Revolution to steal back to his home in Shanghai.

When his mother saw him, she said in dismay, "Oh my poor son! You can't stay here except for this one night. You must go back to Aksu tomorrow. You know you have committed a crime. You have acted against government policy. Your stay here will necessarily involve your family in trouble. Your father might not even allow you to stay here for this one night. Do you under-stand, son? But you must be hungry now. Let me make you a bowl of noodles. Meanwhile, you'd better get ready to hide yourself somewhere."

This reception from his dear mother plunged him imme-diately into the depths of sorrow and indignation. He became so sad and angry at those words that he retorted spitefully, "Mom, you know how much I've suffered. I've traveled thousand of miles to get here. How can you treat me like this? All right, since you want me to go, I won't stay a moment. And I don't want your noodles!!"

Having spoken these words he left immediately. And where did he go then? "Well," he said, "I traveled the city. And I learned to do the skillful thing you are ashamed of. But luck was against me. I was caught at a department store in Tianjing. My

---

[1] The policy of sending urban dwellers to the frontier or rural areas.

name is Huang, by the way. I'm afraid they'll send me back to Aksu."

Huang was indeed sent back to Aksu some months later. But before he left, he revealed to me the true face of a concentration camp on the Pamirs whose secret was kept so tightly from the outside world that very few people, not even the high-ranking Reds, dared to speak about it. As I have now gathered more information about it, I can testify that what he revealed to me is true.

From Huang's revelation and the information I have since gathered, I know that the Concentration Camp on the Pamirs is also called the Tsungling Jail. Whether they call it a camp or a jail, one fact remains: it is a jail without fences or bars. Why so? Because such things are not necessary there. Because no one under ordinary conditions can escape from there to safety without divine aid or miraculous help from others.

Just imagine. The camp or jail is on a plateau as high as five thousand meters. I believe that in the history of mankind no one except Mao Zedong could have thought of a way of imprisoning people there.

It is said that many Nationalist Party soldiers were sent to that secret place after they were captured in the battles with the Reds. In May 1983, many flagrant criminals also began to be sent there to curb the ever-increasing incidence of crime in China.

When sending captives or criminals to the jail-camp, they always take the most convenient route, namely, by way of Xian, Lanzhou, and Hami. After passing Hami, they stop in a small county called Huching where buses are arranged to take them to an unknown place three or four days' journey away. From the unknown place all the prisoners are then forced to walk for about two days before they reach their destination and are able to begin their life on the Pamirs.

Since a captive or criminal is never expected to come back once he is sent to the "Roof of the World," his family starts mourning as soon as they hear he is being sent there. It is not uncommon to see the family of such a prisoner accompany him crying all the way to the station and then see his mother or wife pass out just when he gets on the train.

The train used for these people is very special. There are no seats in its cars because the train is normally used to transport cargo or livestock. The carriages have usually only been remodeled to prevent the "passengers" from running away. Therefore, the doors and windows of the train are usually fit with iron bars. In each car some sixty or seventy "passengers" are stored, guarded by six armed policemen in addition to two plain-clothes agents. All these people share a big iron barrel of water and some biscuits. No one is allowed to leave without permission.

It is said that the many who wish to escape find no way while in the train or in the bus. However, once they start the two-day walk toward their destination, they see their only chance. Many are shot dead by machine guns before they have fled very far.

Life on the Plateau is an eternal torture. Throughout the year the temperature is insanely cold. Just to endure from one day to the next is a big ordeal, especially for those accustomed to the warmth of the South.

The captives or criminals are made to labor there under all weather conditions. The superintendents or officers there are naturally better treated. They have warmer rooms and beds and their work is not very energy-consuming. Nevertheless, they also suffer from the shortage of daily necessaries.

The prisoners are not allowed to correspond with the outside world. In the course of their torturing labor many grow weary of life and commit suicide. And many are executed for doing something wrong, while others are starved or frozen to death.

The officers or superintendents there are paid double wages and when they have finished their service and come back east, they are often promoted to higher positions. However, they often say they would never have served there if they had been free to choose.

I believe this jail-camp on the Roof of the World is the most horrible hell tangible to our feeling and visible to our sight.

After I have learned so many secrets regarding the place, I still stand a bit incredulous. Many perplexing questions still haunt me. How big is the jail? How many unfortunates are suffering there? What are they doing? Building roads of farms? Why did they establish a concentration camp or a jail there in the first place? And why all the secrecy?

I hope some day some reports can get there to answer these questions for us. At least I hope some reconnaissance planes can fly over the area and take some clear pictures. If we believe in human rights and human dignity, we should do our utmost to disclose the secret of the Pamirs.

(Translated by Richard J. Ferris Jr.)

The Day Mao Died

It was around 3 PM on September 9, 1976.

I was sitting thoughtfully on an old sofa, the springs of which were already broken. In fact I had sunk into the sofa, and felt as if I had sunk into a sand-pit. But that didn't hinder my brooding.

Since 1970 I had the habit of spending at least an hour brooding over my past on that particular day to commemorate the anniversary of my release from jail. I just can't forget the time and date (3:05 PM, September 9, 1969) when they told me I was free to go home. At the same time on the same day in 1970, I wrote a poem entitled "3:05 PM" I think the time is already eternalized in my mind.

"Pu Ning, get out your luggage!" Juan, a section chief at the jail, opened the small window over the black door of my cell and gave me the order in a low tone. I looked at his pale face, and felt his command was like the thunder which forebodes the opening of a black coffin in a tale of horror.

God! I had waited for that command for 432 days! What could I say then except "Hallelujah!?" And what could I do except get out my baggage and prepare to leave the "black coffin?"

Forty minutes later I was running frantically to the street to call a rickshaw. I wished to reach home as soon as possible and with dignity. If I had walked home, the two pieces of baggage I carried would have crushed me like two big boulders.

Thirty more minutes later, I appeared in the barbershop near my house. That was the first time in fourteen months that I saw myself in a mirror. But that first impression of myself was everlastingly bad. I found that I did have a thin pale face like a ghost's. I couldn't bear to look at myself in the mirror for long. "I've just come back from a hospital. I had a long serious illness. I almost died." I lied. I thought I owed the barber a decent explanation for my preposterous state and was wary of what would happen if I told him I had just been released from prison.

Year after year, the same scene flashes itself into my memory and unfolds sort of like a film. And to watch the film at the same time every year has become a ritual which I must observe without fail. The film length varies each year but usually lasts about one and a half to two hours, like any ordinary movie. In 1976 however, the film was shorter. My yearly ritual was abruptly interrupted a few minutes before four o'clock in the afternoon.

I was sitting at a table by a window which had two movable windowpanes, the upper one being transparent and the lower one opaque. I remember that it was an especially sultry day. On a day like that I would open both panes of the window unless I was writing. (I opened the entire window to let others see that I, as a released "anti-revolutionary," was not misbehaving. And I kept the lower part of the window closed while writing, no matter how hot it was, because I did not want others to suspect me of being "anti-revolutionary" again.) As I was then not writing but ruminating over a book of literature, the window was entirely open as usual.

A glance outside toward the left revealed Mr. Sun listening to the radio attentively and apparently with nervous tension.

What made him so? I strained my ears to listen. But I heard nothing clear because the radio was not turned up loud enough.

Then a strange thing happened. He suddenly stopped listening, leaped up and walked toward me. Soon I heard him knocking at my door.

I have a poem (poetic manuscripts collected out of jail) which describes my house as being in "the depth of the mountains where neither man nor beast ever reach." Indeed, even after 1972 when I had finally lost the stigma of being an anti-revolutionary, I had very few visitors. The only ones who came to my house were the few close friends I had. Their coming was like the chance falling of some leaves on a distant old pond. Old Sun, though my neighbor, had never paid me a visit before. If he had something (of special concern) to tell me, he often spoke with me in the common yard, never venturing near my house. We often let our conversation be broadcast by the wind to every door in the community. We thought we could thus prove we were guilty of nothing "anti-revolutionary."

The reason why Old Sun and I behaved so gingerly was that both he and I belonged to the "five black categories" of people. In the Hindu caste system, people of the lower castes can still sit together and eat together. But under the government of the Chinese Communists, people belonging to the "black categories" cannot act as freely, because the cadres are everywhere spying on these unfortunates. One suspicious word or act could easily send a member of a "black category" to jail. It is therefore no exaggeration that a man and a woman from a "black category" could live in the same place like husband and wife but never talk to each other for two or three years.

But that day Old Sun broke the unwritten rule. He came over to tell me some big news. But before he gave me the news, he said, "Old Pu, close the lower part of the window." He was still acting prudently.

After I did what he bid, he whispered into my ear, "Mao Zedong is dead!"

"What?" I couldn't believe it.

"Mao is dead. I've just heard it on the radio. He died early this morning."

I came to realize why Old Sun had acted so strangely and cautiously. He asked me to close the window because he was afraid that the news might get me so excited that I'd behave imprudently. He was also afraid, I think, that the news might have just been the product of a broadcaster's madness. Anyway, he wished to tell me the big news secretly without being spied on by others.

To tell the truth, I was really overjoyed to hear the news. I felt like dancing "The Rapid Waltz of the Southern Rose." But before I let things get out of control, I wished to listen to the radio myself.

As soon as I turned on the transistor, I heard the International Anthem and then the news. Meanwhile, I noticed a bright light shining in the common yard. Some people were playing with firecrackers. Mao, the "reddest, reddest, red sun"[1] was like their flames, which could not shine eternally bright.

I rushed back to my own room. I lit a cigarette and lay down smoking it on a rattan couch. I felt as if I were tasting a most delicious fruit. The tidings made me even happier than my marriage in 1965.

It was indeed noteworthy that all Chinese people (and perhaps many foreigners as well), had been concerned about Mao's health and had been anxious to know when he would cease to be. Since the 1950's, people had been talking about the possibility of his sudden decease. Some said, "Fortune-teller Li has just had a close look at his recent photo. He said Mao could hardly survive the winter because his 'yintang'[2] was turning pitch black." Others said, "Astrologer Wang saw an evil star largely dimmed in the sky. He thought Mao might pass away soon." In the spring of 1966, as soon as I entered a friend's house at Hung Kou, he asked me, "Do you know Mao is in East China Military Hospital? They say his case is serious." It was the year the Cultural Revolution broke out. Later that year I saw in the newspaper a photo in which Mao was posing with Lin Biao, Deng Xiaoping, and a visiting political head of Albania. Judging from that photo, Mao was indeed unhealthy, but he didn't seem mortally ill. Afterwards, there were rumors that he had had an apoplexy. But the most interesting rumor was spread by a math teacher who said, "Mao recently passed out all of a sudden while he was in bed with his mistress." In 1975, Mao was still living, for all the rumors (or rather, people's wishes). But judging from the photo in which he posed with Premier Li of Singapore, he was already as disabled as a dead man. That made me decide that he was on his way to see Marx very soon.

---

[1] A saying popular with the Red Guards during the Cultural Revolution. The actual phrasing goes like "Chairman Mao is the reddest, reddest, red sun in our hearts."

[2] The space between the eyebrows.

I had thought that even if Mao could have lived for five more years, I would be able to survive him. If only I survived him, there was hope for a change in my fortune. Now he was gone four years sooner than expected. How could I help but get ecstatic over it?

At five o'clock, I heard the loudspeaker of a nearby factory pronounce the news. I thought I had better go out and see how the people reacted when they heard what was in my opinion the biggest news in the whole history of China.

I stepped out. The first man I saw was Limpy Wu. He sat in the door of his room waving a broken palm-leaf fan. He had a serious face, and was seemingly always in a solemn mood. Yet I could feel with my sixth sense that he was overjoyed like me.

But we did not converse. We communicated in silence. In the meantime, Mrs. Wu commented in a thin voice, "This is the only true equality. No matter who you are, you cannot but take that road."

I glanced around, seeing nobody else in the common yard except Little Wang, who sat on a bamboo chair near his door to cool himself. Little Wang was a worker, noted for his outspoken character. He made a grimace and added, "One should live like that, to live a full life."

Just then, I saw some other people walk into the yard. I immediately pretended to have heard nothing and walked quickly down the street toward the Fish Market Bridge.

From the subtle facial expressions of the people I saw on the street, I knew the news had already spread throughout the city. However, I noticed nobody shed tears, nor appeared really sad. The children were sporting on the sidewalks as usual though the adults appeared still afraid to reveal any mirth.

Many people were indeed astonished to hear the news. But many more had no response at all; they seemed to have been numbed, body and soul, from the long years of ceaseless movements and anti-movements. I believed some had sighed inwardly. But most of them, I believed, had consoled themselves by thinking that now they could say that they had truly tided over the horrible period of the Great Cultural Revolution.

I walked on the street for nearly an hour. But I did not see a single drop of moisture on anyone's face.

The next day I gazed at Mao's picture in the newspaper for ten long minutes. I think I still didn't dare to accept the fact that he was gone and my good fortune was to come. In effect, I was still afraid that the news might only be the result of another rumor. Perhaps the idea that Mao was a great great figure and thus should be deified was still in many ignorant minds. But did it come to my mind at that moment?

In the newspaper picture, Mao was lying in a big glass case, his big body showing its bigness as a dinosaur does. In my cold eyes, that colossal lump still held an-awe-inspiring power. If it rose up again, I thought, it could still trample all of China and shed a torrent of blood as long as the Yellow River. But now his eyes had closed. And it was a consolation to see those two eyes closed so surely tight while his body lay so motionless in the glass coffin. "For all the dread you commanded over the past sixty years, you are come to this, Amen!" I said to him in my heart.

I lit a cigarette and continued to gaze at the picture while smoking. I enjoyed seeing him come to this just as I "enjoyed eating a favorite food." It was a pleasure you could "chew with zest."

No one outside of China, I believed, could imagine how a billion people had been living under the "charm" of that man now lying lifeless in that coffin. "But you are come to this!" I said loudly again to him in my heart.

All the people were commanded to wear crape.[3] But a young worker resisted the orders by saying, "This is sheer nonsense!" He was arrested at once.

Not long after, I heard a rumor that Mao had actually lain speechless on bed for many months before he died. They said he

---

[3] A piece of black crepe as a sign of mourning, often worn as band around the arm.

apparently still had his sense of hearing and could only issue commands by pen and paper.

Some more hearsay which came out still later said that Mao wouldn't have died on that day if his wife Jiang Qing hadn't come to see him. They said she had turned him over in bed to express her tender wifely care, and that had made him expire on the spot, drawing upon herself the suspicion that she had planned to kill "our Great Leader."

Most people were concerned about the future political changes. One of my young friends said, "Jiang Qing might become chairperson of the Party." I thought him naive and said to him scornfully, "You fool, just wait and see." Her days of power, I thought, were numbered as soon as her "great husband" was encased.

My prediction proved true, of course. Today we know the Gang of Four (of whom the leader was Jiang Qing) soon collapsed after Mao's death. Jiang Qing received a death sentence after she was arrested, though the sentence was later commuted to life imprisonment.

But I do not care about the fate of that head of the Gang. For me the day of Mao's death signifies my release from prison, and for many many more Chinese it meant a release from a long insufferable period of pain and terror. It was significant day that every year the arrival of September 9 finds me brooding in my room.

(Translated by Richard J. Ferris Jr.)